DAUGHTER OF THE DEEP

DAVID REDER

Contents

1

CHAPTER 1

It only takes a moment—sometimes, a fraction of a second—before your life turns completely upside down.

This was not one of those moments, but to my taut muscles and pounding heart, it certainly seemed so. I reached up and adjusted my goggles, making sure they were secured around my skin-tight swim cap. Then, wiggling my toes against the rough, grooved surface of the starting block, I mentally prepared myself for the all-consuming race.

"Swimmers, take your marks."

I bent over and gripped the starting block with both hands, fingering the bottom like an outlaw would finger his gun in a showdown.

I can do this.

Narrowing my eyes, I focused on the translucent turquoise water below. The thick black line on the bottom of the pool was visible as a fluctuating geometric design.

Bring it on.

The piercing sound of the buzzer launched me into action. In a heartbeat I dived off the block, arms flying together into a stream-line position. I entered the water flawlessly. One second I was soaring through the air, my leg muscles taut, and the next I was gliding underwater. My legs automatically entered into a powerful dolphin kick, propelling me forward a few yards until I resurfaced. Then my arms followed suit and strained forward, one after another.

Freestyle was my favorite stroke and by far my best. I felt a surge of adrenaline as my whole body worked in unison, my limbs like clockwork, as my mind constantly reminded me to keep in rhythm with my strokes. Before I knew it, the fluctuating black line at the bottom terminated, and I tucked myself into a ball. I performed a quick flip turn before pushing off the wall, gliding underwater for a few yards before breaking out into freestyle once again.

Fast-ter. Fast-ter, I chanted in my head. I. Can. Do. This.

My lungs throbbed with the need for air, but I ignored my oxygen crave and focused on the rush of competing instead. I was almost there. The wall was in sight. My arm strained to reach forward, to brush the tip of the tile and prove that I had made it.

It was all over in a millisecond. I high-fived the wall and jerked my head above the pool. Whipping my goggles off, my gaze automatically flew to the timer positioned at the far side of my lane. As soon as I saw my time, my hopeful smile vanished.

"Excellent time, Bennett!" Coach Davey strode over to my lane and gave me a large thumbs-up. His lips stretched taught against his teeth in a wide smile. "You never fail to impress me, kid."

I clung to the side of the pool, my chest heaving for air. "Thanks," I gasped, "but...was it good enough?"

Coach snorted. "Of course. You have nothing to worry about for the meet this weekend."

"No, it's not that."

His smile turned down a notch. "Ah."

Our eyes locked, and we both knew what the other was thinking. My time was fast, much faster than anyone at Newland High or the rest of the high schools in the area. But it wasn't fast enough to qualify for the Junior Olympics.

"Rayne, how in the world do you do that?"

I glanced over at the swimmer in the lane next to me. It was my best friend, Kimmie, shaking her head as if the fact that I had beat her—again—was unbelievable. "I swear, Rayne," she said, "as soon as you hit the water I can hear the sound barrier break."

"Hey, I'm not that fast," I laughed, but the thought made my stomach flip in anticipation nonetheless. With a little more practice, a couple more laps here and there, some extra training...who knows? The Junior Olympics might not be such a far-fetched dream after all. And after that—the real Olympics! Swimming was my life, and nothing was going to stop me from doing my best.

"Hello...earth to Rayne," Kimmie said.

I shook my head, not realizing that I had spaced out. "Huh?"

"You had that daydream-y look again," she teased. "Don't tell me you were imagining yourself as an Olympic gold medalist."

I splashed her and turned away so she couldn't see the blush creeping up on my cheeks. "No way," I lied.

We swam a few laps to cool down before pulling ourselves out of the pool. After waving goodbye to Coach, who had walked down a few lanes to comment on another swimmer's form, we walked as fast as we could to the changing rooms. The crisp autumn air nipped at our skin, but all I could think about was melting into my warm towel. As soon as that happened, I opted to take a quick shower to get all the nasty chlorine off my skin. I closed my eyes, massaged some shampoo in my stringy hair, and let the refreshing water cleanse me from all the chemicals.

Kimmie waited patiently as I dried off and pulled on my clothes. Together, we grabbed our backpacks from our lockers and swung them over our shoulders. Swim was our last period of the day, and we had a couple more minutes before the dismissal bell rang. Before we headed out the door, Kimmie darted in front of a mirror to check her hair. I chuckled as she attempted to tame her wild curls, which were already starting to dry and pop up in frizzy patches.

With a sigh of defeat, she groaned, "I give up! I wish I had hair like yours, Rayne."

I glanced at my reflection in the mirror. My long black locks were pulled into a tight bun on top of my head. I rarely let my hair down, not only because it got in my way, but because there was something special about it. No matter how often I cut my black tresses, they always grew back faster than before. And, oddly enough, whenever a ray of moonlight swept over my hair, my locks glowed a deep ocean blue. It was something I had discovered as a young girl, but never told anyone besides Dad. As far as I knew, no one else had hair like mine, and it made me feel like an outcast.

"It's not fair," Kimmie muttered, her voice jerking me out of my thoughts.

"What's not fair?"

"How perfect you are."

I rolled my eyes. "Oh, come on. We all have our flaws." And our secrets, I added mentally, as a small tendril of hair fell in front of my eyes.

"Yeah, right," Kimmie persisted. "You're beautiful and you're the best swimmer. I wish I had good looks and athleticism."

"You do have good looks," I argued. "Stop putting yourself down."

"But what about my athleticism?" She made a face. "It's kind of a known fact that I'm the worst swimmer at Newland High."

I opened my mouth, about to reply, but quickly closed it when I realized she did have a point. It would be a stretch to say that Kimmie was a decent swimmer, if even that. Her record showed that she had gotten last place in all the events she entered. Though she had grown to love swimming, she lacked the talent and technique that years of coaching could never impart.

"Okay," I said slowly, "so maybe you're not the best swimmer. So what? We all have our talents."

"Then what's mine?"

"That's easy." I grinned. "You're fearless."

Kimmie broke out into a wide smile. "Well, I guess that's true," she assented.

As we headed out the door and into the bright sunlight, my worn Converse fell into step with her flip-flops. Upon reaching the end of the corridor, she said, "See you tomorrow!"

"See ya." I watched as she headed toward the parking lot, where her mom was waiting to pick her up at the entrance. Meanwhile, I turned left and headed down the breezeway. I stuffed my hands into the pocket of my sweatshirt to ward off the mid-September chill. Just as I rounded the corner to head in the direction of the football field, the piercing sound of the dismissal bell rang out from all directions. Classroom doors immediately flung open, and chattering students poured out like a tumultuous tidal wave.

I quickened my pace, and before I knew it, I had escaped the swirling throngs of students crowding the breezeway. My shoes made slight imprints in the browning grass of the football field.

Before long, I reached the other side and hopped the chain link fence. My cozy, single-story house was only a short walk away, and I licked my lips hungrily at the thought of getting an after-school snack.

"Dad!" I hollered after traipsing across the front yard and jerking open the front door. "I'm home!"

"How was your day?" came the muffled reply. I tossed my backpack and swim gear onto the kitchen table before walking into Dad's office, where I saw him typing away at his computer.

"Oh, same as usual," I replied, reaching over the back of his chair to give him a hug.

He lightly squeezed me back. "Got any homework?"

"Yep." When he continued to type away instead of replying, I added, "So how was work?"

Dad's fingers paused. He sighed and lifted his hands, letting his arms fall to his sides as he spun around in his swivel chair to face me. "It's fine, sweetie. Don't worry about what's going on at work."

"Rough day, huh?"

"Try a rough week. I need to sell at least two more houses by the end of the month, or..."

I waited patiently, but he had lapsed into a thoughtful silence. "Dad."

He smiled faintly and ran a hand through his already-mussed hair. "You always know when I have something else on my mind, don't you?" he chuckled. "Just like your mother."

A tension-filled silence immediately descended on the room. We both paused and awkwardly glanced at anything and everything except each other, trying desperately not to think about her.

I was the first to sbreak the ice. "So what is it?"

"We'll talk about it at dinner, okay? I still have a few other things to work on."

"Aw, Dad..."

"Not now, Rayne. Go ahead and start on your homework. I don't want to see another D in that Spanish class or I'm pulling you from the swim team, alright?"

I stood up straighter. I knew Dad would never go so far as to actually pull me from the swim team—after all, I was Newland High's top female swimmer—but the edge in his voice told me to knock it off or I was sure to pay.

"Okay," I sighed, mentally burying the plethora of questions I had about...well, whatever it was Dad had on his mind. Instead, I busied myself with schoolwork, and by the time dinner rolled around, I had successfully completed homework for all my subjects except Spanish—no surprise there.

Dad was taking out a delicious-smelling pot roast from the oven when I waltzed into the kitchen. My mouth immediately started watering. We were both fortunate that Dad was an excellent cook. I, on the other hand, couldn't even make a grilled cheese sandwich without setting off the fire alarm.

As soon as the table was set, the two of us slid into our seats and began eating. "So what's on your mind?" I asked, trying to sound as nonchalant as possible.

"It's kind of a big deal. Or not. I'm not sure," Dad sighed, setting down his fork to massage his temples. "I might just be making a mountain out of a molehill here."

I waited patiently for him to gather his thoughts. He continued slowly, "Look, Rayne, I know that you love your swim team and all, and you know that I would never willingly take your passion away from you."

"Right," I said, not liking where this conversation was going.

"Even though we live in a nice area and you go to a great school with a good swim team, we can't go on like this much longer. The real estate business is hitting a bump in the road right now. I'm having trouble with our mortgage and...well...and the rest of our debt, actually."

The delicious pot roast in my mouth had suddenly turned to sawdust. "You mean...?"

"Yes."

I forced myself to swallow. The food went halfway down my throat before I started choking. Tears sprang into my eyes.

"Rayne," Dad said urgently.

I grabbed my glass of water and gulped it down. "Okay," I said, "let me get this straight: we're moving."

He nodded slowly.

No. Oh, no. "But where are we going to live?" I cried. "How much longer do we have here?"

"Honestly, hon, I don't know. There's just too much on my mind right now."

I stabbed a chunk of meat with my fork. "How long have you been thinking about this?" I asked, as tears threatened to spring into my eyes again.

"That doesn't really matter."

I knew that was code for a long time, but I kept my mouth shut.

"I'm sorry I didn't tell you earlier, Rayne, but I knew it would be hard to break this to you. And like I said before, I have too much on my mind. First it's the real estate business, then it's our house payments, and then I get a call about Shady Cove—"

I nearly choked on my dinner for the second time this evening.

Dad hurriedly tried to cover his tracks. "That's not what I meant. I wasn't—"

"Is our old house is for sale?"

My hasty guess was proven correct, as Dad heaved a sigh and nodded slowly. "I guess there's no hiding it now."

I sat back, stunned. A million thoughts clouded my mind. How had Dad found out? Why was he even considering moving back to Shady Cove? And who was selling the house? No matter how hard I tried, I couldn't bring an image to mind of what my birthplace looked like. All I knew was that it was situated on top of Redrock Bluff, with a beautiful view of the small beach town and the glittering ocean beyond. But Dad and I had moved away right after the accident. Our home simply had too many memories of her. So why in the world was Dad suddenly thinking about moving back in?

He suddenly stood up. "I'm sorry, honey. I'll be in the office if you need me."

I watched as he methodically rinsed his plate and shoved it in the dishwasher, leaving me sitting alone at the table. I stared gloomily at my half-eaten plate of pot roast.

I had a feeling that everything from here on out was about to change—like Dad and I were on the tip of an iceberg, just waiting for it to fall. And when it did...

Well, there would be no going back.

2

CHAPTER 2

The beeping of my alarm jolted me awake. I groggily lifted my head from the comfort of my pillow and squinted into the darkness. It took me three tries before my hand, blindly flailing over my dresser, finally connected with the alarm. Then I snuggled deeper underneath my blankets and tried to shut out the sound of my dad getting ready for work.

"Rayne?" he called from the hallway. "Are you up yet?"

I opted to remain silent, but that only prompted Dad to rap on my bedroom door. I groaned and turned over in bed, throwing the covers over my face to block out the blinding light that was sure to flood my room at any second.

"Rayne?" Dad called again. "It's time to get up, hon."

"Go away," I groaned, my voice muffled by the pillow.

Dad knocked a few more times. "Rayne Bennett, if you're not out of bed in five minutes, I won't let you swim in the meet tomorrow!"

I muttered something incomprehensible, but tossed off my covers nonetheless and forced myself to get moving. After swinging my legs over the side of my bed, I plodded over to my closet and yanked down some clothes. Fifteen minutes later, after going through the compulsory routine of getting ready for school, I dragged myself into the kitchen for breakfast.

"There's my sleeping beauty," Dad teased. Using his coffee mug, he gestured to the backpack slung around my shoulders. "You won't be needing that today."

"Huh?"

"Here. Eat up. It's going to be a long day."

I stared blankly at the plate Dad slid onto the table. Some scrambled eggs and a few strips of bacon stared back at me. I blinked. "What's going on?"

"I already called Newland High. You're excused for today on account of important family business."

It took a few seconds for the weight of his words to finally sink in. "You mean...I'm not going to school?"

Dad nodded.

"Then why did you wake me up? I could've slept in for once!"

"Ah, but we're going somewhere." A determined look sharpened Dad's face as he spoke. "We're leaving in ten minutes. I would bring a warm jacket and a book if I were you."

"But I don't want to read—"

"Well, you better bring something to do, because it's going to be a long drive." He wiggled his eyebrows at me before disappearing around the corner and into the garage.

I stared uncomprehendingly at my eggs and bacon until the pieces slowly started to fit together. "So we're going to Shady Cove," I told my breakfast. "Well, that certainly came out of the blue. I wonder why Dad is so gung-ho about this moving business."

When the food on my plate didn't reply, I sighed and picked up a strip of bacon. The warm, crispy texture melted in my mouth immediately. As I chewed, I wondered which was worse: missing a day of practice for the swim meet tomorrow, or taking a trip to my birthplace and being confronted with memories of her.

Oh well. Either way, it was sure to be interesting.

"Oh yeah! Life—goes—on!"

Dad and I belted the lyrics to a John Mellencamp song as we rocketed down the highway. Even though the air was biting cold outside, both of our windows had been rolled down, causing my long black hair to whip around my face. We were all laughs and smiles. Dad had finally brought me over to his side, and I was content with ditching school to go on a little adventure.

Three-quarters of the way to Shady Cove, however, my good spirits plunged. It was as if the stormy skies overhead were clouding my feelings, reminding me of my old home—and of her.

"How much longer?" I groaned long after our sporadic singing session was over. I leaned back and stretched out my legs with a yawn.

"We've been driving for a little over an hour and a half," Dad replied, checking his wristwatch. "The town should be popping up here in a few minutes."

I nodded and fixed my gaze on the lush landscape rushing by our window. The more I stared at the rolling green fields and tall, majestic trees, the more it seemed I was entering familiar territory. But along with the scenic countryside came gloomy thoughts. What did our old house look like? It had been thirteen years—a lot could happen in over a decade. I couldn't even remember whom Dad had sold the house to when we moved. But then again, I had only been two. I didn't exactly remember much about my birthplace, only a combination of fragmented memories and secondhand stories.

"Here we are," Dad said softly, pulling off the highway and onto a small dirt road.

"But Shady Cove is a mile that way," I protested, pointing to a sign with bold white lettering.

"Downtown Shady Cove is that way," Dad explained. He pointed up the winding dirt road. "But our house is this way."

I swallowed. Our house. Was it really our house? Was Dad that positive we were going to buy it? But it seemed so far away from everything...no neighbors, no school, no friends. This couldn't be happening.

But the decision wasn't final. I was probably getting ahead of myself. What on earth could possibly possess my dad to make such an irrational decision as to move back to our old house in the middle of nowhere, anyway? It was a crazy idea.

We drove slowly over the thousands of tiny dips and potholes for another half-mile. After what seemed like forever, it finally came into view. The house emerged as a rustic mansion looming over the outlying fields beyond, surrounded on all sides by huge pine trees. A small garden fringed the paved walkway to the front door. All in all, the house looked bigger, much bigger, than I had remembered. It was nothing like the small home Dad and I lived in now. But due to its location and age, I had to admit the mortgage on this house was significantly less.

Dad pulled up next a faded Sedan parked in the driveway. As soon as I set foot on the smooth pavement, a raindrop landed right on my nose. I glanced up at the sky, which billowed with gray storm clouds.

"Looks like it might thunderstorm," Dad observed.

I quietly joined him in the trek to the front door. Everything about this place was big—and slightly intimidating. As if reading my thoughts, Dad slipped his arm around my shoulder, pulling me closer to him. He knocked gingerly on the wooden front door, which gave off a lonesome, hollow sound that echoed sadly.

A few moments later, the door creaked open. A short, frizzy, white-haired lady stood frowning up at us through the pair of pointy spectacles balanced on her nose. "Well?" she snapped in a surprisingly sharp tone.

"Mrs. Barnes! How lovely to see you. I'm Clark Bennett, and this is my daughter, Rayne," Dad replied without missing a beat. He reached out his arm, a dazzling smile on his face, and the poor old lady had no option but to shake his hand and smile in return.

"Oh, forgive me. I forgot all about your phone call last night. Do come in, Mr. Bennett," Mrs. Barnes said in a much friendlier tone. Then she took a good look at me. "And you too, Rayne—my, have you grown since the last time I saw you!"

Dad and Mrs. Barnes made small talk as we sat down on a stiff couch in the living room. The walls were quite drab, with great curtains covering the windows and blocking any sunlight from entering. The flickering candles on the table in the middle of the room weren't helping, either.

"I still go on two walks, one in the morning and one in the afternoon," Mrs. Barnes was saying in her shrill voice. "The view is so lovely from on top of the bluff! But my old bones can't handle the trails as well as they used to, you know."

Dad made a sympathetic comment and nodded.

"I'm gonna get some fresh air," I whispered to him, then bolted before he could say another word. My Converse made a thudding sound on the wooden floor as I sped out of the room. Just as I rounded the corner to the front door, I spotted something out of the corner of my eye.

It was a staircase—a long, winding staircase with a silver railing and forest-green carpeting on the steps. I stood there for a moment, transfixed by my odd discovery. Something tugged at the corners of my mind. The scene was triggering a memory—a long-forgotten, long-buried memory.

Before I knew it, I was standing at the bottom of the staircase looking up. It seemed to go on forever, reaching unseen heights with its sleek silver railing and broad steps. Fascinated, I slowly began to climb the stairs, my eyes wide open in wonder.

There were three storeys. I passed the first two, not really knowing why I was being pulled to the uppermost floor. But as soon as I set foot in the hall, something felt right. I had a feeling that I knew where I was. Trailing my hand along the wall, I walked to the first door on the right and twisted the knob.

I felt like the wind had suddenly been knocked out of me. The open door revealed a large, bright room with turquoise wallpaper and a pristine white desk off to one side. I was surprised that there wasn't a small white bed to match, or a little white table perfect for having a tea party. Where had my furniture gone?

My stomach twisted. My furniture. I turned and glanced out the window, which beheld a stunning view of the ocean. My bedroom. Then I stepped inside and took a good look at every inch of the room, starting with the pint-sized desk perfect for a toddler, all the way to the walk-in closet that seemed a little small for me, but large enough for a two-year-old.

My house. The thought took my breath away. But as my gaze landed on a single picture still hanging on the wall, all fascination ceased. It was like someone had punched me in the gut.

The picture showed a bright-eyed, smiling little girl with long black tresses. She was looking up at a woman with the same eyes and beautiful hair, which could only be her mother. My mother. Her lips were parted in a flawless smile, showing off her white teeth that complemented her tan complexion. She was perfect.

Was it really her?

I backed away slowly, my hand fumbling for the doorknob behind me. As soon as I felt it, I bolted out of the room and slammed the door closed, my heart suddenly pounding wildly in my chest. I darted back down the stairs, all the way to the bottom floor, where Dad and Mrs. Barnes were still chatting pleasantly.

"Rayne! Where have you been? I thought you were outside getting some fresh air," Dad said, a slight warning tone in his voice.

"I—well—I wasn't—"

"Oh, let the girl explore," Mrs. Barnes said with a wave of her hand. "It's been—how long now?"

Dad told her.

"Right, yes—thirteen years since she's last seen the house! You can hardly blame her for wanting to look around."

Dad scratched the back of his neck and forced a smile, but said nothing. When our eyes met, I could tell he was searching for an answer as to why I looked like I had just seen a ghost.

"Um...Mrs. Barnes, could I get a glass of water?" I asked uncertainly, hoping my voice didn't waver. I breathed a sigh of relief when the elderly lady nodded and shuffled into the kitchen. Peeking around the corner, I was surprised to see a modern-looking refrigerator, stove, sink, and cupboards. Apparently the mansion wasn't all gloom and cobwebs.

I tried to not let my mind wander as I sipped my drink. Pushing all thoughts of her out of my head, I drained the rest of my glass and headed back into the living room, where Dad and Mrs. Barnes were shaking hands yet again.

"It was a pleasure seeing you after all these years," Dad was saying. "I'm sorry to hear that you're moving. I know you love it here in Shady Cove."

"Oh, yes, but the house is much too big for a little old lady such as myself! Especially after my husband died..." She grew quiet. "It's just that I can't see myself living here much longer. I've already picked out a nice apartment in the city next to my daughter."

"Good. And I'm sorry about your husband," Dad said sincerely. He cleared his throat when he saw that I had entered the room. "Well, it's time to go, Rayne. I thought we'd have a look around Shady Cove for a bit. Does that sound fun?"

Though walking around a freezing ghost town wasn't exactly my idea of fun, I nodded nonetheless. "Bye, Mrs. Barnes," I said.

To my surprise, the kind woman wrapped me in a large hug. Her frail arms were much stronger than I thought. "Goodbye, dear. I hope you and your father decide to come back to Shady Cove. This house needs some proper owners!"

Dad and I smiled and headed out the door. Several raindrops pelted us as soon as we set foot on the walkway. We both flung our hoods over our heads, then waved goodbye to Mrs. Barnes, who was still standing under the dry safety of her doorway. With raindrops streaking from the sky even faster, we hurried over to our car without a second glance at the house.

Dad eased back onto the dirt road and headed in the direction of the highway. I forced myself not to look at our old house in the side mirror. My heart was still beating rapidly from my little adventure on the third storey.

"So what do you think?"

Dad's question caught me off guard. "What do I think?" I echoed. "Can we not move into that creepy old house? It gives me the willies."

Now it was his turn to be surprised. "Rayne, you grew up there. That's our house."

"But it's not," I argued. "It belongs to Mrs. Barnes—I mean, to whoever the new owner happens to be, which is not us."

Dad heaved a little sigh. "I'm sorry, honey," he said delicately. "I thought you might be excited to see our old place. I'll admit I was a bit hesitant at first too, but Mrs. Barnes has kept the place in great condition—even if she does like to do things the old-fashioned way."

I turned my head and glanced out the window. The rain was pouring down hard now, creating mud puddles in the ruts and potholes in the road.

"Does it bother you that much?" Dad asked softly. "Are you really so against moving back in?"

I didn't reply right away. Instead, I let my thoughts churn for a few moments. "I never expected we would leave our life in Newland," I said tersely. "And I never expected that we would move into some old country house in the middle of nowhere, either."

Dad was silent, but I could tell he was tense because of the way his hands gripped the steering wheel. I sighed and reached for my phone, unwinding its earphones before stuffing the buds in my ears. Then I cranked up the volume as loud as I could stand it. As I simmered silently in my seat, I gradually came to realize that I wasn't mad at Dad. I wasn't mad that he had driven us out to Shady Cove to look at our house. I wasn't even mad at the fact that I had missed a valuable training session for the swim meet tomorrow.

I was mad at myself. I was the one who had wandered up the staircase and entered my old bedroom, who had stared at the fatal picture, and who experienced an emotional breakdown. It was entirely my fault—all of it. But no matter how hard I tried, I couldn't shake the memory of her, infinitesimal though it was. For the first time in my life, I actually admitted that I missed her.

I missed Mom.

3

CHAPTER 3

"So where were you yesterday?" Kimmie asked as soon as I slipped into the women's locker room.

"Oh, nowhere," I replied vaguely.

Kimmie raised her eyebrows.

"Well..." I shimmied out of my clothing to reveal my sleek racing suit underneath. "Actually, my dad took me on a short trip."

"Really? I wish my parents would do that," she said wistfully. "Where did he take you?"

"Oh, you know, for a drive in the countryside. Nothing special." I grabbed my swim cap and goggles, wondering if I should tell her the rest of the news. But no—that would only cause unnecessary drama before our meet, and I couldn't do that to Kimmie. Besides, how likely was it that Dad and I were going to move all the way out to Shady Cove? I didn't want to stir up any false anxiety.

Despite justifying my explanation in my mind, it still felt wrong leaving out the details. Kimmie and I had been best friends since we were in elementary school, and we usually shared everything with each other. I winced and was about to change the subject when Kimmie spoke again.

"I still can't believe you missed an entire school day just for a drive in the country. I mean," she clarified, "I'd rather be anywhere else than at school flipping through textbooks, but why did your dad take you out of school yesterday, of all days? Coach was surprised that his star swimmer actually missed a day of practice. It's unheard of."

"Yeah," I murmured, my thoughts elsewhere. I remembered how Dad and I had driven through Shady Cove, glancing at the quaint little beach shops and watching the gray-blue water seawater hurl itself against the base of the Redrock Cliffs. Long, winding trails snaked down the bluffs to the benign cove where the town had got its name.

The "shady cove" actually was quite shady, as it was situated partly underneath an outcropping of cliff. Looking back, I realized no one had been splashing in the water or lounging on beach towels—the stormy weather had driven everyone indoors.

After observing the cove and the vast enormity of Redrock Cliffs, Dad and I had grabbed a snack at the Shady Cove Café. We had sipped hot chocolate and nibbled on cookies as the storm outside gradually worsened...

"Rayne?" Kimmie's voice shattered me out of my thoughts. "What's wrong—are you nervous about the meet?"

I shook myself out of my reverie. "No, I'm fine. I was just thinking."

Kimmie gave me a worried look before looping her arm through mine. "You're going to do great, as always," she reassured me. "Nobody can beat the lightning-fast Rayne Bennett!"

I forced myself to smile as Kimmie paraded us out the door and into the bright sunlight. The storm clouds had passed overnight, leaving everything smelling fresh and clean. It was a beautiful day for swimming, and as soon as my eyes landed on the sparkling blue water in the pool, my mind immediately kicked into racing mode. I was eager to jump in and get moving, to feel the cool wader gliding past my limbs, to reach out and stroke—

"Good morning, Rayne!"

I turned and saw Coach Davey striding towards me. "'Morning," I greeted.

"Hey, where were you yesterday?" he asked casually. "I was surprised when you didn't show for practice."

"My dad called the school. We had some family business to take care of."

Kimmie grinned, as if to say, Yeah right. 'Family business.'

If only she knew. Fortunately, Coach didn't catch the look of skepticism on Kimmie's face. "Well, I'm just glad you're here and ready to race," he continued. "You two can go on ahead and hop in the pool. Start warming up with your teammates. We have some tough races ahead of us!"

"We do?" Kimmie asked, her smile fading.

Coach nodded. "Don't worry. I have full confidence in you girls."

Kimmie smacked her palm against her forehead. "Oh, man, I forgot we're up against Shady Cove today!"

"Yes, and they have a good swim team this year..."

But I didn't hear the rest of his sentence. How could I have forgotten that I was racing against Shady Cove, of all schools, in today's meet? I swallowed apprehensively. "Come on," I muttered as Kimmie and I headed towards the pool. "It's no big deal."

But as I slid into the far lane to warm up with, I realized it was a big deal. That place had stirred up memories that would have otherwise lain dormant. Just remembering the picture hanging in my old bedroom made my blood run cold. I was petrified. No matter how many times I told myself to snap out of it, I just couldn't. Kimmie gave me another worried look, so I forced myself to smile. "I'm fine," I urged. "Don't worry about me."

"Are you sure? Because you seem a little jittery today."

I just waved her on. Kimmie sighed and pushed off the wall, automatically launching into freestyle. I waited a few seconds before following her, ducking my head underwater and using my legs to push off the wall. I closed my eyes and let the feeling of gliding through water take over. It felt so good, and before long all thoughts of Shady Cove and my old house vanished. After completing my final warm-up lap and pulling myself out of the pool, I let out a deep breath and smiled. It was time to race.

Kimmie and I waited with our other teammates by the side of the pool as the announcer called heat after heat. Finally it was time for the girls' 400 IM—an individual medley composed of swimming butterfly, backstroke, breaststroke, and finishing with freestyle. When the announcer called the names for Heat 1, my entire swim team cheered when they heard, "Rayne Bennett, lane 4."

I grinned and pulled my goggles down over my eyes. After adjusting my swim cap, I stepped up to the starting block in front of lane 4, my gaze fixated on the sparkling water below. Though I was always a tad nervous before racing, I was also pumped up with adrenaline. Swimming was my sport. As my gaze flickered over to my opponents, sizing them up, I told myself I could beat them—and beat them hard. This was my race, and I was going to win.

The referee blew a series of short whistles, followed by one long whistle. I stepped onto the starting block with my right foot forward, left foot back. I was ready.

"Take your marks."

I bent over and gripped the starting block with both hands. Letting out a deep breath, I narrowed my eyes and focused on the shifting turquoise water below. Let's do this.

The buzzer sounded. In a flash my arms extended and my legs thrust me from the starting block. I entered the water in a flawless dive and immediately began dolphin kicking. As soon as I glided near the surface of the water, my arms launched themselves into butterfly stroke. With each powerful pull I surged forward. Upon reaching the wall, I touched it with both hands before twisting my body around and pushing off in the opposite direction.

Now it was time for backstroke. I flew through backstroke and then breaststroke, my entire body focused on one thing—swimming. With each kick, my hunger for winning mounted. By the time I pushed off the wall and was sprinting to the finish, my muscles were fatigued from exertion and my lungs were screaming for air. But I pushed myself to go faster, never once slowing down until my hand slapped the wall and I jerked my head above the water.

"And in first place we have the swimmer in lane 4, Rayne Bennett!"

As soon as I heard the announcer's voice, a huge smile lit up my face. I'd done it—I'd won! I slapped the water with excitement and pulled myself out of the pool.

"Congrats, Rayne!" Kimmie smiled and wrapped her arms around me. "You'll never guess how much you beat the swimmer in second place by!"

"I don't know. What?" Still grinning, I turned and glanced at the scoreboard. My jaw immediately dropped open. The times of all six swimmers were flashing in red numbers. It was unbelievable.

"Five seconds?" I asked dumbly. "Wait, is that for real?"

"You better believe it!" Kimmie squealed.

I rubbed my eyes and gawked at the scoreboard. My time was astonishingly fast—but so fast that I had beaten the second-place swimmer by five seconds? I felt a wave of pride surge within me. That just had to be good enough to qualify for the Junior Olympics!

Coach Davey, who had been standing only a few paces away, reached over to give me a hive-five. "That was phenomenal," he boomed. "You just blew the socks off every person on the pool deck!"

I laughed and shook my head. "I don't even believe it myself," I said truthfully. A shiver of delight ran down my spine. It was almost too good to be true. And yet when I glanced back up at the scoreboard, it was indisputable. Numbers didn't lie. I had never swam faster in my life.

"Amazing job, honey," a familiar voice called.

I whirled around, and a smile immediately lit up my face when I saw who it was. "Dad!"

Despite my being soaked and shivering, Dad wrapped me in an enormous bear hug. "That was your best time by far," he said. "How did you swim so fast?"

"I don't know," I laughed. "But it felt good!"

Dad pulled away and looked me in the eyes. "Rayne, can we talk for a moment?" he asked, his voice dropping an octave.

I glanced over my shoulder at Coach, Kimmie, and the rest of my swim team. "I'll be right back," I told them.

Dad pulled me aside to a quiet corner of the pool deck. His eyes were glowing with excitement. "I don't know how you pulled that off, Rayne, but it was unbelievable." He gave a low whistle. "The

Coach from Shady Cove High even walked up to me with a word of congratulations."

"What? He did?"

"He sure did! Isn't that great?"

I felt sick to my stomach. "Dad..."

"After telling him that we were moving to Shady Cove, he said he would personally ensure that you try out for the Junior Olympics. He really wants you on the Shady Cove swim team, and if you decide to join, he'll do everything he can to help you pursue your swimming dreams. Isn't that great?"

Great? Didn't he understand? I sighed and stared down at my bare feet, watching the endless water droplets trickling down my legs.

And then it hit me. "Wait," I said; "so we are moving back to Shady Cove?"

Dad realized his mistake. "Well...yes. You see, I bought the house."

My heart plummeted. So it was final—we were moving. And Dad taken the liberty of purchasing our old home without consulting me first.

He must have seen the outrage plastered on my face, because he quickly added, "Rayne, honey, I thought you would be excited at the possibility of moving back! And just wait until you meet the new swim coach."

I shook my head. "Not now, Dad. I don't want move there. We left all that behind when we moved here." I angrily blinked away a few tears. "And I like it here, Dad. Newland is a great city. Why can't we just find a smaller home or apartment in Newland? Why do we have to move back to that dumb old house in the middle of nowhere? Why do we have to be reminded of—of—" My hands, which had started gesturing wildly during my little rant, fell limply to my sides. "Never mind. You don't even listen to me anyway."

I was about to turn away when Dad said sharply, "Rayne. Please, just hear me out, okay? I know you're still a little unsure of how to handle this whole moving business, but I also know that nothing makes you happier than swimming. Is that right?"

I nodded mutely.

"This coach is willing to work with you and help you achieve your goal of going to the Junior Olympics. He's trained other athletes, students like yourself who have always dreamed of competing at an elite level, and they've made it. They swam in the Junior Olympics and won medals. So this coach obviously knows what he's talking about, and he sees something in you, Rayne. He sees a phenomenal athlete with the potential for a great future."

Though I was loath to admit it, his words rang true. The thought of being coached by someone who had trained future professionals was appealing.

"But there's a problem," I argued. "We're not moving back to Shady Cove. We can't."

"Is this because of your mother?"

I closed my eyes. "Yes," I admitted, "it is because of her. I don't want to move back our old house simply because you want to relive those memories. They're in the past, and they should stay in the past."

"You can't keep on shoving her away, Rayne," Dad said softly. "She is more a part of you than you realize. Sometimes we have to face those memories instead of pushing them into the darkest corners of our minds."

I knew he was right. But I had tried for so long to forget about her because all it brought was pain. I didn't want to remember her, but I also ached for that motherly role at the same time. It was too much to handle. "Look, Dad," I pleaded, "can we just talk about this later?"

He nodded reluctantly and gave me one more hug. "I'm proud of you, Rayne," he murmured into my ear. "Go enjoy your moment of victory."

I pursed my lips. Moment of victory? Because of him, that moment was lost. I couldn't get the thought of moving out of my head. With a sigh, I peeled off my swim cap and headed back over to Kimmie and the rest of my swim team.

$$4$$

— ◆ —

CHAPTER 4

Try as I might, finding a new house or apartment that was affordable and close to Newland High was next to impossible. Dad joined me in the search, but I could tell his heart wasn't in it. One night, after hours of poring over potential homes, he glanced up at me from his computer with tired eyes and said, "I think we've hit a dead end."

We sure had. I didn't want to call it quits, but there was no other option. Even though Kimmie knew something was up, I couldn't bear to tell her. I was still in denial myself. But every time I passed Dad in his office and saw him fingering a faded old photograph of the mansion in Shady Cove, I knew the truth was inevitable.

I finally told Kimmie one fateful morning, the day after Dad made his final decision to move. It was a heartbreaking day for the two of us. Kimmie cried with me for hours, flicked through old photos and videos of us together, and attempted to give me a pep talk but only succeeded in bringing more tears to my eyes.

Now, one week later, I lay in my bed and tried closing my eyes for the hundredth time that evening. Yet after a few futile seconds of attempting to go to sleep, I groaned and gave up. It had been a long and weary month of looking for a new home, and ever since Dad had officially declared we were moving to Shady Cove, I had been plagued with long, sleepless nights.

Throwing my blankets off, I sat up in bed and let out a deep sigh. It was one in the morning, and my eyes had long since grown used to the darkness of my near-empty room. Only the bare essentials—including my mattress, pillow, blankets, and a few clothes—were left. Everything else had been packed into boxes and moved to Shady Cove.

"It's not fair," I muttered to the emptiness around me. I didn't want to be a downer, but the weight of having to move away from everything I'd ever known was crushing me. Depression had settled on me like a black cloud. I would never again walk the halls of Newland High, dive into the pool next to Kimmie, visit the local coffee shops and movie theater, or take my usual stroll home from school. I was entering a new chapter in my life, one that seemed both frightening and lonely. And I didn't want to turn the page.

As I hugged my knees to my chest, my long ebony locks fell over my face like a glittering sheen, protecting me from the desolation of my deserted room. Just then, a shaft of moonlight pierced my window, illuminating my surroundings for a fraction of a second. A ghost of a smile appeared on my lips as my hair suddenly began to glow, faintly at first and then stronger. Deep ocean-blue streaks intertwined with the midnight ebony of my hair, creating a sort of uncanny luminescence. I ran my fingers through my shimmering hair and smiled wider.

I had discovered this remarkable characteristic when I was a young girl. I had been camping in the backyard with my dad during a sultry summer evening, and when I had stepped outside the tent to look at the stars, I'd realized my hair was glowing. I'd always had long, black hair, even as a toddler, but never knew it glowed blue when exposed to moonlight. It was breathtaking, to say the least, and from that moment on I knew there had to be some connection. Dad's hair didn't glow in the moonlight, so I must have received the trait from her—and for that reason I felt like she was more a part of me.

I reached over for my cell phone to check the time—1:30 a.m. I was about to set it back down when I suddenly caught a glimpse of my reflection in the screen. With a gasp, I tilted the device ever so slightly so I could get a good look at my face.

"My eyes," I whispered into the darkness. They were glowing—there was no other word to describe it.

I didn't know whether to be excited, anxious, or horrified. After a few seconds of studying my reflection, I realized that my eyes were glowing the exact same color as the streaks in my hair—a deep sea blue.

"Amazing," I breathed. Here was yet another unique gift, one that I could only have inherited from my mother! I blinked and rubbed my eyes a few times, then glanced back at my phone. They were still glowing. I had a sudden desire to text Kimmie, but with a pang of guilt, I realized I could never let her in on such a weird and fascinating secret.

Kimmie...Oh, no, tomorrow was the big day—the day I had to say goodbye to all my teachers and friends. It was going to be rough for Kimmie and I. And afterwards, on Saturday morning, Dad and I were leaving for Shady Cove at the break of dawn.

I sighed and glanced out my window at the milky-white moon. My stomach twisted into a tight knot as I realized the peculiar dilemma I was in. I desperately wanted to tell Kimmie about my glowing powers, but now I was being ripped away from her in less than forty-eight hours. I was still puzzled as to why I had never come across anyone else with my powers, including Dad. Even though he knew about my hair, he had instructed me to never, ever tell anyone else. I knew the reason why: I would be labeled a freak.

"Maybe I am a freak," I muttered. As soon as I spoke those words, a light breeze tousled the leaves of the apple tree outside my window, and the ray of moonlight disappeared. The beautiful blue streaks in my hair vanished just as quickly as they had appeared, leaving my tan fingers stroking plain black locks once more.

I hugged my knees tighter against my chest. With a sigh, I wondered how in the world I would survive tomorrow—and then Saturday, the big moving day. A lone tear trickled down my cheek. My life was crumbling, falling through my hands, like millions of grains of sand. And I hated it.

Friday passed with an ill combination of dread and sadness. I went through the motions of going to all my normal classes, and yet it felt anything but normal. My teachers all regarded me with sad expressions, saying, "We're sorry to see you go," and "We'll miss you." A few of my classmates walked up and gave me cookies and brownies. The last period of the day—swim—was by far the worst. Coach didn't make anyone work out or swim laps—instead, my teammates threw a mini-party out on the pool deck, complete with balloons and cupcakes and streamers. I was touched, especially when I spotted Kimmie quietly wiping a few tears off her cheeks when the dismissal bell rang. Coach and I had a bittersweet conversation towards the end of the party, but when I spotted Kimmie sniffling near the entrance to the locker room, I politely excused myself.

My heart went out to my friend. "Hey," I said quietly as soon as she was within earshot.

"Hey." She gave me a sad smile. "So I guess this is the last time we'll stand on this pool deck together, right?" A wry laugh escaped her lips.

"No, of course not, Kimmie. We'll see each other at least once a week—I made Dad promise me that much. And I'll call you every single day to catch up with you and see how things are going. Plus, we can even write letters, just for fun."

Kimmie sniffled again before reaching over and giving me a big hug. "Okay. But it's still hard to believe that you're moving, even after all we've been through together."

"Yeah." I felt some tears of my own pricking at the corners of my eyes. "So...how about coming over to my house right now? We could hang out one last time, since Dad and I are leaving early tomorrow morning and all..."

"Of course! I'd love to, Rayne." Kimmie smiled and wiped another tear away. "Sorry I'm such a crybaby. It's not like you're moving all the way across the continent or anything."

"Don't worry. This is really hard for me too," I said truthfully. With one last mournful look at the Newland High pool, Kimmie and I strode off the pool deck and down the breezeway. We walked arm-in-arm across the browned football field, my worn Converse crunching over the leaves. That's when I knew I would miss Kimmie deeply. She had been my first and only best friend, and now I wouldn't wake up in anticipation of seeing her smiling face at school. I wouldn't have someone to laugh over stupid things and share lunch with. I wouldn't have a swim partner who knew everything about me, from my favorite stroke to my dreams for the future.

"I'll miss you, Kimmie," I said as we sat on my front porch a few hours later, watching the watercolor sunset. "Even though I'll see you next weekend, I'm still going to miss you terribly."

"Me too." A somber look crossed Kimmie's face before she suddenly jabbed me in the stomach. "But you better not find a new best friend to take my place!"

I laughed. "No way—and the same goes for you!"

Kimmie and I laughed and laughed until our stomachs hurt. It felt good to just be sitting here, watching the beautiful sunset. "You know I would never let anyone take your place," she said honestly. "Remember the pact we made in fourth grade?"

"You mean the one where signed in ketchup because neither of us wanted to prick our fingers and sign in blood?"

"Yeah, that one." Kimmie and I shared a secret smile before both of us said aloud, "Rayne and Kimmie—best friends forever."

My heart was heavy when I finally said goodnight to her. The sunset was long gone and Dad was finishing up some last-minute packing as I ambled to my room. My steps felt like lead, and my shoulders were weighed down by a burden I didn't want to bear.

"So long, Newland," I murmured.

The next morning I awoke to what sounded like a saber-toothed tiger scraping its claws across my bedroom door. My eyes immediately flew open. "What in the world?" I muttered. When the hideous noise continued after a few more seconds, I threw off my blankets and staggered over to the door. Flinging it open, I realized it was only Dad dragging a ridiculously huge box down the hallway.

"Oh! Rayne, you're up!" he exclaimed. "Good, we should leave in about thirty minutes."

I rubbed my eyes, hoping that by the time I glanced back up Dad would be gone and this would all be some sort of dream. But it was real, and Dad was still standing there with a goofy grin on his face. I groaned. "Are you serious?"

Dad cheerfully ignored the aggravated tone to my voice and continued to pull the box across the floor. I winced and covered my ears at the awful sound. How could this day get any worse?

As I would soon find out, though, today would get a lot worse. Not only was I running on a mere three hours of sleep, but I put my sweatshirt on backwards and spent two minutes trying to shove my left foot into my right shoe. Then Dad happened to burn my waffles and spill my orange juice all over my lap. By the time we finally got into the car, the box on the top of the pile in the backseat slid off, causing my laptop to fall out and get chipped against the door.

It was safe to say today officially sucked. I dragged myself into the front seat of the car and sulked the entire drive to Shady Cove, not even bothering to stretch my legs when they started to cramp from two hours of sitting. I didn't lift my eyes to watch the last trails of the sunrise, either, even after Dad remarked that it was the best sunrise he'd ever seen.

If he was trying to cheer me up, it wasn't working. Not even the anticipation of new adventures, new friends, and a brand-new start could excite me. In fact, it did just the opposite—it filled me with dread.

"Come on, Rayne," Dad urged. "Admit it—you're excited we're moving back home!"

I pursed my lips. Home was back in Newland. Shady Cove, on the other hand, was a nightmare of memories.

Yet it was nearly impossible to miss the glowing excitement on Dad's face when we finally pulled up to our castle of a house. "We're here!" he exclaimed, leaping out of the car and gazing at the house as if it were packed full of hundred-dollar bills. He pulled out a key from his jeans pocket, jogged across the lawn, and unlocked the front door. "Tada!" he yelled, loud enough for me to hear from where I was still seated in the car.

Dad grinned at me, obviously expecting a smile in return. I merely frowned. "Oh, come on, honey. Look alive!" he said, walking back to unload the car. "Come help me unpack, and then you can see which room I've picked out for you."

My heart started racing after he said that. I had the horrible feeling that he had picked the room—my old bedroom. The one with the picture. The one with the memories that were so raw, they nearly tore my heart in two. I couldn't go back in there.

Fortunately, my new bedroom was completely different from the one I had wandered into when Mrs. Barnes still lived here. Dad proudly led me into a beautiful, spacious bedroom on the second floor. He had spent hours renting U-Haul trailers and moving all our stuff into the house over the past week, so I wasn't surprised to see a pile of boxes already in one corner. But the picturesque furnishings tore my gaze away from my meager belongings, making my jaw drop open in shock. My new bedroom was complete with turquoise curtains and a matching bedspread, along with a roomy walk-in closet and my own bathroom. Dad said it was the second-largest of the four bedrooms in the house, with his being the biggest.

"Why don't you start unpacking your things?" he suggested. "Just holler if you need some help moving the furniture."

"Alright." I plopped down on my new bed. The bedroom was nice, for sure. Okay, so maybe that was an understatement. The bedroom was awesome. But a part of me still yearned to be back in our cozy one-storey house in Newland.

I pursed my lips and traced the design on my bedspread with a finger. After sitting in silence for a few minutes, letting everything soak in, I slowly got up and started rummaging through some boxes. I pulled out a few articles of clothing and a couple pairs of shoes before stopping. I wasn't really motivated to start unpacking.

At that moment, I desperately wanted to be anywhere but here. I turned and glanced out the window as the sound of a faint roar reached my ears. I had no clue what the roar could be, so I leaned out the window and glanced right and left, wondering where it was coming from. That's when I realized it wasn't nearby; it was below.

It was the ocean. The faint roar was the sound of waves crashing against the base of the cliffs. Though this house wasn't built on the very edge of the Redrock Cliffs, it was close enough that one could easily hear the pounding waves on a stormy day. There must have been a powerful swell causing the large waves to hurl themselves against the rocks.

I had the sudden urge to walk over to the edge of the cliffs and see the ocean up close. The feeling was so strong that I immediately turned around and walked straight out of my bedroom. It wasn't until I was outside the house that I realized what I was doing—and by then it was too late. As Dad appeared from behind the car, cradling a large box in his arms, his expression brightened when he saw me.

"Hi honey. Need some help unpacking?"

"No," I said quickly. "I'm just...just...going for a walk, I guess."

Dad's eyes lit up at the mention of a walk. "Hey, that's a great idea," he said. "Have fun, and make sure you stick to the trails. Be careful."

I shoved my hands into my sweatshirt pocket, meandered over to the side of our yard, and began following a little goat trail that wound towards the edge of the cliffs. Before long, the scraggly grass and bushes gave way to rocky ground and ugly weeds. Then the trail took a sharp turn and began to dip down, allowing me a partial view of the ocean below.

"Whoa," I breathed. Maybe going for a walk was a better idea than I'd thought. Standing on the tip of Redrock Cliffs gave me a beautiful overlook of the horizon, the broad rugged bluff, and the vast expanse of the sea. I felt another tug on my heart and continued walking, making sure to keep one hand on the makeshift railing as I made my way down the hairpin trail.

After twenty minutes of huffing and puffing, I finally reached the bottom. The trail ended with a flight of steps painstakingly cut out of the cliffs before opening out to a breathtaking view of the beach. It was smaller and somehow more picturesque than Shady Cove—maybe because it appeared to be virtually untouched by humans. Only the swishing tides and raging storms could reach this protected area of the beach. Surrounded by the cliffs on three sides and the ocean on the other, the little cove was like some sort of private beach. Maybe Dad and I owned this beach—who knew? After all, we had our own trail leading straight to it. How cool would that be?

I slipped out of my shoes and socks and buried my toes in the warm sand. A salty gust of wind whipped my hair around my face. I realized for the first time since I had arrived in Shady Cove, I was smiling. There was just something about this place—something so rugged and remote and unique—that it warmed my heart and made me feel more alive than ever.

I walked across the golden sand dunes to the water's edge, silently watching the surge of the tide and the crashing waves only yards away. The foaming crests of the waves seemed huge as they swelled to nearly ten feet in height. They slammed down onto the surface of the water with a deafening roar that should have scared me to death, but for some reason didn't. If anything, I felt invigorated by watching the shifting ocean, which seemed more alive and potent than I had realized. Despite the huge waves and the churning waters, I had the sudden urge to dive in and experience what it felt like to glide underwater. Something told me it would feel different than merely stroking across a swimming pool.

But I stopped myself. The skies overhead were darkening with the threat of another storm. A distant rumble of thunder raised goosebumps on my arms, so I hurried back to my shoes and slipped them on before making the long uphill trek to the house. My little ocean swim would have to wait for another day.

5

CHAPTER 5

Unfortunately, I didn't get the chance to go swimming for the rest of the weekend. A fierce storm hit Shady Cove, pelting the small town with rain and rumblings of thunder. The ocean swirled and boiled like a giant foaming whirlpool. I spent most of my time indoors unpacking and watching raindrops skid down my window. The exhilarating feeling that the ocean had given me slowly dissipated until it was only a faint memory in the shadows of my mind.

I didn't even realize I had to go to school until Monday morning rolled around. I moseyed into the kitchen to find that Dad had made me a steaming plate of pancakes and sausage. "Here's a big breakfast for your big day at school!" he announced.

It took me a few seconds to process what he had said. "Huh?"

"It's your first day at Shady Cove High, remember?"

My eyes grew wide. "High school? Today?" I had completely forgotten.

Dad's smile vanished. "I'm sorry, Rayne, but you have to go. You can always finish unpacking after school."

"No, it's not that." I sighed and glanced down at my bare feet, which were slightly covered by my trailing pajama bottoms. "I just don't want to go." It would be like walking into a room full of strangers. I wouldn't know anybody, and they wouldn't know me. There would be no Kimmie to say hi and laugh with while eating lunch. There would be no one to mess around with on the pool deck or in the locker room. I would be all alone.

Of course, I didn't dare speak my thoughts aloud to Dad. But they drifted across the forefront of my mind nonetheless. For the next ten minutes I pushed my pancakes and sausage around my plate absentmindedly until I was bored. Might as well face the inevitable, I thought grimly, heading back upstairs to get dressed. I wasn't exactly a "fashionable" person—my usual clothes consisted of jeans, a T-shirt, and my trusty Converse. So I dressed quickly and did my hair up in a sloppy bun, then stuffed my swim cap, goggles, and racing suit into my backpack with my other school items. Dad was already in the car by the time I walked out the front door.

"I don't start work until tomorrow," he said as I slid into the passenger seat. "So when we get to the school, I'll walk you to the office and help you get situated."

"Okay." My stomach was queasy with anticipation the entire drive to Shady Cove High. The school was only a few miles from our house, so Dad said tomorrow I would have to start riding my bike because he had to work. I wasn't exactly looking forward to bumping my way down a pothole-ridden dirt road.

After the highway took a sharp dip, the sleepy town of Shady Cove came into view. With the glittering ocean as a background, I saw multiple neighborhoods nestled around shops, schools, and a few green parks. Dad coasted down the long hill until we were eye-level with the entire town, the ocean no longer visible behind the many houses and buildings. A short drive later, we pulled up in front of a gleaming gray-and-white school with a neatly trimmed lawn and freshly paved parking lot. The entire structure appeared to be brand new, from the spotless double doors of the main entrance to the stunning track and football field. Even from a distance, Shady Cove High looked impressive.

Dad pulled into a parking space, turned the key, and jerked it out of the ignition. To my surprise, though, he didn't unbuckle his seatbelt.

"Um...aren't we going to get out of the car?" I asked, my gaze flickering to the dozens of students streaming towards the main double doors.

"In a minute." Dad let out a deep breath before placing a hand on my shoulder—an uncharacteristic gesture that took me by surprise. "Listen, hon, I just want to take a moment to let you know that I care about you. I know how much you're struggling with the move. It can be hard to leave all your friends and your swim team. I totally understand."

Then we should have stayed in Newland...

He took a deep breath. "Rayne," he said, "I've noticed that you haven't been the same fun-loving, carefree girl you normally are. Even though moving to Shady Cove has been hard on you, please listen to me. A positive attitude changes everything."

I nodded stiffly. "Alright." Jerking open the door, I stepped out into the bright sunlight and pulled my backpack over my shoulders. "But no promises," I warned.

Dad slid out of his seat. "All I'm asking is that you try to be more optimistic. Just for today. Shady Cove High is a great school, and I know you'll have a good time if you open up and allow yourself to have fun. Okay?"

"Yeah." I averted my gaze from his, squared my shoulders, and began the trek towards the main double doors. Dad fell in step behind me, and I had the feeling this was going to be a long day.

"Mr. Bennett," the secretary gushed as soon as we entered the office. "Good morning! And this must be Rayne. Nice to meet you."

We dutifully shook hands, and I fidgeted anxiously as the secretary explained my schedule and had Dad sign some papers. "One of our student guides will give you a brief tour around the school," she continued. "You might be a tad late to first period, but I've already notified your teacher ahead of time, so don't worry."

I smiled weakly. "Great."

Dad scribbled his signature on one last paper before handing it back to the secretary. "Well, that's that," he said. "Have fun, Rayne. I'll pick you up after school." He gave me a brief hug and flashed me a smile before disappearing out the door, leaving me standing awkwardly clutching my schedule to my chest.

Fortunately, the secretary broke the uncomfortable silence by ushering in a petite girl with short blonde hair. "Here's one of our student guides," she explained. "This is Sage. She'll show you around the school."

With one look at Sage, I knew she had a bubbly personality. Her broad smile and bright blue eyes positively gushed warmth and friendship. "Hi!" she exclaimed, sticking out her hand. "I'm Sage Thomson. Nice to meet you."

"I'm Rayne," I said, reaching out to shake her hand uncertainly.

"Take care, girls." The secretary waved as Sage pulled me out the door and into the crowded hallway. It was a completely different atmosphere from the stuffy, quiet office. Students laughed and talked and clogged the hallway. The sound was amplified even more by the metal lockers and stone walls of the school.

"So what grade are you in?" Sage asked. I could barely hear her voice above the pandemonium.

"Tenth," I replied. "You?"

"I'm a sophomore too," she said. "They usually pair up new students with guides who are in the same grade. Mind if I take a look at your schedule?"

"Be my guest." I handed Sage the piece of paper and let her point out my different classes as we zigzagged through the throngs of students. She led me outside to the track, football and soccer fields, and the pool. "All sports are during the last period of the day," she explained. "I'm on the swim team too, so you can meet me in the women's locker room during sixth period."

"Sounds good." From the outside, Shady Cove High looked ginormous, but now that Sage had given me this brief tour, I realized it was actually quite small. I caught a glimpse of the pool as Sage and I headed back indoors, and my heart took a little leap. The shimmering water looked so inviting. I couldn't wait for sixth period, where I could finally put on my racing suit and dive into the crystal-clear water.

Unfortunately, my first five periods went by painfully slow. The day seemed to drag on and on without any clear ending in sight. Every time I entered a new class, I was forced to go through the same ritual—greet the teacher, introduce myself to the class, take a seat next some kid in the back, and endure fifty-five minutes of pure torture. School wasn't exactly my strongest suit—especially Spanish. I was clueless when it came to foreign languages.

On the bright side, I ended up seeing Sage in my biology and Spanish classes. She was more than willing to partner up with me for our cell research project, which was a relief. When it came to group projects, I didn't want to be the awkward new kid who had to be assigned a group from the teacher.

By the time lunch rolled around, I was both physically and mentally exhausted. My teachers had even been kind enough to load me down with extra homework so I could "get caught up" with the class. Hooray for me.

With a weary sigh, I grabbed my lunch and from my locker before following the mob of students heading for the cafeteria. I was glad that I didn't have to wait in line to buy lunch, so I quickly slid into the nearest empty table and pulled out my phone. Stuffing my earbuds in, I chose my favorite song and let the noise around me fade into the background. I admit it felt a little strange eating alone for the first time with no one to talk to. Loneliness overwhelmed me when I pictured Kimmie sitting at our favorite lunch table back at Newland High, talking and laughing with some girls from our swim team. Or was she just as lonely as I was? With a sigh, I was about to pull out my phone again to text her, when I suddenly heard my name.

Sage was waving from a few tables down. "Rayne!" she called again. "Hi!"

I waved and forced a smile. I didn't really feel up to hanging out with Sage and her friends, but then again, I didn't want to be known as the weird girl who ate lunch by herself. So without a second thought, I gathered my things and walked over to Sage's group. She introduced me to her friends, many of which were on the swim team. One of them even recognized me from the meet a few weeks ago.

"Aren't you the one with that super fast time?" a girl with a long brown ponytail asked.

"Hey, Marley's right!" Sage exclaimed. "You swam the girls' IM in a record-breaking time, didn't you?"

I blushed, but it felt good to be recognized for my swimming talent. "Yeah," I said, "I guess that was me."

"It was totally you," Marley pressed. "You are so fast!"

"Yeah," Sage giggled, turning to her friend, "you would know. You came in second place in that heat."

Marley rolled her eyes. "Okay, you got me. I had to race against Rayne. She beat me by—what was it? Five, six seconds? She was so far ahead I couldn't even see her wake!"

All the girls laughed, and I felt my smile widen as I looked around the group. Everyone was so charming and friendly. Swim would definitely be my favorite period of the day, by far.

Lunch was over quickly, and then it was off to one more class before swim. My mind kept wandering during English, but I finally made it through and rushed to my locker as soon as the bell rang. I met up with Sage and Marley in the locker room as we slipped into our suits. They were as talkative and charismatic as ever, and we were deep into another conversation by the time we strolled onto the pool deck.

"Rayne Bennett?" a deep voice called.

It was the coach. The three of us paused, but Sage didn't miss a beat. "Meet you in the pool, Rayne!" she chirped. As she and Marley headed over to an empty lane, I quietly stepped over to where the Shady Cove swim coach was standing.

"Hello, Rayne, I'm Coach Hansen. It's a pleasure to meet you." He extended a large, leathery hand, which I shook timidly. "I'm so glad you and your father are here in Shady Cove. He might have told you what I have in mind for your swimming career."

"Yeah, he did."

"Great. Then you know that I am one hundred percent on your side." Coach Hansen smiled. "And we already know that you are an extremely talented swimmer—in fact, one of the fastest I've ever seen on a high school swim team. It's your dream to make it to the Junior Olympics, correct?"

I nodded. Coach Hansen laid one of his leathery hands on my shoulder. "Believe me, Rayne," he said, "I will do my best to help you achieve that dream."

Even though he gave me a fatherly smile, I was still intimidated. "Okay," I stammered. "Thank you."

Coach Hansen laughed and withdrew his hand. "I see you've already made friends with Sage and Marley. Why don't you hop into their lane, and they'll show you what we do for our warm-up?"

"Sure." I gratefully turned around and scurried over to the side of the pool. After pulling my goggles into place, I slid into the refreshingly cool water and waited until Sage and Marley finished their first lap. They were already breathing hard by the time they reached my end of the lane.

"Hey, glad you could make it," Marley said. "All done talking with Coach?"

"Yep. He said you two could teach me the warm-up."

"Of course. It's easy." Marley smiled and launched into a brief explanation of what to do. Before long, I was gliding through the water and reveling in every stroke I took. It felt amazingly good to wipe all thoughts from my mind except swimming. There was nothing to focus on but the pull of my hands through the turquoise water, the powerful kick of my legs, and the feeling of gliding, gliding, gliding.

After our warm-up, Sage, Marley, and I listened to Coach as he called out what to do next. "Everyone go grab a kickboard. Let's do four laps freestyle kick, four laps frog kick."

I pulled myself out of the pool and headed over to a bin filled with kickboards and other swimming equipment. Just as I reached in to grab the nearest one, someone suddenly jerked it out of my hand.

"Watch it, new girl," came a low tone.

I glanced up in surprise at the tan brunette giving me a warning look. "I was only trying to grab a kickboard," I said slowly.

"Well, this one's taken," she replied icily. "You need to learn your place."

I raised an eyebrow, but I wasn't really in the mood to pick a fight on my first day of school. So I sighed and grabbed another kickboard, making sure to give the rude swimmer a proper stink eye as I stormed back over to the pool. What a jerk.

"Rayne?" Sage asked, giving me an alarmed look as soon as I jumped back into our lane. "Why were you giving Madeleine a death glare?" She jerked a thumb towards the girl who had provoked me.

I shrugged. "She ripped my kickboard right out of my hands. What's her problem?"

Sage gaped at me. "Do you even know who she is?"

She and Marley exchanged glances. "That's Madeleine Hansen," Marley explained. "The coach's daughter. It's best not to get on her bad side."

"Too late," I said, cracking a grin.

"It's probably because she knows what you can do. She's afraid you're going to steal her spotlight," Marley continued. "She's one of our fastest swimmers, but you can easily beat her in any stroke."

"We call her the Mad Hansen," Sage butted in. "Never to her face, of course."

I smiled mischievously. "Well, maybe it's time somebody did."

"No!" Sage and Marley exclaimed in unison. Their bewildered expressions quickly vanished as soon as I said I was kidding. Then the two of them broke out into relieved laughter. Marley pushed off the wall and began kicking, with Sage and I trailing behind. But I couldn't shake the glare that was boring into my back. Glancing over my shoulder, I realized my fear was confirmed.

Madeleine Hansen was still shooting daggers at me with her eyes. I ignored her and focused on my kicking once again. I didn't know what I had done to provoke "the Mad Hansen," but it looked like I would just have to tread carefully. Whatever happened, I wouldn't let the coach's daughter ruin my love of swimming. Nothing could take that away from me.

6

—— ◦ ——

CHAPTER 6

"So how was school?" Dad asked as I slid into the passenger seat of our car.

"Not that bad, actually," I admitted.

"Make any new friends?"

"A couple." I turned my attention to the congested parking lot as Dad pulled out onto the street. Students were heading in all directions, and I wondered if the 300 or so teenagers who attended Shady Cove High all knew each other. The nearest town was thirty miles away, so it wasn't like there were any students who attended the school from out of town.

And then there was me—the new kid who happened to get on Madeleine Hansen's bad side the first day at school. I winced, remembering how she had glared at me with a look that could lift road kill. And all because she was worried that I was faster than her?

I turned my attention forward and realized we were already on the highway heading back home.

"And how were your classes?" Dad asked.

"No big deal, except my teachers loaded me down with tons of homework. What do they expect me to do—magically complete two months' worth of homework to get caught up with the class?"

"Exaggerating much?" he chuckled.

"Maybe. But still, I have a crazy amount of homework, more than I usually got at Newland."

"Well, you better get started on it as soon as we get home," Dad said. "There's no use procrastinating."

"Yeah...I guess you're right." I sighed and propped my elbow up on the armrest. The landscape that flew by the window made my heart beat a little faster—tall pine trees and large bushes gave way to rocky cliffs, and beyond that, the ocean. I grew even more agitated as we neared our house. Something was pulling me to the cliffs, and I felt the desperate urge to jump out of the car and take off at full speed to the ocean. So as soon as Dad parked the car, I grabbed my backpack and made a beeline for the goat-trail leading to the private beach.

"Hey!" Dad called. "Where are you off to so quickly?"

"I'm just going for a quick hike. There's a nice spot up ahead to do some schoolwork," I called back. The lie rolled off my tongue smoothly and effortlessly, like a knife through water.

"All right. Just don't be gone too long," Dad agreed. I waited until he disappeared inside the house before taking off down the rugged dirt trail, skirting rocks and bushes and scraggly weeds in my haste. I was huffing and puffing by the time I reached the edge of the Redrock Cliffs and gazed down at the churning ocean far below. Just the sight of the sparkling blue-green water ignited my heart and made my whole body pulse with renewed energy.

I flew down the last portion of the trail, skipped the final three steps, and jumped onto the sand. I quickly slipped my backpack off my shoulders before pausing to catch my breath. Sweeping my gaze over the private beach, I realized it was even more beautiful than I had remembered. The golden sand dunes shimmered in the sunlight and complemented the deep blues and greens of the ocean. The waves were no longer huge and crashing, but smaller and gentler, making swimming seem more feasible than the last time I had been here.

I tore off my jacket, shoes, and socks before shimmying out of my jeans and T-shirt. I was still wearing my damp bathing suit from earlier. My whole body buzzed with excitement as I strode towards the inviting water. I slowed upon reaching the shoreline, savoring the feeling of squishing my toes in the wet sand. My extremities were tingling in anticipation of what was to come.

I took a deep breath and dove in. The first sensation that overwhelmed me was that of piercing coldness, chilling all my bones and making my teeth chatter underwater. Ignoring the goosebumps sprouting on every inch of my body, I opened my eyes and was delighted to find that I could see, even if it was a little blurry. Particles of sand and bits of seaweed drifted past me. Rays of light streamed towards the ocean floor, illuminating the hazy underwater world. Then I felt myself being dragged backwards and realized a wave was surging overhead.

I scissor-kicked my way to the surface and broke through, gasping for air. I hadn't realized how long I had been underwater, but it seemed way too short. Just as another wave was about to crash on top of me, I sucked in a deep breath and dove back under.

Swimming in the ocean was nothing like swimming in a pool. It was like I was a part of something so alive, something that surged and swirled around me. I swam deeper and trailed my hand across the sandy seafloor, smiling as bits of sand floated upwards in a hazy cloud.

But all too soon, I ran out of breath again and was forced to swim back up for air. This time I glanced back at shore and realized that a current had pulled me farther down the beach, almost completely out of the small cove. If I didn't swim back soon, I would be dragged along the cliffs and lose my chance to reach dry land. I didn't know where the next beach was—it could be miles down the coast.

So instead of diving under and swimming along the seafloor, I swam freestyle along the surface of the water. I fought my way through the wind chop until I reached the spot where I had originally entered the water. I continued this cycle of drifting and swimming until my throat was parched from salt water. Then I reluctantly headed in to shore and changed back into my dry clothes.

I was in a daze as I made the long uphill trek to the house. My mind was consumed with images of diving underwater, watching the waves break over my head and the sand swirl beneath my feet. Though I desperately needed a drink, I would rather spend more time swimming in the sea. But Dad would be wondering where I was, and for some reason I felt uncomfortable telling him that I had been swimming in the ocean. There was a sort of forbidden thrill that came with the sea, as if I shouldn't be there but longed for it anyway.

Just before entering the house, I squeezed out my long black hair and wrapped it up in a tight bun. Hopefully Dad wouldn't notice it was wet.

"Rayne? Is that you?" he called as soon as he heard me walk in.

"Yeah." I followed his voice to the dining room, where I saw him sitting at the table flipping through some old photo albums. My eyebrows immediately shot up in surprise. I had never seen those before...where had he gotten them?

"What's that?" I asked, coming up behind him and peering at the pictures over his shoulder.

"Oh, just some old photos from back in the day. Nothing special." Dad quickly closed the album and slid it across the table. But my fingers had been resting on the corner of one of the pages, preventing the album from closing completely.

"Rayne," Dad warned.

But I had already pulled the album towards me and flipped it open. As soon my eyes alighted on the pictures inside, I froze. The very first photo showed a younger version of Dad with his arm wrapped around a beautiful woman with long black hair—hair just like mine. Her dazzling smile was the epicenter of the picture.

Tiny tears sprang into my eyes. I touched her face with the tip of my finger. "Dad...why haven't you shown me this before?"

"I found the album while I was finishing unpacking," he replied slowly. "I had forgotten about all these photos."

I swallowed. I had seen a few pictures of my mother before, but nothing like this—not an entire album filled with memories of her. Sadness pricked at my heart.

Dad's voice was thick when he said, "It's hard to remember. Sometimes I don't want to think about her. But other times..."

I backed away. "Is that the reason we moved here? So you could relive those memories?"

"Not exactly—"

But I knew that was the main reason. Living in a less expensive home was merely a plus. The real reason Dad had narrowed down his search to Shady Cove was because he wanted her back.

I chewed on my bottom lip. "Dad, she's not coming back," I said quietly, my voice cracking. Two tears streaked down my cheeks.

He leaned back in his chair, and I saw a strange light in his eyes. "Why are you so sad, Rayne?" he asked wearily. "Why does this make you so bitter? These are normal feelings to have when a loved one passes away, I know, but you need to learn to confront them after a time. You can't keep dwelling on them. Memories are meant for treasuring those happy moments and learning from the bad ones. They aren't meant to be pushed away and forgotten."

But I don't have any memories of her, I wanted to say. Only fragments.

I held my father's gaze for a long, tension-filled minute, admiring the strange thoughtful peace on his face, before turning around and heading upstairs. I felt like I had been cheated. Not only did I grow up without a mother, but now I had been whisked into an entirely new life because of Dad's crazy whim. If he thought returning to my birthplace would spark memories, then he was right. But, like I had already discovered, those memories were more painful than pleasant.

All night long I drifted in and out of sleep. My dreams were more like nightmares, causing me to toss and turn in bed. I finally woke up at the sound of the front door closing, causing the entire house to shudder with the reverberations.

My skin prickled with goosebumps as I sat up in bed. I listened, my eyes gradually adjusting to the darkness, as Dad noisily made his way through one of the rooms below me. I heard a strange thud, and then the unmistakable hiss of the gas fireplace. Before long, a faint crackling sound could be heard, and I pictured him sitting in a chair gazing at the dancing flames.

I quietly slid out of bed and pulled on my robe. As I padded down the stairs, a sliver of moonlight from a nearby window suddenly illuminated part of my hair, causing those familiar streaks of deep blue.

I found Dad in the living room. He glanced up but remained motionless as I stood in the shadows. "Hey," I said softly.

"You should be in bed."

"I know." I bit my lip and stepped forward, my hair immediately glowing in the pale moonlight. Dad's eyes widened as he took in the network of beautiful blue streaks interwoven in my hair.

"It's been a while since I've seen that," he said softly. I gave him a wry smile and took a seat next to him, part of my hair falling over my eyes. I quickly pushed it away and glanced down. Dad was fingering something shiny in his hands, and upon closer inspection I realized it was his wedding ring.

The room suddenly felt a bit colder, despite the blazing fire only a few yards in front of us. Dad silently slipped the ring back onto his finger. He squeezed my hand reassuringly.

I drew in a sharp breath. "You know, I've been doing some think ing..."

"Yeah? About what?"

"This." I ran my fingers through my long black tresses. "I've always taken it for granted. A unique gift. But what if there's something wrong with my hair?"

"There's nothing wrong with it. Your hair is beautiful."

"But how did it get this way? Why was I born with glowing hair, and no one else was? I mean, your hair doesn't glow like mine." I pointed to his natural brown curls.

Dad was thoughtful. "Sometimes it's better to take things as they are," he said finally. "Sometimes we just have to accept what we have, and not ask questions."

"Dad," I pressed, "I don't want a textbook answer. I want real answers." I gazed into his eyes, searching. I had a feeling he knew. He had to know. So why wasn't he telling me?

Dad glanced away, simultaneously removing his hand from mine. He got up and started to pace the room. I stood up as well, turning my face towards the window and letting the moonlight hit me full on the face.

Dad immediately stopped pacing. "Rayne?" he asked urgently. "What—" He bent down and grasped my face with both hands. "Your eyes," he gasped.

I could feel the heat simmering just beneath my eyeballs. "I know," I said simply.

"I don't believe it." Dad ran a hand through his mussed hair and took a seat again. "Oh, Rayne...this is more complicated than you think."

"Why?"

He lapsed into silence.

I tapped my fingers impatiently on my thigh. "Dad, please. Why do I glow in the moonlight?"

"I don't know," he said, running a hand down his jaw.

"Just tell me," I pleaded. "I've lived with this secret my whole life. Don't I deserve to know?"

"Yes," he admitted, "but I'm just not sure you're ready to hear it."

"Try me."

"Rayne..."

I begged him until he finally assented. "All right," he sighed after a moment of deliberation, "it's because of your mother."

"I kind of figured that," I said slowly.

"Well, now you know."

"But that's not all there is, right? That can't—"

"Rayne." Dad's tone was stern and commanding. "Enough with the questions. Like I said before, you're not ready to hear this. Just be satisfied with what I told you, okay?"

"But—"

"But nothing. Now go back to bed and get a good night's sleep. You have school tomorrow."

I opened my mouth, ready to fire another volley of questions, but thought better of it and clamped my jaw shut. "Fine," I muttered. I retreated back into the shadows, my hair and eyes fading from their luminescent glow.

"Good night, Rayne," Dad said softly as I began to climb the stairs. I murmured a reply as I headed back up to my room. I flung off my robe and climbed into bed, pulling the covers tightly over my shivering body. But sleep was evasive, as my thoughts were fixed on one thing and one thing only: what were Dad's secrets, and why was he keeping them from me?

It was a mystery that I was determined to solve.

7

CHAPTER 7

ONE WEEK LATER

I slid into my seat just as the bell rang. Señora Ramirez, my Spanish teacher, looked at me and tsked. "That was another close call, Rayne," she warned. Her lilting accent carried across the room, and a few students turned their heads to glance at me. Feeling my cheeks redden from the unwanted attention, I nodded and tried my best to look apologetic. In reality, I could care less if I arrived late to class. Spanish was my least favorite subject, mainly because it was my worst. Learning a foreign language did not come easy to me.

"Take out su tarea and pass it forward, por favor," Señora Ramirez instructed the class. As soon as everyone had passed up his or her homework, she handed out a worksheet for us to do while she corrected.

I twirled my pencil around with my fingers as I stared at the paper in front of me. I had a vague idea what some of the words meant, but for others I had no clue. I groaned and sunk lower in my seat.

Time passed slowly. I had only filled in ten of the twenty questions on the worksheet by the time Señora Ramirez stood up to command the class' attention.

A feeling of dread settled in my stomach. I reread question 11 multiple times, but I couldn't think of the answer for the life of me. Verb conjugations swirled around in my head.

I glanced up and swept my gaze anxiously around the room. Almost every student was finished, their papers lying face-down on their desks. Only a few continued to scribble frantically in order to finish before time was up. I knew I needed to do the same. My pencil hovered over the remaining questions, ready to circle at random, when Señora Ramirez suddenly announced, "Time's up!"

A few students grumbled while others yawned and mechanically passed their papers forward. I inwardly cringed as I handed my worksheet to the person in front of me. Señora Ramirez is going to kill me. I only answered ten questions—ten stupid questions! Why can't I remember this stuff? I had tried my hand at studying, but since I had the attention span of a lightning bolt, it was impossible for me to focus for more than a few minutes. And Spanish was like trying to study an error code on a computer—it was just a jumble of characters that made absolutely no sense.

By the time class was finally over, I slung my backpack over my shoulder and walked over to Sage's desk. "Hey," I sighed.

"Hi." She cocked her head and regarded me carefully. "Had some trouble with that worksheet?"

"Yeah. I'm clueless when it comes to speaking another language."

"Ugh, I know how you feel. Sometimes—"

"Rayne," Señora Ramirez called, beckoning me over to her desk.

I sighed. "Gotta go. See you later."

Sage gave me a reassuring smile before heading off to her next class, and I warily stepped up to my teacher's desk.

She held up the worksheet that I had struggled with earlier. "Rayne, I don't understand. You had veinte minutos to complete this paper, and yet only the first ten questions are answered."

"I'm sorry, Señora Ramirez...I just need to study my vocab some more."

"No! Vocabulario is not the problem. You need to focus in class and pay attention. Less talking, y más escuchando. ¿Comprendo?"

I blinked.

Señora Ramirez shook her head sadly. "Less talking and more listening, Rayne. This is your second year of Spanish, ¿sí?"

I nodded.

"Then you should not have so much trouble remembering words and phrases from last year. Take some extra time tonight to study, and remember when you come to class tomorrow that you need to stay focused. It all comes down to effort. ¿Comprendo?"

I swallowed nervously. "Yep. More effort—got it." As soon as Señora Ramirez dismissed me, I bolted from the room like a dog from its leash. I headed straight for my locker, knowing that I only had a few minutes to get to my next class. If I came in late, that meant another lecture from another teacher, as well as a possible detention. Yikes.

"Rayne! Over here!"

I spun around, and a relieved smile broke out on my face when I saw Sage running towards me. "Hey, what's up?"

"I just had a great idea!" she gushed. "I know you're having trouble in Spanish, so I talked to my friend Luke. He's fluent in the language. The only reason he's in our Spanish class is for an easy A." Sage was talking so fast, she had to pause and gulp in a breath of air. "So guess what?" she continued breathlessly. "He said he can tutor you after school!"

I rubbed my eyes tiredly. Was there a Luke in our class...? I couldn't remember. "Look," I sighed, "I appreciate the offer, but tell your friend that it isn't necessary. I might be beyond hope."

Sage didn't miss a beat. "No, I insist! Luke would love to tutor you. He's really smart and easy to get along with."

I shifted uncomfortably from one foot to the other. "No, it's not that—"

Sage glanced down at her wristwatch. "Oops! Hey, I'll see you in biology. I have to get going to my next class. I'll just tell Luke that you'll meet him in the library at three. How does that sound?"

"Wait, what?"

A group of passing girls suddenly called Sage's name, and her attention was diverted. She beamed her dazzling smile at me and called, "See you soon!" before being whisked away.

"Oh great," I muttered. Had I just gotten myself a tutor? But I didn't even want one! What was Sage thinking? What was I thinking?

I felt my cheeks grow hot as I slammed my locker closed. Who was this Luke guy anyway? I hastily scanned my memory for any person named Luke in my Spanish class, but I came up empty. Having only attended Shady Cove High for a week, I still couldn't remember the majority of my classmates' names.

Frustrated, I plodded over to my next class. I kept my head down and my hands shoved in my pockets, forcing my way through the crowd. Suddenly, a voice shouted, "Hey, watch where you're going!"

Startled, I looked up and realized I had almost experienced a head-on collision with another girl. But it wasn't just any girl—it was

Madeleine Hansen, and she stood with her arms crossed, blocking the doorway to my class.

"What are you doing here?" I asked, more curious than angry.

"I'm just dropping some stuff off for Mrs. Brown. Are you in this class?"

Her tone was anything but friendly. "Yes," I said, narrowing my eyes, "so can you move?"

Madeleine smirked. I rolled my eyes. I was fortunate not to have had any run-ins with "the Mad Hansen" over the past week, but it looked like my luck had run out.

"Look, Madeleine, you'll save both of us a headache if you just step away from the door," I pointed out.

Suddenly, Mrs. Brown bustled towards us. "Excuse me," her shrill voice said. "I'd like to get through."

Madeleine immediately stepped aside. "Sorry, Mrs. Brown!" she chirped. "Rayne and I were just talking. Did you know we're both on the swim team?"

I gawked at her. Madeleine continued to smile sweetly at the teacher until she walked away, and then her face morphed back into a nasty glare, which she focused on me the entire time I walked to my desk.

My blood boiled. What an immature, two-faced teacher's pet! It took everything in me to quietly sit down, unzip my backpack, and ignore Madeleine's provocations. Though the school day was not yet halfway over, it already felt like I had suffered through a very, very long day.

To make things worse, I never got a chance to talk to Sage in biology class. I needed a way to cancel my tutoring session, but I had no clue who this Luke guy was or what he even looked like.

Sage was my only option, but so far she had succeeded in being inconveniently unreachable.

By the time lunch finally rolled around, my stomach was growling with hunger. I eagerly stepped into line to buy some food from the cafeteria, which looked surprisingly tasty compared to my experience with Newland High's caf food.

"Anything to drink?" the lunch lady asked after I had piled several items onto my tray.

"I think I'll have water. Thanks." I watched as she reached into a mini refrigerator and pulled out a water bottle. Then, without thinking, I reached over and grabbed a straw and a packet of salt. With my hands full, I plodded over to my usual table and took a seat.

"Is Sage here?" I asked Marley, who was busy unzipping her backpack and taking out her lunch.

"Nah, I haven't seen her. I think she's helping in the office. She's an aide, you know."

"Right." I took a bite of my pizza, trying to shove down the bitter disappointment welling up within me. "So," I tried again, "do you happen to know anyone named Luke?"

"Luke?" Marley's brow scrunched in concentration. "I don't think so. Why?" Her eyes sparkled with mischief.

"No reason."

"Oh, sure."

"I'm serious!" I set down my slice of pizza and grabbed the packet of salt, emptying it into my water bottle. With my straw, I stirred the particles around until they dissolved. "I just need to get ahold of this Luke guy because Sage set up a tutoring session for us."

"What?" Marley gaped at me.

"A tutoring session," I repeated. "It's for Spanish. I—"

"No, not that." Marley pointed to my water bottle. "I'm talking about this. What in the world are you doing?"

I glanced down and immediately stopped stirring. "Oh...nothing." I hastily dropped my straw onto the table. The two of us stared at the tiny grains of salt swirling around inside the bottle.

"Okay, I'm going to ask an obvious question here: why did you put salt in your water?"

"Because I'm thirsty?"

"For salty water?"

Oh. Right. My face scrunched up into a look of disbelief. What was I doing? Trying to cover my tracks, I said lamely, "It's for a science project. We're trying to see if salt dissolves in water. You know, for chemistry."

Marley raised an eyebrow. "I thought you and Sage were in biology."

"Yeah, well, we touch on other things too." I quickly put the cap back on the water bottle and stood up. "At least I know that salt dissolves in water. Experiment done!" I gave a forced laugh and headed over to the nearest trash can.

Marley blinked a few times and shook her head. "Okay," she chuckled, turning back to her food.

I smiled weakly. After making sure no one was watching, I hastily uncapped the bottle and took a long, deep draught. My taste buds were on fire from the salt, but it felt incredibly good. It was the most refreshing drink I had ever tasted. I studied the murky water eagerly, wondering why I hadn't thought of drinking saltwater before. Why did everyone else consider it so disgusting?

I took one more quick sip before dropping the bottle into the trash. Then I walked back over to our table and resumed eating my lunch like any normal high school student would. But the thoughts that were flying around my head were anything but normal. What was happening to me? First my hair, then my eyes, and now my taste buds?

"Rayne?"

I snapped back to reality. "Huh?"

Marley stared at me worriedly. "Are you doing okay?" she asked. "You seem a little out of it today."

I smiled reassuringly. "Couldn't be better."

If only she knew...

8

CHAPTER 8

I rapped my fingers impatiently on the wooden table. My feet were kicked up on a nearby chair while the contents of my backpack were scattered all over the table. I checked my phone for the umpteenth time and sighed noisily. Thanks a lot, Sage! I could have been well on my way home instead of stuck in this smelly library waiting for a guy who might not even show up.

Earlier, I had gotten the chance to talk to Sage during swim class, and I made it crystal-clear that I had no interest in being tutored. But Sage meekly replied that Luke had already cleared his schedule for me, so it was now between he and I.

"Just meet him in the library and tell him face-to-face," she'd suggested.

"But don't you have his number or something? Can't you tell him for me?" I had protested.

Despite my pleading, Sage was convinced it was too late to go back on her word. So, with a sigh, I resigned myself to my fate. That's why I had been sitting in the library for fifteen minutes, completely and utterly bored out of my mind. I decided to give Luke two more minutes. Then, if he still didn't show up, I would leave.

Suddenly, the front door swung open, and the librarian smiled up at the newcomer. "Can I help you with anything?" she asked.

"No thanks." The student—a tall, tanned boy with brown hair—smiled and shook his head. "I'm just meeting someone here for tutoring."

The librarian nodded in understanding, and the boy swept his gaze around the room. I immediately wished I had a book to hide my face. Despite my previous intentions, I suddenly didn't know how I was going to tell this guy that our tutoring session was off.

The boy, upon realizing that I was the only student in the room, casually stepped up to my table and said, "You must be Rayne."

Darn it. I swallowed the lump in my throat and sat up straighter. "Yeah. And you are...?"

"Luke Sanchez. Nice to meet you." He stuck out his hand, and I shook it a bit reluctantly. "So," he said, taking a seat across from me, "Sage said you needed some help with Spanish."

I stared at him. He didn't even have an accent. Only his chocolate-brown eyes and shaggy brown hair hinted that he was Hispanic. And maybe the way his nose was slightly pointed and his face was perfectly chiseled. And possibly how his mouth curled up into a sort of half-smile when he talked. And—

"You do need help with Spanish, right...?"

I immediately glanced away, trying to ignore the deep blush rising on my cheeks. "Yes! Yes, I'm terrible," I said hastily. "Terrible at Spanish, I mean. I'm pretty good at other things."

His lips quirked up into a smile.

"I—uh—do you play any sports?" I asked, changing the subject.

"Sports?" he echoed. "Nah. Not really my thing."

"Oh. I thought you might, because you're really...ah..." I winced. "Muscular?"

Luke tried in vain to suppress a laugh. "Thanks," he chuckled.

I ducked my head in embarrassment. My cheeks were now flushed scarlet. Since when had I become such a dunce? The words had just popped out of my mouth before I could stop them.

"I should probably get going now," I said nervously. "Sorry for wasting your time." And sorry for making this way more awkward than it should be.

"Wait, you're leaving?" he asked, crestfallen.

I fumbled for the right words to say, but all I came up with was, "I don't need a tutor."

Luke studied me carefully. "I thought you said you were terrible at Spanish."

"Well, I am," I admitted.

"Then you're not wasting my time," he said. "Not even close."

"Alright." I tucked a stray of my still-damp hair behind my ear. The rest of it was done up in a sloppy bun, leaving a few tendrils hanging down to frame my face.

Luke smiled, and I added, "I'm not sure how long you can handle my awkward social skills, though."

He shrugged. "And I'm not sure how long I can keep staring at a pretty girl like you."

I nearly choked on my own saliva. "What?" If my cheeks had been scarlet before, then they were blood red now.

Luke shifted uncomfortably in his seat. "Sorry. That was out of line."

"It's okay," I said, even though I was even more confused and embarrassed now.

We sat in another awkward silence for a few seconds. Finally, Luke stuck out his hand and suggested, "Hey, why don't we start over?"

I nodded.

"Okay, I'm Luke," he said.

I felt a smile creep up on my face. "I'm Rayne," I said, and we shook hands and laughed.

"There. Now that that's over with, should we get to work on your Spanish?"

"Sure." I flipped through my scattered papers until I found the worksheet from earlier. Señora Ramirez wanted me to redo it for homework tonight. "Let's start with this one," I suggested.

Luke turned the paper sideways and skimmed the instructions. "Oh, hey, I remember this. It's just some fill-in-the-blank stuff. Pretty simple."

"Yeah, but way too confusing."

"Having trouble remembering verb conjugation?"

"I guess."

"Do you remember how it works?"

"Don't take the same word and just change it around?"

"Right." Luke grinned. "It's when you take a verb, like estudiar, and change it to match the subject."

"Oh, yeah."

"Good. It's a start." Luke shifted his chair to sit diagonally from me, and I hoped I didn't smell too strongly of chlorine. Or sweat. I wrinkled my nose.

"—the verb ir."

"Huh?" I snapped back to reality.

Luke glanced up, and our eyes met for a brief second. "I said, 'it looks like this worksheet is focusing on the verb ir.'"

"Oh. Right."

"So how would you conjugate it to fit the first sentence?"

I shifted my gaze to the worksheet and stared at question #1. The words swam before my eyes. I took a wild guess and blurted out a random answer.

Luke corrected me patiently, but it took multiple tries before I finally understood what he was saying.

"Let's try this again," he suggested. "Look at question two."

This time, I thought I knew the answer, but it turned out I was wrong again. Frustration was beginning to settle in.

Luke smiled wryly. "I think it's time to go back to the basics." He pushed the worksheet away and pulled out a scrap piece of paper. "Okay," he said, taking out a pencil. "Listen carefully."

One hour later, Luke had successfully taught me the basics of verb conjugation and helped me complete Señora Ramirez's worksheet. It was hard to believe that it was already past four o'clock. Although my brain was fried and my eyes were dead tired from concentrating for so long, I had to admit that Luke was a great teacher. He was patient and willing to put up with my slow learning, but he was also charming and comical at the same time. Once I got over my embarrassment from earlier, I actually had a great time.

"So," Luke said, swinging his backpack over one shoulder, "same time and place tomorrow?"

"Sure," I replied without missing a beat.

"Great. I'll see you tomorrow, then." He grinned and waved good-bye before heading out the door. I smiled in return as I gathered my belongings, shoving multiple papers and binders into my bulging backpack.

By the time I made it outside, I realized my bike was the last one chained to the rack. The school was nearly empty and felt like a ghost town. I quickly unlocked my bike and hopped on the seat, pedaling towards home. It wasn't until I was riding down the dirt trail that I realized I had made a huge mistake. The whole reason for meeting Luke at the library was so I could tell him I didn't need tutoring. But now the complete opposite had happened—Luke was tutoring me again tomorrow.

"Good grief," I muttered. What had happened to my firm resolution from earlier? Then again, I had certainly benefited from his help. Maybe the tutoring wasn't such a bad idea after all.

I glanced up, expecting to see my castle of a house looming high above the horizon, but instead I realized I was heading straight for the edge of a cliff. I screamed and slammed on my brakes, quickly swerving to the right and coming to a complete stop. My heart beat rapidly as I stepped off my bike. "That was a close one," I breathed, peering over the edge of the cliff at the swirling ocean below. Waves slammed against the rocks in a spray of glittering foam.

I swallowed nervously. How could I have let myself get so sidetracked? I nearly rode straight off a cliff! And what was I even doing here, anyway? I was supposed to be heading home, not to the entrance of the trail leading to the private beach.

There could only be one explanation: the ocean was pulling me back in. Its invisible undertow was drawing me to the seashore once again. I could feel its pull on my heartstrings like thousands of invisible fingers, tugging at me, urging me to come swim.

I let out a shaky breath before slipping off my backpack and placing it next to my bike, which was lying in the tall scraggly weeds behind me. "Well, I'm here now," I murmured. "Might as well..."

The shock from my near-death experience soon gave way to relief. The familiar buzz of excitement took over as I raced down the steep trail. As soon as I reached the bottom, I quickly peeled off my clothes and darted into the water in my bathing suit. While the sand was blazing hot, the ocean was freezing cold, chilling my limbs to the point where I could hardly move. But once I began swimming, my muscles warmed up and made the cold seem a little more bearable.

I took a deep breath and dove under an oncoming wave. It surged over my head like a billowing white cloud, causing sand to shift underneath me. I closed my eyes and relaxed my arms and legs, allowing myself to float with the rhythm of the sea until my lungs ran out of air and I was forced to swim back to the surface.

I frowned. The need for oxygen made staying underwater extremely inconvenient. I wondered if I could train myself to hold my breath for a longer period of time. Then I would be able to swim underwater for minutes rather than a few measly seconds. I smiled and took another deep breath before diving back under. This time, I counted in my head as I closed my eyes. I felt waves crashing above me and seaweed brushing against my legs. My lungs began screaming for air, but I gritted my teeth and forced myself to stay underwater. Then, just when the need to breathe became unbearable, I bolted to the surface.

"Forty-three seconds," I gasped. "I can only hold my breath for forty-three seconds." I let out a wry laugh. Well, that left a lot of room for improvement.

For the next half hour I continued to practice holding my breath, sometimes for so long that I nearly passed out. I finally decided it was time to take a break when black spots started to dance across my vision. I staggered out of the water, the world spinning in front of my eyes. Before I knew it, I had collapsed on the sand and emptied the contents of my nauseated stomach.

I groaned and clutched my hair. I felt extremely lightheaded. Maybe I shouldn't have held my breath that many times in a row, I thought miserably. My record had been a minute and two seconds, but without a watch it was hard to know the exact time. Plus, the more I had practiced holding my breath, the more it made me feel dizzy and exhausted.

I lay on the warm sand for a few minutes until my head felt a little better. Then I meandered over to my clothes and got dressed, my arms and legs shivering from being exposed to the cool evening air. I barely had the energy to make it up the trail to my bike, and my vision was cloudy and constricted by a massive headache.

By the time I finally dragged myself through the front door, it was nearly five thirty. I dumped my backpack on the dining room table and grabbed a water bottle from the refrigerator. After glancing over my shoulder to make sure Dad was nowhere in sight, I grabbed the saltshaker as well. I took a seat at the kitchen table and stirred some salt into my water, swirling it around until the entire bottle was cloudy. I gulped the entire thing down, letting the refreshing taste run down my throat and satisfy my taste buds. Once again, I was enthralled. Who knew saltwater could taste so good?

"Rayne?"

I jumped in my chair, nearly spitting out my mouthful of water. "Oh, Dad! Hey, I didn't see you there." I laughed nervously.

But he wasn't amused. "I've been waiting for you to come home from school! Where have you been for the last two hours?" he demanded.

"I had a tutoring session," I explained, "in the school library. I needed some help with my Spanish."

Dad's stern expression transformed into one of relief. "Oh," he said simply. "I tried calling you a few times, but you wouldn't answer. Did you turn your phone off?"

"No, I think it was on vibrate...but it may have gotten shoved to the bottom of my backpack."

Dad nodded and was about to turn away when he suddenly paused and cocked his head. "Say, why is your hair so wet? I thought swim practice was over two hours ago."

"Um, we ran a little late. And then I didn't squeeze it out very good."

"Well, next time use a towel," he called over his shoulder.

"Will do." As soon as he left the room, I let out a sigh of relief and rubbed my eyes tiredly. The saltwater had definitely helped clear my head and gotten rid of some of the dizziness.

Feeling slightly refreshed, I headed upstairs to get started on my pile of homework. Just as I plopped down on my bed, my phone suddenly vibrated. I pulled it out and realized it was a text from Sage: Ready 4 the meet this weekend?

The meet? I had completely forgotten about it. That was a first. Why didn't I remember something so important as a swim meet?

The answer came to me immediately: the ocean. It seemed like that was the answer to all my problems recently. Something was constantly pulling me back to the crashing waves and mysterious underwater world of the sea. Yet I had never felt that way before. I used to be obsessed with swimming and racing...and now my thoughts were consumed with swimming in the ocean.

I sighed and quickly texted a reply to Sage, something along the lines of You bet I'm ready, even though my stomach twisted at the thought of a swim meet this weekend. I would rather spend the entire weekend diving under the waves and swimming in the sea until my arms gave out.

I glanced at my phone. It was almost time for dinner, and I still hadn't done any schoolwork. So I before I could be distracted any further, I pushed my phone away and grabbed my backpack. It was time to get busy.

9

CHAPTER 9

My arms strained forward and my legs kicked furiously on overdrive. I cupped my hands and dug deep into the water. With every stroke, I drew closer to the wall and to finishing the race. As soon as I touched the tile, I jerked my head up and whipped off my goggles. I glanced at the lanes on either side of me and smiled when I realized no one else had reached the wall yet.

First place again!

Even though this had been a practice race, I was thrilled. The real test would come this weekend during the meet.

"Fantastic work, Rayne!" Coach Hansen congratulated me. He reached down and extended a hand to help me out of the pool.

"Thanks," I wheezed, climbing out onto the pool deck. I placed my hands on my hips, waiting for my pulse to go down to normal.

"You never fail to surprise me," he continued. "Keep up the phenomenal work. I have a feeling we're going to do great in the next meet, especially"—here he lowered his voice—"with you as our star swimmer."

I laughed nervously. "Thanks...I sure hope so."

Once Coach Hansen left to critique the other swimmers, Sage and Marley came up to me with huge smiles on their faces. "Teacher's pet!" Marley teased.

I rolled my eyes good-naturedly. "Yeah, right."

"Oh, come on. It's so obvious," Sage put in. "Coach is always saying good things about you, and he rarely ever critiques you unless he's in a nitpicky mood."

"Not true."

"It is so true," she argued. "You're his favorite swimmer. Everybody knows that."

"Yeah, including the Mad Hansen." Marley jerked a thumb towards the swimmer scowling at us from lane 3. "Apparently she doesn't like coming in second place."

"It was just a practice race." I shook my head. "She needs to cool her jets."

"She hates you with a passion. I don't think cooling her jets is an option," Marley chuckled.

"I don't see how that's funny." Sage crossed her arms over her chest. She leaned in and narrowed her eyes. "Last year," she murmured, "Madeleine had the guts to beat up a guy from the swim team. He gave her a rude comment, so she gave him two black eyes and a broken nose."

My eyes widened. "Are you serious?"

"Dead serious. All I'm saying is, you better not do anything to get on her nerves," Sage warned. "She's a loose cannon if I ever saw one."

I swallowed nervously. "Yikes," I murmured, remembering our little confrontation in front of Mrs. Brown's class the other day.

"So do you guys have any plans for the weekend?" Marley asked, swiftly changing the subject. The three of us immediately forgot all about Madeleine and jumped right into a new conversation. We were talking at full volume as we entered the women's locker room.

"Hey, why don't you guys come over to my place after the swim meet?" I suggested.

"Sure," Marley said automatically.

"Of course! Let me just double-check with my parents first," Sage added.

"Great." I finished changing into my jeans and T-shirt before combing out my long black hair. I was about to wrap it up into another bun when Sage suddenly cried out.

"Rayne!" she exclaimed. "I've been meaning to tell you, your hair is so beautiful. I can't get over it."

"Oh, this?" I held up one of my locks. "Well, thanks. Most of the time it just gets in my way."

"Because it's so long?" Marley asked, stepping up to admire my hair. She ran her fingers through it and grinned. "Hey, when we come over to your house this weekend we should try something with it."

"Oh my gosh, yes," Sage gushed.

"Okay," I agreed reluctantly, quickly sweeping my hair up into a bun. I pinned it neatly against the back of my head, causing Marley and Sage to frown.

"Can't you leave it down for once?" Sage asked.

"Like I said before, it gets in my way." I bent down and grabbed my belongings, not really wanting to give away the real reason I never showed off my hair. I was afraid people would poke fun at me because of how dark and lengthy it was. No one else even came close to having hair like mine—and not just because it could glow in the moonlight. Since it was extremely dark and straight, falling down my back like an ebony waterfall, it turned heads whenever I wore it down. My hair was sure to bring me unwanted attention.

"Fine," Marley sighed, "but just remember, we're fixing it up at your house on Saturday!"

"All right." I grinned and waved goodbye to my two friends before stepping out of the locker room. It was that time again—time for another tutoring session in the library. I was eager to see Luke again, but also reluctant to make a fool of myself like I had last time.

"Rayne!" called a voice.

I turned around, surprised to see Coach Hansen waving and beckoning me over from the entrance to the locker rooms.

"Yeah?" I asked, retracing my steps.

"I have something to ask you," he said, betraying a hint of excitement in his voice.

"Oh, okay."

"What would you say to an after-school training session? It would be one-on-one, aimed at getting you prepared for the Junior Olympics."

It wasn't what I was expecting. "Well..."

"You don't have to decide right now, of course. Go home and ask your dad about it. Training would only take an extra hour after school." He smiled broadly. "Promise me you'll think about it?"

"Of course." We said goodbye, and I headed in the direction of the library with an entirely new dilemma on my hands: tutoring, or training? After mulling over my options for a few moments, I suddenly stopped and realized the exquisite irony of the situation. If, a few months ago, my former coach had offered me this opportunity, I would have jumped on it in a heartbeat. But now—well, now swimming wasn't my top priority. It was bizarre to think about it that way, but I knew in my heart it was true. Though I still enjoyed racing, it wasn't my ultimate passion. It didn't consume my every thought.

And that was a peculiar feeling.

"Hey, Rayne," Luke greeted me as soon as I set foot in the library.

I smiled, all thoughts of swimming suddenly gone. "Oh, hey," I called.

He was sitting at a table in the middle of the library. "Sorry I didn't get a chance to talk to you in class today," he said. "How'd you do with the verb conjugations?"

"Much better," I replied truthfully.

Luke beamed. "Great! I was afraid you might not have understood it completely, since...you know."

I gave him a quizzical look.

"Well, this is my first time tutoring someone in Spanish, so I'm not exactly the most seasoned teacher, if you know what I mean."

I wasn't exactly sure how to reply, so I took a seat and began rifling through my backpack. Maybe as long as I kept my mouth shut, I wouldn't make a fool of myself.

"So," Luke said, clearing his throat, "let's take a look at tonight's homework."

I couldn't help but wonder if something was on his mind. For some reason he was acting a little differently today. But Luke removed all doubts from my mind as soon as he launched into my first lesson. For the next hour, as we worked on Senora Ramirez's assignment, I realized I was already improving greatly on my understanding of the Spanish language. Things were falling into place, piece by piece. Yet at the same time, I was falling for Luke's charm. I caught myself gazing into his chocolate-brown eyes once or twice instead of the words he was writing on my paper. I found myself studying the way he gestured during his explanations rather than absorbing the information I desperately needed to know.

Fortunately, the tutoring session was still fairly productive. Luke helped me finish my entire homework packet for the weekend, which cleared up my schedule immensely. For that I was extremely grateful. "Thank you so much," I said as Luke and I packed our belongings and got ready to leave.

"No problem. Good work today." He slung his backpack over one shoulder. "I guess I'll see you Monday?" he asked, a little hesitantly.

"Yeah. See you then." I watched as he headed towards the door, heaving a little sigh. Oh, darn it. "Luke!" I called.

He paused and turned back to face me.

"Why—why are you doing this?" I asked cautiously.

"What, tutoring you?"

I nodded.

One corner of his mouth turned up, and he shrugged lightly. "I don't really know. I like to help people out, but I also like teaching. I've always wanted to be a professor, or a tour guide, or someone like that."

"And you're really willing to help me out every day after school?"

"Well, that's kind of what I wanted to talk to you about," he admitted. "If it's okay with you, we don't have to meet here every single day after school. We could make this a Tuesday/Thursday thing or whatever."

My heart did a little skip at the thought. Having tutoring only on Tuesday and Thursday would leave me more time to swim in the ocean—but then again, it would open the door for a Monday/Wednesday/Friday training session with Coach Hansen, which I knew Dad would probably push me to do.

Before I could stop myself, I blurted, "No."

"No?"

"Let's keep meeting here every day after school."

He paused. I couldn't read his expression, so I backtracked and said, "We don't have to if you don't want to."

"No! No, that's totally fine."

"If you ever get tired of tutoring, we could always do a group study or something, I guess."

"Right. That would be fine. I'm not very busy after school since I'm not in any clubs, and I don't play any sports."

"Me neither. Well, except for swimming, of course, which I guess is considered a sport."

Luke chuckled, and I suddenly realized what I'd said. I mentally face-palmed myself.

"Well, I guess I better get going," he said, shifting his weight. "Good luck tomorrow."

"Thanks." I smiled. "Wait, how did you know about the swim meet tomorrow?"

"Sage," he replied automatically.

Of course. The two of them had been friends for a long time, apparently—maybe even as far back as elementary school.

I waved and headed out the door, my heart still aflutter with thoughts of Luke, and tutoring, and Luke...

"You better hurry if you want to make it on time!" Dad hollered, nearly shoving me out of the car.

"I'm going, I'm going!" I huffed, fumbling to grab my swim bag from the backseat.

"We would have gotten here on time if you didn't go on that hike," Dad grumbled. "Where did you go that took two hours, anyway?"

"Nowhere." I finally got ahold of my swim bag and yanked it out, then darted quickly out the door. "Bye!" I hollered. I didn't wait for a reply—I ran as fast as I could to the locker room and changed into my racing suit in record time. I was still trying to shove my swim cap over my sloppy bun as I stumbled onto the pool deck. By the time I reached Coach and the team, I was nearly twenty minutes late. My heat was near the end of the meet anyway, but I should have been on time to warm up. I had lost track of time while swimming in the ocean earlier that morning. My new record for holding my breath was two minutes—a surprisingly long time, considering that I had only been practicing for a few days.

"Rayne!" Coach Hansen hollered.

"Sorry I'm late," I gasped, out of breath from my short sprint. "I got here as soon as I could."

His expression softened. "Well, I'm glad you're here. Go ahead and warm up," he said in a kinder tone.

Knowing that I had just swam in the ocean for two hours straight, I replied, "Actually, I'm fine."

Coach raised an eyebrow. "Are you sure?"

"Positive."

He hesitated. "Fine, but I'm taking your word for it. We don't want our number one swimmer pulling a muscle."

He had a point, but seeing as I had been swimming two to three times more than normal without any ramifications, I figured I would be fine.

"So what did your father say about the after-school training session?" he asked.

I cringed, suddenly realizing that I had yet to talk to Dad about Coach Hansen's offer. I said the first thing that came to mind and explained, "Well, I actually have other commitments that I need to keep. My grades have been slipping, so I'm seeing a tutor directly after school."

"Oh. How many days a week?"

"Every day."

Coach frowned. "Well...I guess that can't be helped." He sighed thoughtfully. "Maybe I can set aside some extra time during swim period. While the other kids are doing their laps, I can work with you one-on-one."

I nodded eagerly. "Of course. Thank you." Then, remembering Madeleine, I wondered if maybe that wasn't such a great idea after all. How would she handle a special training session created specifically for me?

"Won't that make some students feel left out?" I asked carefully.

Coach Hansen laughed loudly. "Left out? Of course not, Rayne! You're Olympic material. And Olympians always make sacrifices for their sport. Consider this a minor sacrifice on my behalf."

I nodded again. Coach took a step back, his encouragement sufficiently renewed, and said, "Well, I think I'll go ahead and talk to your dad about some extra training. Hopefully we can work something out."

"Yeah. Hopefully." As soon as he left, I immediately turned my attention to searching for Sage and Marley amid the sea of faces that made up the Shady Cove High swim team. Once I spotted them, I rushed over.

Upon seeing me, they both dropped their conversation and exclaimed, "Rayne! Where were you?"

"Sorry I'm late, I lost track of time," I said breathlessly.

"Well, good thing you just got here! Your heat is coming up in two minutes," Marley explained.

"What?"

"They had to rearrange the schedule," Sage clarified.

"Oh, great." I sighed and pulled my goggles over my swim cap, letting them rest on my forehead. "I guess I'd better head over to the starting blocks, then."

"Good luck!" Marley called.

"Go kill 'em, Rayne!" Sage hollered.

I couldn't help but chuckle at Sage's uncharacteristic comment as I made my way over to the side of the pool. It was time to get in the zone. Even though I had gotten an extremely late start, I still needed to cool down and mentally prepare myself to race. I shook out my arms and did a few light stretches, all the while staring at the turquoise water lapping at the edges of the pool.

Before long, the announcer called my race and heat, and I stepped up to the appropriate lane. I could hear my teammates cheering me on as I pulled my goggles down over my eyes. I let out a deep breath as the announcer continued to call out the names of the current swimmers—four from Shady Cove High and four from St. Paul's, the opposing school. But my heart stopped when Madeleine Hansen's name was announced.

I closed my eyes, already picturing her permanent glare fixated on my face. If I were any other swimmer, I would let Madeleine beat me so I didn't have to suffer through another week of her glares and bad attitude. But I wasn't just any swimmer—I was Rayne Bennett, the best swimmer on the pool deck. And this was my race to win.

The referee blew a series of short whistles, followed by one long whistle. The sound pierced the cool autumn air, silencing most of the commotion on the pool deck.

I stepped onto the starting block with my right foot forward, left foot back.

"Take your marks."

I bent over and gripped the starting block with both hands. All right, I thought, narrowing my eyes and focusing on the shifting blue water beneath me. Let's do this.

There was silence for about two seconds, and then the buzzer sounded. The race was on.

10

CHAPTER 10

The water felt refreshingly cool when I dove in. As I glided forward, it enveloped my figure like a liquid blanket. My arms and legs were drawn taut in a streamline position. I dolphin-kicked my way to the surface and launched into freestyle as soon as I broke through. My whole body flew into action and propelled me forward. Faster! I coached myself. Faster...

In order to complete the 400 freestyle, I had to swim up and back twice. With each lap I pushed myself to go faster, never once glancing over my shoulder to see where the other swimmers were. I focused solely on myself, not worrying whether or not someone was going to pass me. It felt like no time had even elapsed when I slapped the tile and finished the race.

My chest heaved as I gasped for air, but a smile broke out on my face nonetheless. I whipped off my goggles and waved to Marley and Sage, who were jumping up and down, screaming my name.

"And first place goes to the swimmer in lane 5, Rayne Bennett, from Shady Cove High School!" the announcer bellowed. Hoots and hollers erupted from the crowd as I pulled myself out of the pool.

Sage and Marley were the first to dash over, immediately wrapping me in a large bear hug. "I'm positive you just broke a school record," Sage said in awe. "That was amazing! How do you swim so fast?"

"I don't know," I laughed. "I just swim!"

"Words of wisdom," Marley said solemnly, before letting out a laugh of her own. "But seriously, I'm glad you put you-know-who in her place."

Uh-oh. I turned and glanced at Madeleine, who was scowling at me as she climbed out onto the pool deck. "She's gotten first place one too many times," Marley explained. "It always goes to her head. I'm glad someone beat her for once!"

"And by a whopping six seconds!" Sage added.

I ducked my head shyly as my friends continued to rave about the race. Then someone placed their hand on my shoulder, and I glanced up to see my father smiling down at me. "Dad!" I cried.

"Hey, honey. Fantastic race," he congratulated me, giving me a brief hug. "And guess what?" He waved his phone animatedly in the air. "I got it all on video! Come take a look!"

Marley, Sage, and I crowded around him to watch the replay. The camerawork was a little shaky in the beginning, and Dad's voice could constantly be heard cheering me on in the background, but it was entertaining nonetheless. It was interesting to see myself in action for once. I realized I did look pretty fast, especially with my streamlined form, long limbs, and taut muscles glistening with water droplets. "Wow," I breathed.

"Wow is right," Marley exclaimed. "I mean, look at yourself! You only took five breaths the entire race!"

We all froze upon realizing the truth of her words. Sage, Marley, and Dad glanced up from the video to gape at me. "Hey, she's right," Sage said, awestruck. "How did you hold your breath for that long?"

"I've been training," I admitted, caught off guard by the question. I hadn't even realized I had held my breath for that long until Marley pointed it out. I guess all that training in the ocean had paid off.

"Training?" Dad echoed. "Since when?"

"Well, I don't know...maybe since last week? I started forcing myself to hold my breath for longer periods of time. You know, during swim practice," I explained, stretching the truth a bit. If Dad had known I was actually swimming in the ocean, he might not let me go hiking along the cliffs again. The crashing waves and dangerous current didn't exactly harbor safe conditions—and yet I had been in the ocean so many times that I was familiar with it by now.

"That's insane," Marley gasped as Dad replayed the video. "I wish I could hold my breath like that!"

I was starting to feel a little queasy, so I quietly edged away. I slipped into the women's locker room and changed into my clothes, knowing that the 400 freestyle was my only race for today. Usually I swam in two or three races, but lately I hadn't been that interested in swimming—in a pool, that is. Now the ocean was a completely different matter.

I paused with my T-shirt halfway over my head. I glanced down and realized I had a rash just above both hipbones. "Stupid swimsuit," I muttered, tenderly rubbing the sore areas. I winced as my fingers brushed across the reddish-pink surface.

If anything, the tender spots felt like strawberries, the kind one gets from falling off a skateboard or bicycle and landing on the concrete. It reminded me of when I had skinned my knee as a little girl, leaving a reddish-pink area on my kneecap.

"Ouch," I muttered, accidentally pressing against one of the tender spots a little too hard. What could I have done to injure myself like that? It was possible that my swimsuit was getting too tight...

Whatever the problem was, it would have to wait. I quickly slipped my T-shirt all the way on and headed back out to the pool deck. It was time to watch Marley and Sage swim in their races.

By the time the meet was over, it was almost two-thirty in the afternoon. Sage and Marley had both gotten third place for the 400 breaststroke and 200 backstroke, respectively. As I waited for them to change clothes, I quickly texted Kimmie, reminding her that I would see her tomorrow. Dad had promised to drive me back to Newland at least once a week to see my old friends, and today's swim meet had left an aching hole in my heart. Hanging out with Marley and Sage on the pool deck reminded me of how Kimmie and I would laugh and talk together. I wanted to see her so badly.

Once Sage and Marley were dressed and ready to go, we all piled into Dad's car and headed down the highway to my house. As soon as they caught sight of our massive home, they immediately burst into a flurry of questions. "It's huge! How many rooms do you have in that thing?" "Do you really own all this property?" "How big is your room?" "Do you have a walk-in closet?"

Dad and I shared a knowing smile through the rearview mirror. "Yep," I laughed. "Our house is pretty big, isn't it?"

"'Big' is an understatement," Marley snorted.

As soon as Dad parked the car, the four of us filed out, and I was obliged to give my friends a tour of the house. I showed them the living room, office, kitchen, and dining room on the first floor; the bedrooms and bathrooms on the second floor; and I briefly described the spare bedrooms and game room on the third floor (with the exception of my old bedroom). I didn't want Sage and Marley to see the picture of her on the wall—that would be asking for a plethora of unwanted questions.

Fortunately, we kept ourselves occupied for the next few hours as we watched TV and messed around in the game room. Dad ordered pizza for an early dinner and even promised to buy us a gallon of ice cream afterwards. I felt like the happiest girl in the world. Rarely did I enjoy sleepovers, since Kimmie had never been a big fan of them, so bouncing off the walls with Sage and Marley was a whole new experience for me. They made everything fun, including braiding my hair and sneaking onto the roof to watch the sunset. As we lay on the cool shingles, our breath coming out in warm vapors against the chilly night air, I suddenly felt queasy once again. My gaze drifted over to the ocean, which was tinted pink and orange from the sunset. I felt another pull on my heart, immediately wishing I was diving under the waves.

Before I knew what I was doing, I said, "Hey, we should sneak down to the beach tonight."

"All the way to Shady Cove?" Marley asked, incredulous. "But that's miles away!"

"No, just to the private beach down there." I pointed to the edge of the cliffs. "There's a little trail that I found. It leads to a secluded cove. We could sneak out with flashlights after dark."

"I don't know...isn't that a little scary?" Sage asked nervously.

"My dad has a huge lantern. You can easily see everything within a ten-foot radius," I said, remembering how we had used that lantern during camping trips.

"Let's do it," Marley said eagerly. "What time should we go?"

"Midnight," I suggested.

"That's so creepy." Sage shuddered. "Why can't we go now and get it over with? What if there are wild animals that come out at midnight?"

Marley chuckled. "There aren't any wild animals in Shady Cove, silly—unless you count the squirrels."

"And we can't go right now anyway," I added. "I don't think my Dad will want us hiking down a trail in the dark. We have to sneak out." Once again, I felt that familiar forbidden thrill that came with the ocean. I couldn't wait to go back to my private beach and feel the sand between my toes, hear the waves pounding on the shore, feel the wind tousling my hair, and—

"Rayyyyyne!"

I immediately snapped back to reality. "Oops, Dad's calling me." The three of us giggled as we clambered down the roof and through the window of the game room. Sage was the slowest, and she barely made it back inside before Dad burst into the room.

"There you are," he said. "I was wondering what flavor ice cream you girls wanted me to get."

The three of us were still giggling from our secret escapade on the roof. Dad eyed us warily. "What's the matter?"

"Nothing," I said quickly, causing Sage and Marley to giggle even louder. "Can you get us Neapolitan?"

As soon as my father left the room, we shared a knowing smile and burst into another fit of laughter. For the next couple hours we had a movie marathon in the living room while bundled up in sleeping bags. Dad went to bed around 11:30 after I had convinced him we would get a good night's sleep.

"You don't have to worry about us," I reassured him. "After this movie's over we'll go right to sleep."

He was a little skeptical at first, but after Sage and Marley promised they wouldn't stay up the whole night talking, he assented. The three of us grew more and more excited as midnight grew nearer.

"Okay," I said when the clock struck 11:55. The desire to swim in the ocean was overwhelming now. "Follow my lead," I instructed Sage and Marley, quietly stuffing a few pillows into my sleeping bag to make it look like someone was snoozing underneath the covers—just in case Dad decided he wanted to check in on us. The girls copied my movements, and before long we were ready to sneak outside.

The three of us bundled up in sweatshirts and coats, knowing it would be freezing out on the cliffs. We left the TV on to hide any extraneous sound before slipping out the front door. I carried Dad's huge lantern in one hand, but we agreed not to use it until we were well away from the house, just to be safe.

"I feel like a ninja," Sage whispered as we stumbled towards the edge of the cliff.

Marley chuckled. "I feel more like a secret agent," she said.

Before long, we reached the start of the downhill section of the trail, and I lit the lantern to illuminate the way. It was extremely bright, and the three of us stared in awe, watching as our warm breaths exhaled against the chilly night air.

"This way," I said, stepping in front and leading my friends down the trail. The cold was seeping in quicker now, biting any exposed skin and making us shiver.

"How much farther?" Sage asked after a few more minutes of hiking.

"Just a little." I ignored the fact that we had at least ten minutes to go, maybe even longer. A freezing gust of wind shook our coats and sent Marley's beanie flying into the air, but I pressed on. I was consumed with the desire to see the ocean and dive under the waves. I just had to keep going.

"Rayne!" Sage suddenly gasped.

"I already told you; we're almost there," I retorted.

"No, it's not that," Marley interrupted. The worry laced through her words made me pause. "Sage meant—I mean—it's your hair."

I quickly glanced up at the night sky. I gasped when I saw that the billowing clouds overhead had parted, allowing a sliver of moonlight to dart through. I immediately dropped the lantern and threw my hood over my hair. I made sure to keep my eyes downcast so they couldn't see my glowing eyeballs, either.

Marley and Sage gaped at me. "What was that?" Sage asked, shocked.

"Nothing. It was nothing." I suddenly realized I was freezing cold, and the previously overwhelming need to swim in the ocean was ebbing away like a flowing tide. "You know what?" I sighed. "This is stupid. Come on, let's go back."

I grabbed the lantern and pushed past my friends, feeling like a complete and utter fool. What had I been thinking? I had led them out to the edge of Redrock Cliffs, only to let them see the glowing streaks in my hair! Now I was sure to be called a freak at Shady Cove High. How could I have let this happen?

"Sorry, guys," I muttered as soon as we were back inside my warm, cozy house. I peeled off my layers and sank down on the couch, angry with myself for giving into my impulses once again.

Marley and Sage didn't move. They didn't even take off their coats and sweatshirts. "Okay," Sage said finally, letting out a shaky breath, "what happened back there?"

"Nothing happened," I said automatically.

"Oh, sure. Like watching your hair turn blue before our eyes is 'nothing,'" Marley pressed. "There has to be an explanation."

I didn't say anything. I merely buried my head in my hands, my mind swimming with all kinds of excuses, but not one of them sounding suitable for the situation. My stomach felt like it was turned upside down.

"Rayne?" Sage asked quietly. "Is this why you don't like to show off your hair?"

I was about to say "no" when I realized that I could use Sage's words to my advantage. Heaving my most realistic sigh, I admitted, "Yes."

"Then why does it turn blue?" Marley demanded.

"Promise you won't tell anybody?"

Sage and Marley nodded solemnly. I then jumped into an explanation that would hopefully satisfy their questions. "Well," I began, "years ago, I went through this phase where I wanted to dye my hair blue. But during a dare at my old high school, I was forced to use glow-in-the-dark dye."

My friends swiftly exchanged glances. I panicked when I thought they weren't going to buy it. After all, it didn't take a genius to realize the whole glow-in-the-dark hair dye excuse didn't explain why my hair had been normal the first twenty minutes we were romping down the trail.

But to my relief, Marley let out a loud laugh. "You didn't!" she exclaimed.

"You saw it yourself." I switched on the light and let down my hood.

"That's crazy," Sage murmured. "At first I thought your hair was magic or something."

I laughed nervously.

"Hey, let's turn off all the lights," Marley suggested. "Can we see your hair glow again?"

"Marley!" Sage hissed. "Can't you see Rayne is upset?"

I put on my best puppy dog eyes, and Marley gave a little sigh. "Sorry," she murmured. "If it makes you that uncomfortable, then I don't want to put you on the spot."

"Thanks," I replied weakly. An awkward silence descended on the room, and the walls flickered from orange, to blue, then to black. Credits began scrolling on the TV in front of us.

Sage cleared her throat. "So, how about another movie? Anyone want to watch Pirates?"

"Sure." Marley plopped down on her sleeping bag, and I gingerly removed my pillows before slipping into mine. I didn't even breathe until the new movie started playing and my friends' gazes were fixed firmly on the TV. My hands were still shaking from our little adventure. My secret had been close to being discovered—much too close. I couldn't afford to be as careless next time.

11

— • —

CHAPTER 11

Guilt gnawed at my insides the entire evening. I felt horrible at having to lie to Sage and Marley. But what else could I do? There was no way I could come clean and tell them that my hair—and eyes—glowed blue in the moonlight. That was just crazy. They wouldn't believe it—and even if they did, they would probably think I was some sort of freak of nature.

I shuddered and huddled deeper into my sleeping bag. I hadn't slept a wink all night, whereas Marley and Sage had fallen asleep around two in the morning. There were sure to be dark circles under my eyes.

I glanced up at the wall clock. It was nine in the morning, and Dad was noisily moving around downstairs. I suddenly remembered that we were supposed to drive to Newland today. My heart leaped in my chest, and I eagerly shimmied out of my sleeping bag. Kimmie and I texted every single day and called each other at least three times a week, but that still couldn't heal the aching hole in my heart. I needed to see her in person, just like I used to see her every day at Newland High.

When my gaze drifted over to the window, I frowned. I felt Marley stir from where she was sleeping just inches away from my feet, so

I didn't move a muscle. But my mouth dropped open of its own accord. What in the world...?

White. The yard, the sky, everything, was completely white. It wasn't snow. The worst weather Shady Cove received was a thunderstorm, hail, and a little frost. No, the culprit was fog—an extremely thick blanket of fog that had decided to settle over the town last night.

I crawled out of my sleeping bag as silently as possible, cautiously stepping over Sage and Marley's sleeping bodies to reach the window. The pane was cold to the touch—ice cold. As far as the eye could see, the house was shrouded in white. I could barely even make out the ground below. There was no way Dad—or anyone, for that matter—could drive in this thick cloud.

I grumbled my way into the kitchen, where I poured myself a glass of water (along with a pinch of salt) to soothe my scratchy throat. Dad shuffled into the kitchen a few moments later, just as I drained the last drops of my drink. "Good morning!" he said brightly.

"What's so good about it?" I muttered, gesturing to the window. "Just look at all that fog."

"There's no need to be upset," he reasoned. "We can wait a few hours and see if it clears. The fog should blow away by noon at the latest."

"I hope so." I stood up and rinsed out my glass before placing it in the dishwasher. "Oh, and if Sage and Marley ask, I put glow-in-the-dark dye on my hair."

Dad's eyebrows shot up in surprise. "What?"

"They saw my hair glow last night," I admitted. "I had to give them some sort of excuse."

He ran a hand through his hair. "Oh, Rayne..."

"I know, I know. I'm sorry."

"Are they awake?"

"Not yet."

"Did you even get any sleep last night?" Dad folded his arms across his chest.

"Not really. But Sage and Marley slept like logs."

"Well, once they're up and they've eaten breakfast, let's see how the fog looks. I suggest you take a long nap if we can't make it to Kimmie's today." The corners of his lips turned up into a smile. "Those bags under your eyes make you look like a raccoon."

"Gee, thanks, Dad." I rolled my eyes and headed toward the stairs. "Hey, if Marley or Sage wakes up, tell them I'm in the shower."

Dad assented, so I took that as my cue to leave and gratefully headed toward the warm shower awaiting me. The morning was chilly, much chillier than usual, and I knew the fog was to blame. But Dad's logic had given me some hope. There was still a possibility...

Once the hot water was running and I was standing in the shower, my stomach began to feel queasy again. I frowned and glanced down at the tender spots above my hipbones. They were still red and sore to touch, but strangely enough, the hot water didn't sting one bit. What did hurt was rubbing some cream on the surface after I got out of the shower. I had to bite back a scream because the pain was so intense. After that, it hurt to get dressed, so I was forced to wear baggy sweatpants and a loose T-shirt so I wouldn't aggravate the sore areas.

By the time I made it back downstairs, Marley and Sage were awake, and Dad was flipping pancakes on the griddle. It smelled delicious, and I realized I was ravenously hungry despite the queasy feeling in my stomach. Since the pain had intensified after trying to put cream on my tender spots, I was forced to eat breakfast in a slightly hunched-over position, trying not to double all the way over.

"Is something wrong, Rayne?" Sage asked, noticing I looked a little uncomfortable.

"No, I'm fine. I just have a slight stomachache," I reassured her. But 'slight' was a gross understatement. Though Dad's pancakes were delicious, I was unable to finish even my first one. My torso felt like it was on fire. After apologizing to my friends, I weakly climbed the stairs to my bedroom. Sage and Marley eyed me worriedly as Dad followed me, helped me into bed, and tucked me under the covers.

"I'm going to take the girls home," he said. "Just stay here and try to get some sleep."

"But the fog," I protested. "You can't see anything."

"I'll just have to drive slow. Fortunately the town is only a few miles away, so it shouldn't take more than twenty minutes max." He laid a hand on my forehead and frowned. "Hmm...on second thought, I think I'll stop by the pharmacy, too. You might be coming down with something."

Marley and Sage warily stepped into the doorway to say goodbye. "I hope you feel better, Rayne," Sage said kindly. "Thanks for having us over."

"Yeah, thanks for the fun time. See you soon!" Marley said.

"Bye," I murmured weakly. I closed my eyes and tried to drift off to sleep, listening for the rumble of an engine as Dad pulled out of the driveway. The house was silent as a graveyard after that, yet no matter how hard I tried, I was unable to keep my eyes shut for more than a few minutes. My mind began to wander, from the strange spots on my hips, to the swirling white fog outside, to the waves that I imagined I could hear churning against the bottom of the cliffs. I suddenly felt the need to see the ocean and dive under its blue-green surface. "Not again," I groaned, trying to shove the impulse away. But it only came back stronger. I knew I would never get some rest unless I made the trek to the cliffs.

The desire to see the ocean overwhelmed the pain in my torso, so I slid out of bed. With each step I took towards the sea, the less I focused on my pain. I pulled on a sweatshirt and grabbed my swim bag on the way out the door. Then, with a deep breath, I marched straight into the fog. If anything, it had only thickened since this morning, yet I didn't have to fear losing my way. My brain automatically remembered where the trail was, even if I couldn't see more than three feet in front of me. Before long I found myself meandering down the side of the cliff and toward the private beach.

"Finally," I breathed as soon as my feet hit the soft, warm sand. I sank to my knees and dug my hands into the sand, savoring the feeling of millions of grains running between my fingers. It felt amazing to be back, almost like I had returned home after a long journey. I let out a sigh of contentment before changing into my swimsuit and heading to the shoreline.

Though I could barely see the waves, I had no problem hearing them as they crashed and slammed onto the surface of the water. The ocean was freezing cold as I began to wade in, but once I dove completely underwater, my body gradually became used to the temperature. I found that I now enjoyed the cool water, even more so than the hot shower I had taken earlier.

I smiled as I glided underneath the waves. I closed my eyes and let the saltwater sink into every pore of my body, leaving me feeling refreshed and rejuvenated. Even the sore areas above my hipbones no longer throbbed in pain. I did a few happy somersaults underwater, blowing some air bubbles along the way so I wouldn't get water up my nose.

When I opened my eyes, I was shocked to find that the underwater world no longer appeared hazy and blurry. Somehow I could see perfectly. In fact, it seemed as though I could see more clearly than I could with goggles! Everything was crystal-clear and sharpened to perfection, as if someone had taken a snapshot and edited the picture to make it look dazzlingly clear.

I was thrilled. "Whoa," I exclaimed, the word coming out in a plethora of bubbles that escaped between my lips before floating to the surface. I giggled and swam deeper, mentally counting the seconds I was holding my breath: 54.

My newly discovered talent of seeing underwater made the ocean seem even more alive than ever. Every inch of the sea was illuminated, from the golden sand to the brilliant green seaweed. I even spotted a few minnows darting past my nose, their sleek gray bodies glinting like pieces of silver.

138. I did a few more somersaults just for fun, then placed my hands behind my head and let myself sink to the bottom. The surface of the water slowly grew farther and farther away, and I watched as waves surged and swelled overhead. From this perspective, they looked like billowing white clouds when they broke. It was breathtaking.

170. I smiled when I realized I was going on three minutes—three whole minutes without taking a breath of air! My lungs weren't even craving oxygen yet. I felt perfectly at peace with my surroundings, and for the first time I actually wanted to swim deeper into the ocean. I wanted to swim farther out from shore, where the waves

rolled by unbroken, and where I could see sea otters and dolphins and other animals in their natural habitats.

But not today, the voice in my head warned. I reluctantly swam up to the surface and trudged into shore, knowing that Dad would be returning home shortly. I was supposed to be in bed, sick with a stomachache.

With this thought in mind, I quickly changed back into my sweatpants and T-shirt. Despite the thick fog, I wrung out my long hair the best I could. I swept it up into my normal bun before heading back up the trail, forcing myself to quicken my pace so I could get home before Dad did. If he caught me, I had no idea how to explain where I'd been.

I had a little trouble finding my way back, but I continued to shuffle along the goat-trail until a dark shape loomed in the distance. I could faintly make out the outline of my house as I stumbled towards it. I hoped desperately that Dad wasn't back yet.

I let out a sigh of relief when I jerked open the front door. Everything was just as I had left it, and Dad was still gone. I headed upstairs and squeezed out my hair with a towel before slipping back into bed. The covers were warm and cozy, and my torso still hurt a tiny bit, but it was nothing compared to the freeing feeling of swimming in the sea.

As I waited for Dad to come home, I pulled out my phone and texted Kimmie, saying that I wouldn't be able to see her today because it was extremely foggy. A few minutes later, she replied in the affirmative, saying that Newland was covered in fog as well.

I told her I would try to come next weekend. As soon as I hit the send button, I suddenly heard the front door open, and Dad came jogging up the stairs moments later.

"Rayne, honey, how are you doing?" he asked, coming over to my bedside.

"I'm a little better," I replied. "My stomach doesn't hurt as bad."

Dad smiled with relief. "Good. Still try to get some rest, okay?"

"Okay."

"You realize we won't be able to visit Kimmie today, right?" he said apologetically.

I nodded. "I just texted her."

"I think the fog is getting worse, if anything." He heaved a sigh and leaned over to give me a kiss on the forehead. "Let me know if you need anything, hon."

"Alright." I reached for my headphones as he closed the door on his way out. With soft music playing in my ears and memories of the ocean drifting across the forefront of my mind, fatigue took over and I fell into a dreamless sleep.

"Almost late again, Rayne."

Señora Ramirez eyed me coldly as I sprinted into the classroom. "Sorry," I murmured, brushing past her and sliding into my seat. As soon as I took off my backpack, the bell rang, and my Spanish teacher shook her head at my near-tardiness.

"Take out su tarea and pass it forward, por favor," she instructed. I smiled faintly as I passed up my homework, knowing that my tutoring sessions with Luke were paying off. For the first time this year, I actually had a C in the class. Dad promised to buy me a new swimsuit if I raised my grade to A, but I had a feeling that would never happen. The only A out of all my classes was in swimming.

"Hey, Rayne," a voice suddenly said, close to my ear.

I jumped in my seat. "Wait, Luke? What are you doing here?" Normally everyone sat in the same seats from the beginning of the year, and Luke just happened to be on the opposite side of the room from me. But today, he took the opportunity of sliding into the seat of an absent classmate.

He chuckled. "I know, I know. We usually sit far away from each other, but I never get the chance to say hi to you. Then again," he added, lowering his voice, "you're always coming in late."

I felt my cheeks grow red. "I'm not late."

"Whatever you say," he replied breezily. "Well, the real reason I came over here is to tell y—"

"Señor Sanchez!" Señora Ramirez snapped, making both of us jump. "What are you doing out of your seat?"

"Sorry. It won't happen again," he said quickly, backing away from my desk.

"Well, whatever it is, it can wait until después de la clase," Señora Ramirez ordered, her steel gaze directing Luke back to his seat.

I glanced down and realized he had slipped a scrap of paper onto my lap without me noticing. Once Señora Ramirez had her attention turned back to the whiteboard, I flipped the paper over and saw a phone number scribbled on the front. A smile tugged on the corners of my lips.

As Señora Ramirez jumped into the next lesson, my thoughts were focused on everything except Spanish. Why would Luke give me his number? Was this strictly for tutoring purposes, or could it precede something more? And what had he wanted to tell me? I knew it was more probable that Luke had given me his number for a practical reason, since he was my tutor and all, but it was more fun to think that he might have a "thing" for me. I clutched the piece of paper and smiled to myself.

Suddenly, I felt a tap on my shoulder. I glanced up and realized someone was passing me a note. I grabbed it and made sure Señora Ramirez wasn't looking before unfolding the paper. On the inside were the words: I can't make it to tutoring today. Visiting my grandma after school. – Luke

I frowned and quickly scribbled a reply: Alright. Is that what you were trying to tell me earlier?

As soon as Señora Ramirez's back was turned, I folded the piece of paper and passed it to my classmate, nodding in Luke's direction. In a few minutes I received another note: Yeah. I also wanted to see if we could go to the Café after tutoring tomorrow. How does that sound?

I grinned. Sure! I wrote, my pencil hovering over the empty space after the exclamation mark. I finally opted not to put a smiley face at the end. Better keep things as professional as possible, even though the fact that he had given me his number and asked me to the Café were pretty suggestive.

After passing my note back to my classmate, I glanced over my shoulder and realized Luke was smiling at me. I smiled back, and our eyes locked for a brief second. What was this boy up to?

12

CHAPTER 12

"So let me get this straight—Luke gave you his number and asked you to go with him to the Shady Cove Café?" Sage asked as we walked out of the locker room.

I shrugged, trying to play it cool. "Pretty much."

"So how is that not a date?" Sage threw her hands up in the air. "This is breaking news, Rayne!"

"Breaking news? What'd I miss?" Marley demanded as she jogged up next to us.

"Rayne's got a date with Luke Sanchez," Sage explained.

I shook my head vigorously. "It's tutoring, not a date."

Marley wiggled her eyebrows up and down suggestively. "Are you sure? Because it sounds like a date to me."

"I'm positive." I crossed my arms over my chest. "I'm beginning to think that Sage is the one who set me up with him in the first place."

Marley's gaze swung over to Sage, who smiled coyly. "Maybe," she admitted, "but that doesn't mean you won't make a great couple."

"For the last time," I said, "there's nothing going on, and this is not a date!"

"Ooh, touchy subject," Marley teased. "But I've gotta admit, you and Luke do look great together." She laughed and high-fived Sage.

I sighed in defeat—it was useless to try and convince them of something once they ganged up on me.

"See you guys later," I said, pulling away from them and jerking open the front door of the library.

"Bye!" Sage called.

"Have fun on your date!" Marley added.

I felt heat rush to my cheeks as I entered the library. "It's not a date!" I hollered over my shoulder, but my two friends had already turned the corner, their giggles reverberating off the walls. I sighed and turned back to face the endless rows of books and computers that made up the high school library.

Then I froze. The librarian was glaring at me with a stern expression, and Luke was trying not to laugh from where he sat at a nearby empty table. I ducked my head shyly and shuffled over to his table, utterly humiliated.

"So," he said, trying to hide his amused smile, "I see it's pretty clear that we're not going on a date."

"Ha ha, very funny."

"I mean, we can make it a date if you want to..."

Huh? I tried to ignore the millions of butterflies that had suddenly exploded in my stomach at his words. Was he legitimately asking me out, or was he merely teasing? I swept my eyes over his face, but no reaction gave his true thoughts away. I finally decided my best tactic was to switch tracks. "Well," I said vaguely, "what exactly were you planning to do at the Café?"

"That depends—do you like food?"

I grinned. "Duh."

"And hot chocolate?"

"Of course."

"And a walk on the pier?"

"Hmm, isn't it a little chilly out?"

"You can always wear my hoodie."

I was literally smiling from ear to ear now. I was sure my heart couldn't handle another ounce of excitement, I was so thrilled. "Alright," I agreed. "Let's go!"

"Now?" Despite the question, Luke didn't seem one bit surprised. If anything, he seemed just as eager to get going as I was.

"Yes, now!" I urged. "You tutor me every single day after school. It won't hurt to miss one day, right?"

Luke grinned. "Right."

We slid out of our chairs at the same time and made a beeline for the exit. As soon as we were outside the library, we laughed and raced each other to the parking lot, ignoring the looks from students who were still waiting for their rides. We finally slowed and walked side-by-side for half a mile until Main Street came into view. I was shivering from the slight chill in the air, so Luke took off once again, insisting that a short sprint would warm me up immediately. I tried my hardest to catch him, but he was ahead of me the entire time.

"Slowpoke," he said when I finally caught up to him at the intersection.

"Hey, I'm not a marathon runner! I'm a swimmer," I protested, breathing heavily. Much to my chagrin, I was winded.

"Yeah, but doesn't that mean you should be in shape?" Luke countered.

"Trust me, I'm in shape," I said airily.

The walk signal turned on, so we stepped off the curb.

"Anyway, I heard you're a pretty good. At swimming, that is," Luke added.

"Oh. I don't know. I guess you'd just have to watch me and find out for yourself." As soon as the words came out, I immediately regretted them. What was I doing—trying to be a flirt?

Fortunately, Luke plowed ahead. "But it's true you beat Madeleine Hansen, right?"

I winced. "Does the whole school know about that?"

"Probably." He shrugged. "News travels fast in a small town—and even faster in a small high school."

"Oh."

"You don't sound too excited. You should be thrilled, Rayne!" He grinned. "Madeleine has been one of the top athletes since junior high. She's practicably unbeatable—that is, until you came out of nowhere and destroyed her."

"I don't think that's necessarily a good thing."

"Why not?"

"Well, ever since my first day at Shady Cove High, she's been out to get me."

He laughed dryly. "Yeah, she has a bit of a temper."

"But on the first day? Seriously?" I shook my head. "I know her dad is the swim coach and all, but it's not like he's giving me special treatment or anything." I suddenly clamped my mouth shut. Maybe that was my problem after all. Coach Hansen had been trying to find a time to train me for the Junior Olympics, and he did show me a lot of favoritism during practice. Was Madeleine furious over that?

"You know," I added, "I heard she beat up some guy from the swim team last year. Is that true?"

"Yeah."

"What was her motive?"

"I don't know. Nobody is one hundred percent certain why she does the things she does. I guess she had a grudge against him or something. They were fighting in the hall, he gave her a little shove, and then she went all King Kong on him."

I swallowed nervously. This conversation wasn't exactly the most comforting thing to hear at the moment. "So...do you think Madeleine would beat me up?"

Luke gave me a strange look. "I doubt it. Why would she beat you up just for being a better swimmer than her?"

"I don't know." I sighed and glanced down at my Converse, wiggling my toes underneath their worn surface.

"We're here," Luke suddenly announced. He gestured toward the small building up ahead. With a smile, he held open the door to the Café and ushered me inside. Just before entering, I got a whiff of a salty sea breeze and realized we were fairly close to the ocean. I immediately felt that familiar tug on my heart.

"So what do you want to eat? Pick anything you want."

I quickly snapped back to reality and scanned the menu. The playful font was displayed in teal and silver lettering. It seemed like those were the theme colors of the entire building, from the walls to the tiles to the colorful rugs on the floor. Though the Café was small, it was light and airy. Quaint seemed the best word to describe it.

"Hmm," I said at Luke's prodding, "I think I'll have one of the sandwiches."

A few moments later, we were at the front of the line, and the effervescent cashier took our orders quickly and brightly. I pulled out my wallet from my jeans pocket, but Luke slapped down a twenty before I could pay. "It's on me," he said, smiling.

"Are you sure?"

"Of course." Luke turned to the cashier. "Oh, and can we have two hot chocolates with marshmallows and whipped cream?"

I felt a blush creeping up on my cheeks. This was the first time a guy (other than Dad, of course) had paid for my meal. Had Sage and Marley been right?

For the rest of the time in the Café, I felt like I was in a dream. Luke and I sat across from each other in a booth and chatted casually as we ate our sandwiches and sipped our hot chocolate. The food was delicious, the atmosphere pleasant, and the company charming. "If only Kimmie could see me now," I murmured with a half-smile on my lips.

"What?"

I suddenly realized I had just spoken my thoughts out loud. "Oh, nothing," I said quickly.

Luke gazed at me inquisitively, so I confessed, "I was thinking about my friend back in Newland."

"Oh." He settled back in his seat. "That must be hard to move away from all your friends."

"Yeah, but at least I've made new ones." I felt a slight pang of guilt at my words, remembering what Kimmie had said the night before I moved away:

"You better not find a new best friend to take my place!"

I laughed. "No way—and the same goes for you!"

Kimmie and I laughed and laughed until our stomachs hurt. It felt good to just be sitting here, watching the beautiful sunset. "You know I would never let anyone take your place," she said honestly.

Had I broken my promise to my best friend? Were Sage and Marley slowly replacing the place in my heart where Kimmie had been?

"Rayne?" Luke asked, reaching out to touch my hand. "Are you okay?"

I sucked in a deep breath. "Yeah, I'm fine. I just—I just miss my old home."

Luke was silent for a few moments. I stared down at my half-empty cup of hot chocolate, watching as the last of the whipped cream swirled around in the center of the drink. "So," he said suddenly, "do you still want to take that walk on the pier?"

I immediately brightened at the thought of strolling along the ocean. "Sure. Let's go." We gathered up our trash and threw it away before heading outside. I carried my cup of hot chocolate in both hands to warm my skin as we walked down the sidewalk. There was a light breeze blowing in from the sea, making it even colder than the air around Shady Cove High. True to his word, Luke took off his hoodie and placed it over my shoulders as soon as we reached the pier.

We strolled across the wooden boards quietly. The only sound was the crashing of waves below us and the lapping of water against the pilings of the pier. The wind was even stronger here, and my bun bobbed loosely against the back of my head. Our conversation had lapsed into a pleasant silence as we headed to the end of the pier.

We huddled over the railing together and watched the murky blue water swirl against the pilings. "Are you cold?" Luke asked.

"No," I lied. The truth was, I had goosebumps on every inch of my body, but I didn't want to spoil the moment. This had been a wonderful afternoon.

"Hey," I exclaimed, pointing at the water. "Dolphins!"

"Where?" He scanned the ocean but couldn't find anything. "I don't see any."

"They're swimming right underneath us." I leaned over the railing and watched as one dolphin after another suddenly began breaching under the pier. Luke stared in awe. The dolphins seemed to smiling at us as they leaped out of the water and splashed back in. I immediately wished I could be swimming with them.

"Come on," I said, pulling on Luke's sleeve. "They want us to play. Let's go in to shore and see if they'll follow."

Luke gave me a puzzled smile. "So you're a dolphin whisperer?"

"Not that I know of," I laughed. "Come on! Let's get closer to them!"

We ran all the way back to shore, jumping off the last section of the pier where it was only a few feet off the sand. Luke paused while I ran all the way to the water's edge, my heart beating rapidly with excitement. "What are you waiting for?" I called over my shoulder. "They're coming!"

Sure enough, the pod of dolphins that had been breaching underneath the pier were directly in front of me, playing in the waves. Their sleek silver bodies glistened under the setting sun as they leaped high into the air before crashing back into the water, sending foam spraying everywhere. I smiled as I watched their acrobatics. My heart longed to be in the ocean swimming with those amazing creatures, but I was forced to hold myself back. Not here. Not now.

"Wow," Luke breathed, coming up behind me. "That's amazing. Why did they follow us into shore?"

"They wanted to," I replied simply. "They're trying to get us to come play in the water."

Luke gave me a strange look. "You baffle me sometimes," he said. "Are you sure you're not a dolphin whisperer? I mean, how do you know they want us to play with them?"

His question caught me off guard. How did I know?

"I just know," I answered truthfully, if a little ambiguously. I had known when the dolphins were underneath the pier, and I had known why they followed us into shore. It was instinct.

Luke drew closer to me, and we watched quietly as the dolphins began to swim farther and farther away, until they were no longer breaching but swimming underneath the surface, out of sight. The sun was beginning to dip behind the horizon, casting watercolor streaks of orange and yellow across the surface of the water.

"You're different, Rayne," Luke said suddenly. His voice was thoughtful. "I can't explain it, but somehow you're different. In a good way, of course."

I turned to face him. "Thanks for today. I had a lot of fun." Then, with slight hesitation, I added, "We should do this again sometime."

"Totally," Luke said to my relief. "Should we meet at the Café again on Saturday?"

I grinned. "Of course."

"How about one o'clock? Is that a good time?"

"Yes," I said immediately. I didn't have a meet this weekend, so spending the afternoon with Luke would be a perfect way to pass the time. I didn't care that he hadn't officially asked me out on a date. I didn't care that Marley and Sage would tease me mercilessly if he did. All that mattered was standing here, on the soft glowing sand, watching the dazzling sunset mirrored on the glassy surface of the water. I wanted to savor this moment like the sweet hot chocolate that was still melting on my tongue.

13

CHAPTER 13

Somehow, I survived Sage and Marley's endless rounds of interrogations the following day. They fired question after question at me, all of which I answered as tactfully as possible.

"Did he make a move?"

"No."

"Did you even hold hands?"

"No."

"Did you snuggle in the booth?"

"No."

"Did he smell good?"

"What?" I laughed. "Oh, wait, I remember—he smelled like a fresh bakery on a spring morning."

Sage rolled her eyes. "You're hopeless, Rayne," she sighed.

"I sure am."

"You know he's never going to ask you out again."

"Correction: he never did ask me out in the first place."

"Whatever." Sage shook her head sadly. "You two would have made a great couple."

"Not."

Sage playfully shoved my shoulder, and I shoved her back. I knew she was disappointed in me, but I wasn't about to tell her that Luke and I were meeting at the Café again on Saturday. She and Marley would jump all over the news.

Speaking of Marley...

As Sage and I rounded the corner towards the pool complex, I asked her where the third member of our trio was.

"I dunno." Sage shrugged. "She was here at lunch."

"That's weird. I wonder where she is." I glanced over at Sage's wristwatch as we entered the women's locker room. "We better hurry. Swim starts in two minutes." I hurried over to my locker, but as soon as I pulled it open, I let out a sharp cry of astonishment.

"What?" Sage asked, scurrying over. "What's wr—" Her eyes grew wide when she saw what had happened. "Oh no. Rayne..."

We both stared in disbelief at the contents of my locker. I gingerly picked up my goggles, which had been cut in two, most likely by a sharp razor. My towel was frayed and cut in multiple places. My cap had even been slashed down the middle. But the worst damage was done to my racing suit. I could barely even distinguish the bright colors and markings as a veil of tears began to cloud my vision.

"That jerk," I muttered, not even bothering to wipe my eyes as I pulled my personal belongings out. I stared at them incredulously, not believing that this had actually happened. Madeleine had gone too far this time—much too far. My blood boiled with rage. "She has no right," I said fiercely, slamming my locker closed. "Who does she think she is? Why is she doing this to me?"

"You can use my extra swimsuit," Sage offered quietly.

"It wouldn't fit. I'm four inches taller than you," I muttered, cradling my head in my hands. Something had snapped inside of me at the sight of all my swim equipment destroyed. Did Madeleine Hansen have a disorder or an anger management problem? Because who else would do such a thing?

I glanced over at Sage, whose mouth was still parted in shock. "Do you have an idea?" I demanded. "Any idea as to why she would do this?"

"I don't know," Sage said softly, calmly.

I stared at my locker, fists clenched. "How are you not even angry?"

"Rayne, believe me, I'm just as upset as you are," Sage said quickly. "But if Madeleine did this out of anger, why do you think being angry is the solution?"

"I have a right to be angry."

"But—"

"Look," I said, exasperated, "I don't want to argue right now. This is between Madeleine and I." It was hard to believe that she had the audacity to break in (though it was just as likely that I had forgotten to lock my belongings, as usual). But even harder to believe was the fact that she had destroyed my belongings. Why the sudden outrage? Or had it been building up all this time?

I swallowed. I had saved up for three months last summer in order to buy my racing suit, and now it was worthless. And my favorite pair of goggles...

Anger simmered within me. Madeleine would pay—she had to pay.

"W-what are you going to do?" Sage stammered.

"Watch me," I said, heading for the exit.

"Rayne!" Sage cried anxiously. "Where are you going?"

"I'm telling Coach Hansen what happened!" I hollered over my shoulder. Several girls glanced up at me as I barreled past them.

"But he won't do anything about it! He never does! And if Madeleine finds out that you tattled on her..." Sage trailed off into silence.

I turned around. "Well, someone has to stop her from bullying, and it might as well be me." With that statement ringing through the now-silent locker room, I stormed outside and headed straight for Coach Hansen, who was pacing the pool deck with his hands on his hips.

"Coach," I said coolly, trying to bite back the anger rising within me.

"Rayne!" His eyes immediately lit up when he saw me. "How are you? Have you considered squeezing some training sessions in between your tutoring after school?"

"Actually, Coach, that's not what I want to talk to you about." My voice suddenly grew calm—eerily calm. "Are you aware that ever since I arrived at this school, your daughter has had it out for me? Are you aware that she has held a grudge against me for the past two weeks?"

Coach Hansen blinked.

I fumbled for the right words. I needed to be strong—to stand my ground. "Are you aware that Madeleine broke into my swim locker and destroyed everything inside?" I demanded.

"Rayne," he said, concerned, "this is a serious charge. Are you sure?"

His question caught me off guard. Was I sure? I hadn't seen her do it, and the locker rooms didn't have security cameras...

I suddenly felt foolish. "She's—she's—" Then I stopped again. I couldn't exactly say she's a bully without sounding like a scared little kid. But the fact only angered me even more.

"Madeleine beat up someone from the swim team," I said, switching tactics. "How'd she get away with that one?"

Coach narrowed his eyes. "She got a detention, of course. Why—"

A detention? Not an expulsion, or even a suspension?

My expression must have betrayed my thoughts, because Coach cleared his throat and said firmly, "Rayne, this is none of your business. What's done is done."

"But it is my business," I pressed. Students were trickling onto the pool deck now, watching our little argument with curious expressions. "Madeleine is...well...she's uncontrollable! She vandalized my personal belongings and destroyed something that is precious to me. She ripped up my racing suit, my goggles, and my towel—and it must have been with a razor or a pocket knife, which isn't even allowed on school property—and I know it was her because no one else has had it out for me the short time I've been here." I took a deep breath, hoping that Coach Hansen felt the full weight of my words. He had to believe me.

But he merely laughed. "Oh, Rayne..."

I bristled against his nonchalant attitude. "Never mind," I muttered. I would handle this with a different, more mature, adult—maybe another teacher, or even the school principal himself. I turned around and stomped out of the pool complex, ignoring the strange looks thrown my way. The mob of swimmers in front of the locker rooms parted to let me through, but their attention was diverted when Madeleine suddenly entered the pool deck.

We both paused. She lifted her eyebrows, watching, waiting. The sly little smile playing on the corners of her lips told me that she knew. She knew my anger and frustration, and she knew what was coming next.

"You!" I spluttered, not knowing what else to say.

"Have a problem, Rayne?" she sneered. She folded her arms and stepped closer to me.

"You know what the problem is," I said. "Now own up to it."

She tossed her head like one who has the upper hand, and knows it. "Make me."

By now the entire girls' swim team was watching. They kept an equal distance away from Madeleine and I, but I knew they were more terrified of her than of me. And that's when I realized I was playing right into Madeleine's hands. She wanted a fight, and she wanted to provoke me. I unclenched my fists, took a few deep breaths, and replaced my anger with calm authority.

"Let's settle this in the office," I said.

Madeleine saw my relaxation and heard the new tone in my voice, and her eyes darkened. "What?" she snapped.

"I said, we need to take this to the—"

But I didn't even have a chance to finish my sentence. Madeleine was on top of me in less than a second, and the two of us tumbled to the floor. I winced in pain when my head made contact with the hard linoleum tile of the locker room. Madeleine took a swing at me, but both my arms were raised over my face, protecting me from her blows. There was a lot of commotion (and a few startled screams) until I felt someone pull Madeleine away from me.

"Rayne! Are you okay?" Coach Hansen was holding his daughter back while the guidance counselor bent over me anxiously.

"Yeah," I groaned, sitting up and looking around me. My hair was tangled, and my clothes were wrinkled and disheveled. Everyone stared at me with wide eyes while Madeleine thrashed in her father's arms.

"Did you see what she did to me?" she shrieked.

I raised my eyes to meet Coach Hansen's. I held his gaze until he finally looked down at his daughter and said, "We need to talk."

"What? No, you need to talk to her!" She pointed an accusing finger at me.

Coach quickly pulled Madeleine aside, and the guidance counselor helped me to my feet. "Let's get you cleaned up in the office," she said gently, yet she had a firm tone to her voice. As we left the locker room, I heard the murmur of voices escalate behind me, and knew that Sage's was probably among them.

I was herded down the hall and into the office, where the secretary glanced up at me through her wide-rimmed glasses. "Hello, Rayne!" she chirped.

I smiled weakly. "Hi."

"How are you?"

"There was a fight," the guidance counselor deadpanned, ushering me into an empty room and motioning for me take a seat. "Do you need to see a nurse?" she asked, a little more kindly.

I shook my head, even though my head throbbed and my arms were sure to be littered with bruises.

"All right. I'll be back shortly," she replied, before closing the door and leaving me alone.

Suddenly, my phone rang. I glanced at the door, figured I was safe for a few more minutes, and then pulled the device out of my pocket. To my surprise, it was Sage.

"Rayne!" she exclaimed as soon as I answered. "Are you okay?"

"Yeah, I'm fine. You worry too much about me," I chuckled, even though I was sure to have a few bruises from the fight.

"Good. I was so scared, I had to—" She suddenly paused.

A thought came to me. "Sage, were you the person who ran and got the guidance counselor?"

"Well...yes."

"But...why? I had it all under control."

Sage laughed. "Under control? Rayne, Madeleine was beating you up!"

"It was proof against her," I argued. "It showed her true colors to her father."

"So what?" Her pitch rose a notch. "Was this some sort of experiment for you?"

"No. I just didn't want her to get away with it like she has before!"

From outside the room, I saw the secretary turn her head in my direction, so I quickly looked away. In a much quieter voice, I added, "I didn't want Madeleine to get off the hook this time. She needs to be put in her place."

"But provoking her was the wrong way to go about it."

"I didn't try to provoke her. She—" I suddenly paused. What was the use of explaining, anyway? I heard the fear, the confused terror, in my friend's speech. "Sage, what makes you so scared of her?"

She suddenly grew silent. Static crackled through the speaker.

"Sage?" I asked quietly. "There's something you're not telling me, isn't there?"

"I'd rather not talk about it," she mumbled.

"Well, okay..." I knew it was only fair to give her some space, but I had the feeling that her relationship with Madeleine went farther back than I'd realized.

Sage muttered something incoherent, but finally gave in to my plea. "All right," she sighed, "it started back in sixth grade."

I pressed my phone harder against my ear.

"I had just joined the local swim team, and Madeleine was already the star. She's always been the star. I guess her favorite lane was lane 1, but I didn't know that, which was my first mistake. I was a pretty decent swimmer from playing in the ocean during the summertime, so my swim instructor told me to hop into the big pool—which was where Madeleine and the rest of the 'good' swimmers were.

"I jumped into lane 1, since all the other lanes were already full, and I figured the girl in lane 1 wouldn't mind sharing hers with me. But Madeleine had claimed it all to herself, because when I hopped in next to her, she grew really upset. She splashed me with her kicks and even kneed me underwater a few times. I was too scared to complain. It just didn't make sense."

I waited patiently as my friend collected her thoughts. She let out a shaky breath. "Anyway, after swim class Madeleine pulled me aside and said she wanted to help me with my technique. I was new and all, and since she was so much bigger and stronger than me, naturally I said yes. That was my second mistake."

For the first time since she had started speaking, Sage's voice wobbled. "She punched me, Rayne. And not just once or twice, but multiple times. I lost count because my eyes grew puffy and closed over. I couldn't see for two whole days." A lone tear trickled down her cheek, and my heart immediately went out to her.

"Oh, Sage," I whispered. "I never knew..."

"She hurt me physically, Rayne, but she also scarred me for life. I just don't want the same thing to happen to you."

"Did Madeleine get in trouble?"

"No one ever found out."

"What? Not even your parents?"

"I told them it was a stray dog. They didn't believe me, of course, not for a second. But I didn't want to tell the truth because I was afraid Madeleine would make me suffer all over again."

I let out a low whistle before settling back in my seat. "What's wrong with this girl?" I asked. "Why would a sixth-grade girl beat up another sixth-grade girl? And just for swimming in her favorite lane?"

"I researched it a few years later," Sage explained. "I couldn't figure it out until I read about a disorder called ASPD—antisocial personality disorder: someone who breaks the rules and has no respect for others."

"That sounds like her, all right."

"I guess she would have to be on medication for something like that, but I'm not sure."

"Well, if she is, the meds aren't working," I muttered.

"So what are you going to do now?" Sage asked.

I blew a whoosh of air between my lips. "I have no idea," I admitted. "At least it's clear that Madeleine initiated the fight, not me. That fact alone should prove to her father that she hates me, and it also acts as evidence that she was the one who destroyed the items in my locker."

"You think?" she asked hopefully.

Just then, the door suddenly flew open, and the guidance counselor stepped in wearily. I immediately ended the call and slid my phone into my pocket. Fortunately, the counselor didn't seem to notice, as she said, "I'm sorry to have kept you waiting. Mr. Hansen and I were talking with Madeleine."

"So...is she suspended?" I asked hopefully.

"Yes."

I couldn't help but smile. Finally, Madeleine got what she deserved!

"For how long?" I added carefully.

"Three days."

Three days? My smile immediately vanished. "But...but she attacked me!"

"Mr. Hansen told me that you verbally attacked his daughter, and that you provoked the fight."

"No, no, that's not—"

"There were witnesses," the counselor continued firmly, "and we have decided to suspend you as well."

Angry tears pricked at the corners of my eyes.

"The principal is on his way," she continued. "In the meantime, I want to warn you that your suspension will probably be for one day."

I nodded stiffly. Fantastic—this was going to be a long and very painful afternoon.

14

CHAPTER 14

Dad was not going to be happy; I knew that much. I also knew that the school had called him while he was at work and informed him that I was suspended for a day. Unless I pleaded my case, I knew he would ground me. But I desperately hoped Dad, of all people, would understand.

When I came home after school, I found him pacing in the living room.

"Rayne!" he thundered as I meekly stepped through the doorway. "You are in such big trouble, young lady!"

I shuffled over to him, already feeling guilty in anticipation of the conversation to come. "Dad, I'm sorry, but it's not what you think."

"Then tell me what you think. Explain what went through your head when you got in that fight."

"Well, there's this girl at school who has been picking on me," I began slowly. "And she's been picking on other kids, too. Her father, Coach Hansen, is oblivious to it all—"

"So you verbally attacked his daughter?"

"No! Madeleine attacked me. I mean—" With a frustrated sigh, I covered my face in my hands and tried again. "Look, first I brought the situation to Coach Hansen, hoping he would understand. But he wouldn't listen to me. He didn't even care. He—"

"Rayne, what on earth were you thinking?" Dad cried in exasperation. "Hansen is your ticket to qualifying for the Junior Olympics! What—"

"I told him that Madeleine was causing trouble at school," I continued, raising my voice. "He didn't do anything about it, so I walked away. Then Madeleine came up to me and started the fight."

"The school claims you started the fight."

"No! That's a lie," I gasped.

Dad ran his fingers through his hair, gazing at me long and hard. His mouth was set in a firm line. "Rayne, the school called and told me that you're suspended on the grounds of verbal assault, provoking a student to violence, and involvement in fighting on school grounds. How am I supposed to understand that? You've had no reason to fail me before."

I suddenly realized Dad was hurt, deeply hurt. He was right; I had never had a cause to disappoint him in such a way.

"Listen to me," I pleaded. "I may have gotten carried away, but I never assaulted anyone, and I did not provoke the fight."

He pursed his lips. "What am I supposed to believe?" he asked finally.

"Believe me," I pressed.

But he had already turned his back on me, arms folded across his chest. "We'll talk about this later, Rayne," he said wearily. "Whether you provoked the fight or not, you were involved in it. I'm grounding you for the next three days—your suspension day tomorrow, plus the weekend—and I'm taking away your phone."

For the second time today, angry tears sprang into my eyes. That's not fair! I wanted to scream. I didn't do anything wrong! But what good would it do to win this argument, anyway? My actions were clearly stressing Dad out. I hated to see him this way.

And then it hit me. Coming around to the other side of him, I demanded, "What about Kimmie? You promised I would get to see her."

"Rayne, I already said you're grounded, and that's the end of it."

"But—"

"But nothing. Your coach called me earlier and said he was very disappointed in you. He's not interested in training a swimmer who is prone to acts of violence."

In any other situation, I would have laughed out loud at his words. I was prone to violence? What about Madeleine? Was he blind?

But Dad clearly trusted the adults at my school more than his own daughter. I shook my head and backed away towards the door. "Okay. If you don't want to hear my side of the story, then fine."

I grabbed my backpack and ripped it open, throwing my torn swimsuit, cap, towel, and goggles to the ground. Dad stared in disbelief, but I didn't wait to hear what he had to say. I dashed out the door and headed for the cliffs. I didn't look back even once as I sprinted down the goat-trail, only pausing when it started sloping downhill, trying not to lose my footing. The wind whipped my hair out of its sloppy bun, causing it to stream behind me like a tangled waterfall, sometimes falling in front of my eyes. I pushed a few strands away and stumbled down the rest of the trail until I reached the private beach. Then, kicking my shoes off, I sprinted across the sand, never slowing until I reached the water. A wave slammed into my face as I dove in, and the freezing cold pierced my skin like an icy arrow.

I swam and swam until my limbs felt like they were going to fall off. I never once came up for air, but it wasn't like I needed it anyway. I just wanted to get away from it all and be by myself, thoughtlessly drifting on the tides of the ocean. I sunk to the bottom, where I dug my hands into the clusters of seaweed and sand, and gazed up at the rays of light fluctuating in the water.

Maybe I was wrong. Maybe I overreacted. I sighed, unleashing a torrent of bubbles that floated lazily upwards. I wished I could go back to the moment when I had opened my swim locker and found my destroyed belongings. But then what? Would I have really done anything differently?

Suddenly, I sensed a presence beside me. I turned, expecting to see a pair of dolphins, but I saw nothing—just the light rays streaming underwater and the seaweed floating with the current. That's weird, I thought. Something told me that dolphins were nearby, but where?

That's when I heard the clicks. They came low and soft at first, before increasing in frequency and becoming higher-pitched. Before I knew what I was doing, I pushed off the sandy bottom and made some clicking sounds in return. A few seconds later, two hazy shapes appeared in the distance, rapidly approaching. I swam towards them and was delighted to find that they were the two dolphins, just like I had predicted!

The dolphins clicked excitedly when I reached them. I smiled and clicked in return, trying to imitate their sounds, hoping I was doing it correctly. The dolphins seemed to smile in reassurance as they circled underwater.

Follow us, they seemed to say, clicking and ushering me forward as they continued to swim. I followed them for ten minutes, not really knowing where I was going, but feeling safe next to these majestic creatures. There was nothing but sand, water and seaweed for miles in all directions, yet I knew that I was safe with these dolphins. I hadn't even made it more than half a mile from the private beach, anyway.

Almost there, the dolphins clicked. I realized we were heading back towards the cliffs as we swam through a large underwater arch made of rugged red rock. I glanced at my surroundings in awe. The sand sparkled beneath me and the water shimmered with an unearthly glow. I noticed we were swimming through some sort of cave, as the rock walls slowly grew smoother and darker.

Come see! Come see! The dolphins turned and clicked excitedly at me. I smiled and followed them as they swam towards the surface, circling up and up until we broke through. I was surprised to find that my lungs weren't screaming for air, nor was I completely out of breath. Was it really possible that I had held my breath for that long?

I glanced up, delighted with my new discovery, but paused when I saw where the dolphins had led me. We were inside a massive cave surrounded on all sides by smooth, slippery rock. Near the entrance a large pile of smooth stones was resting on the seafloor. Up above, water shimmered off the cave walls like the turquoise aurora borealis. I tilted my head back and saw that there were only a few pinholes of light streaming through the top of the cave, barely illuminating this magical grotto.

"Wow," I breathed. "This is so cool."

The dolphins raised their heads above the water, seemingly smiling at me. I smiled back and said, "Thank you for taking me here. Is this your home?"

They suddenly disappeared back underwater. I ducked under the surface and listened to their clicks, studying their behavior carefully. You must know, they seemed to say with urgency. You must find out.

Find out what? I asked curiously.

In reply, the dolphins swam over to a small cleft in one of the cave walls. They clicked excitedly until I followed them and strained to see what was inside the cleft. I could barely make out a thin, silvery lettering carved into the back of the tiny hole. I pressed my face closer against the cave wall, shivering at its cool, slimy surface. The harder I looked, the better I could make out what the words said: The sea holds many secrets.

I felt a chill run down my spine. Who would spend time carving this? And how would they even hold their breath long enough to stay underwater? I backed away from the cliff rock and swam up to the surface, glancing around at the solid cave walls. Clearly, there was no way out except through the underwater tunnel the dolphins had led me through. It was impossible for any other human to reach this secret grotto, unless they were using scuba equipment. Was that how had the message had been carved onto the wall?

Puzzled, I dove back under to where the dolphins were still watching me expectantly. I read the mysterious message one last time: The sea holds many secrets. Then I gasped, suddenly realizing there were two more words carved in smaller letters below the message. I squinted until my eyes hurt, but as soon as I read the words I felt my entire body go numb with shock.

Miranda B.

It was impossible. It couldn't be real. Had all of this just been a dream? I felt myself reeling backwards, the words swimming before my eyes, making me feel nauseous and claustrophobic. I stopped treading water and let myself sink to the bottom of the grotto, stunned.

Memories came flooding back. They were unleashed like a raging torrent, surging and swelling in my mind's eye. A little girl playing with her mother on the beach...watching the waves crash on the shore...being picked up by her father...tucked into bed by her mother...listening as a sweet voice read her a bedtime story...waking up with a sinking feeling...something was wrong...something was wrong...the little girl didn't understand...she was gone...why was she gone?...driving away from the house...tears and sadness and a deep aching for someone who could never be replaced...

I suddenly pushed off the sandy bottom and swam as fast as I could out of the secret cave. I felt tears spring into my eyes, but they were lost in the overwhelming blue of the ocean. I didn't stop until I had swam completely out of the tunnel and broke through the surface, suddenly surrounded by billowing storm clouds overhead and choppy whitecaps all around me.

The dolphins appeared a few moments later, clicking anxiously. You know! You know! they cried.

I squeezed my eyes shut, forcing out a few more tears. Why? I asked mournfully. Why did you bring me here?

You had to know. You will find out soon, they replied.

"But I didn't want to know!" I screamed, burying my face in my hands while the waves kept me afloat. I sobbed, trying to shove the memories back into the shadows of my mind, but failing whenever I remembered the secret message etched onto the cave walls.

"I'm sorry," I told the dolphins.

They clicked compassionately before ducking back under the surface. I let out a shaky breath before following them, ready to head back home. I suddenly felt extremely weary from all I had been through.

I was surprised when the dolphins paused a short distance away from the entrance to the underwater tunnel. Judging by the movement of sand and discoloration of the water, there was a current just a few yards away, heading to some unknown depth off in the distance.

What? Are we going somewhere else now? I asked the dolphins.

Not now. You will go when you are ready, they replied.

What is that supposed to mean? I frowned and studied them carefully, but their clicks only repeated the same message over and over again. I finally gave up and stretched out my hands in a gesture of farewell. Will I see you again?

When you are ready, they clicked, swimming closer to me and allowing me to rub their rostrums affectionately. I smiled and watched as they pulled away after a few seconds, swimming into the fast-flowing current and disappearing from view. I floated quietly in the water, staring at the shifting blue-green depths of the sea that stretched out like an endless canvas in front of me. Then I began the long swim back to the private beach, knowing that the sun would be setting soon and Dad would be wondering where I was.

I emerged out of the water ten minutes later with my wet clothes plastered against my skin. I staggered onto the warm sand, exhausted and confused. I was overwhelmed with questions now—questions that could only be answered by one person.

Dad. I needed to talk to him. I had a feeling he knew the reason why my hair and eyes glowed, so he had to know the reason for my love of the ocean and the strange but beautiful connections I had with it. I was prepared to tell him how I swam in the sea almost every day. I was willing to take whatever punishment he might throw at me. No matter the cost, I needed those answers. I needed to find out what was really going on.

I started walking towards my shoes and socks, which I had flung near the entrance to the trail. I winced in pain when my wet T-shirt rubbed against the tender spots above my hips. "Ouch," I muttered, carefully lifting my T-shirt up to expose the sore areas.

I gasped. Whereas the areas had been a light pinkish-red color before, they were now a deep, translucent blood red. It was unlike anything I had ever seen before. I gingerly extended a finger and poked the strange surface. To my utter surprise, the red suddenly disappeared as faint flaps skin—my own skin—folded over it.

I screamed in horror. What was that? What was happening to me? I closed my eyes and counted to ten, willing my pulse to go down to normal. Then I opened my eyes and looked back down at my hips. After studying them carefully, I realized I had seen something like this before—on fish.

They were gills.

The situation was so bizarre that it was almost hilarious. Gills? My head swam. How had I developed gills? Was that why I could hold my breath for so long? But it was impossible! Humans couldn't develop gills, could they?

My mind whirled with thoughts. There was only one way to find out the answer. I quickly grabbed my shoes and socks, not even bothering to put them on. There was no time to waste. I bolted up the goat-trail and made it back to the house in record time, my legs burning from overexertion. I sprinted straight into the living room, wet clothes and all, and stood breathing heavily in the middle of the floor.

Dad glanced up from where he was sitting on the couch, deep in thought. "Rayne!" he exclaimed. "What—"

"You have to tell me," I interrupted. "Dad, I have to know." I thought back to the mysterious message engraved on the cliff walls: The sea holds many secrets. Then I remembered the name, the dreaded name, that had caused the unleashing of so many memories.

Dad and I stared at each other for a fewseconds. The only sound was my heavybreathing. Then I spoke. "Mom's still alive, isn't she?"

15

CHAPTER 15

Dad stared at me. I stared back at him. We must have stared at each other for a full ten seconds before he finally cleared his throat and said, "No. Yes. I don't know."

I narrowed my eyes.

"Why are you sopping wet?" he demanded.

I glanced down at my clothes. "Well...I was swimming."

"Where?"

"In the ocean." I held my breath and waited for Dad to scream at me, to tell me that it was extremely dangerous and that I should never go near the water again. But all he did was shake his head slowly and deliberately.

"I should have known," he muttered. He let out a low whistle. "Rayne, please answer truthfully when I ask you this. It's very important." He leaned forward. "Did anything happen to you? Anything...well...out of the ordinary?"

Like growing gills and talking to dolphins and drinking saltwater? I swallowed nervously. For a few moments, I debated what to tell him. "Well," I said carefully, "I guess you could say I have this connection with the ocean. I can't stay away from it."

There. That was the most normal thing I could say at the moment.

Dad furrowed his brow before taking my hands in his. "Are you sure, honey? Please, if there's something you're not telling me, say it now. This is very important."

I backed away slowly. "Why? Do you know something?"

Dad hesitated before answering. "Yes and no. It's a tricky situation, Rayne. But you're sure nothing else happened while you were in the ocean?"

I hesitated for a brief second. "I'm sure."

He let out a sigh of relief. "Good. Just promise me you won't go swimming in the sea again, alright?"

"What?" I tore my hands out of his grasp. "That's impossible. And you still haven't answered my questions."

"This is for your own safety, Rayne. You have to understand."

"How I can understand when you won't even give me any answers?"

"Answers to what?"

"Why my hair and eyes glow blue in the moonlight. Why I have this connection with the ocean. Why I love swimming so much. And—and why you lied to me about her." I swallowed the lump that had formed in my throat. "You said she was dead, but I know that's not true. Why haven't you told me? Why can't you open up and talk to me about this? Is it because you can't trust your own daughter?"

The tears shimmering in Dad's eyes caused me to regret my words at once. "I'm sorry, Rayne," he said huskily, "but I don't think you're ready. I haven't been lying to you this whole time; I've been protecting you."

"Protecting me? From what?" I clenched my fists in desperation. "Stop talking to me in riddles and explain some things! Please."

Dad sighed and took a seat on the couch. He held his head in his hands and sucked in a deep breath before letting it out slowly. I crossed my shivering arms over my chest as I waited for him to respond.

"She was a swimmer," he said finally, his voice hollow. "Your mother, I mean. She loved to swim, but she loved the ocean even more."

I felt my heart breaking at his words. Memories flooded in like a tidal wave, but I didn't try to stop them this time. Dad's voice grew more and more alive with each sentence, and tears began streaming down his cheeks as he spoke. "She was the most beautiful thing I had ever set eyes on. Ever since the first day we met, she had me under her spell. She was amazing. Because of her love of the ocean, we decided to move to this quiet seaside town, in this old house, dreaming of starting a family and filling the rooms with our children.

"You were life's gift to us, Rayne. We were delighted to have a child just as beautiful as her mother. We were the happiest family on the coast, without a doubt, and we spent all of our free time together. I felt like the luckiest dad in the whole world.

"But it didn't last for long. You were just a toddler when the accident happened." He paused and made a steeple with his fingers, resting his chin on his hands. I had to strain to hear his next part of the story, as his voice became low and barely distinguishable.

"She disappeared one day and never returned. She was on her daily swim in the ocean, like usual, and then she was...gone. I never saw her again."

I chewed on my bottom lip to keep myself from crying. My voice cracked as I said, "So we moved to Newland."

"Yes." Dad nodded slowly. "The memory of Miranda was too fresh in my mind. I couldn't bear to face living in the same house as her, so we moved. But when I saw how much you resembled her, both in appearance and in spirit, I started to regret the decision. I realized you shared her love of swimming, and you were extremely talented at it—just like your mother."

I smiled through my tears.

"But when it became too hard for me to pay our mortgage, I saw that another house was for sale in Shady Cove. Believe me, Rayne, I was against moving back here at first, just like you. But I realized it would feel like Miranda was still with me—with us—if we were back in our old house. I still miss her terribly, but somehow living in Shady Cove makes it a little better. It makes facing the memories more bearable."

"So that's the reason for those." I glanced at the photo albums sitting on the coffee table.

"Yes." Dad reached over and picked one up, turning the pages slowly. He smiled sadly at each photo as he relived the moment in his mind's eye. "I wish she was still with us."

"So do I," I whispered, sitting down next to him and placing my hand on his arm. "Thank you."

"I had to tell you someday," Dad said wryly. I could see his forehead was crinkled deep in concentration, as if he was debating whether or not to say something else. He finally closed the photo album and stood up. "Well, I better start dinner. It's getting late. And we have a long day ahead of us on Saturday."

"What? We do?"

Dad flashed me a quick smile before disappearing into the kitchen. "We're going to see Kimmie."

My mind was still spinning with everything Dad had told me. I could hardly sleep that night as I tossed and turned in bed, my thoughts drifting back and forth from the ocean, to her, and to the mysterious message etched onto the cave walls, followed by Miranda B. I had a powerful feeling that she was still alive. She was still here, somewhere on this earth, and I could feel her presence as strongly as if she was sitting right next to me.

Before long, fatigue overtook me, and I found myself drifting off to sleep. Since I was both physically and mentally exhausted, I experienced no dreams or nightmares—just one long, blissful sleep. I awoke the next morning to a sharp pain in my side, and realized that I had slept in an awkward position that aggravated my gills.

My gills...would I ever get used to the fact? But it was true, I knew, as I lightly traced the smooth skin over my hipbones. They were real, just like the dozens of other weird things that had happened to me as of late. I knew it all tied in to her somehow—after all, Dad had said she had loved the ocean and used to be a great swimmer. But was he really telling the truth? Had she really died? Or was she kidnapped, lost at sea, or—I gulped—had she run away?

I couldn't bear to think of Mom that way. Dad made her seem like such a beautiful, amazing person, someone who would never think of abandoning her family and leaving them to grieve. And yet my conscience told me she was still alive. She had to be alive. But where?

My mind was overwhelmed with all these questions. Since I was suspended for today, I relaxed in bed and did some homework before Dad headed off to work. Then, as soon as the coast was clear, I headed for the cliffs.

The ocean was as refreshing and inviting as always. I spent nearly the entire afternoon swimming in the sea, enjoying the use of my newfound gills and perfect underwater eyesight. I finally dragged myself out of the water to allow myself enough time to dry off before Dad returned home. Fortunately, he didn't ask what I had been doing all day. My conscience pricked at me, reminding me of Dad's instructions not to return to the sea, but I pushed it away. How could I go against my own passion?

Dad and I didn't talk much during dinner that night. He seemed deep in thought, as if weighed down by an invisible burden on his shoulders. I was lost in thought, too, but I didn't dare ask him about Mom again. Dad was in a strange mood.

My mind was still consumed with questions the next day, too, when I woke up after another long night's sleep. I felt a little better after showering and getting dressed, so I made my way downstairs to where Dad was making breakfast. I smiled when I remembered we were going to see Kimmie today.

"Good morning!" I chirped, sliding into a seat at the table.

"'Morning." Dad grinned as he cracked open an egg. It sizzled as it hit the frying pan. "You sound pretty excited today," he noted.

"We're driving to Newland. Of course I'm excited!" I exclaimed. "And the weather outside is perfect—nice and sunny, with no fog in sight."

"The forecast said it's going to rain tonight. As long as we leave within the hour, you and Kimmie can spend the afternoon outside until the storm rolls in."

He cracked another egg, and this one sizzled even louder as it landed inside the pan. He cleared his throat and turned to face me. "Listen, Rayne...about the past couple days. I've been thinking, and I'm sorry for getting on your case about the fight at school. You don't deserve to be grounded."

His words surprised me. "Oh, Dad, it's fine."

"No, it's not fine. I was upset and overwhelmed with a lot of things, and I took the fight too seriously. It wasn't your fault, honey. I should have known you would never do something like that." He sighed heavily. "I've had to make some tough decisions over the past few years, and I'm sorry that I haven't been the best parent."

"You're a great parent, Dad," I protested.

He wrapped his strong arms around me. "Thank you, honey," he murmured, planting a kiss on the top of my head. "If it seems like I'm holding back from telling you something, just know that it's for your safety. Before your mother...well...before she disappeared, she asked me to promise that I keep you safe. And every day I struggle to keep that promise, Rayne. The world is more dangerous than you think."

"Dad..."

"I know that at your stage in life, everything is about fun and games—"

"Dad."

He placed his hands on my shoulders. "Honey, you have to understand that—"

"Dad!" I pointed to the stove. "The eggs are burning!"

His serious expression immediately morphed into one of surprise. "Oh!" he exclaimed, quickly turning around and using his spatula to flip the eggs. I chuckled.

Dad smiled sheepishly. "You do get what I'm saying, though, right?"

"Of course. You don't have to worry about me."

Though he gave me an anxious look, he let the subject drop and continued to scramble our eggs. My mind persisted to wander all throughout breakfast, debating whether or not to bombard Dad with more questions. But as soon as he finished eating, he headed upstairs, leaving me alone with my thoughts. I was busy running through multiple scenarios about the message on the cave walls: The sea holds many secrets.

Could my mother have written that message before her disappearance, trying to communicate something to her family? Or was it more plausible to believe that she had written the message after disappearing? In grave danger and unable to show her face, she could have etched the mysterious message in one last plight of communication.

I shook my head and took one last bite of breakfast. I was getting too far ahead of myself. For all I knew, my mother was completely fine and in no danger whatsoever. She could have been a teenager when she wrote that message, many years ago. After all, Dad never told me where she grew up. She could have lived right here in Shady Cove her whole life.

But something told me she had written the message, and she had written it for me. She was still alive, and she was trying to get my attention. Why else would the dolphins lead me to that secret underwater grotto beneath the cliffs, where no human could go?

"Rayne!"

I jumped in my seat, startled at hearing Dad's voice. "Huh?"

"We need to get going. Are you ready?"

"Almost." I quickly dumped my dishes in the sink and scurried upstairs to finish getting ready. I came back into the living room a few moments later, dressed in my usual T-shirt and jeans, carrying a sweatshirt in case it got cold later tonight. I knew I didn't want to be caught in short sleeves when the storm rolled in.

The drive to Newland seemed to take forever due to my excitement. I couldn't wait to see Kimmie. My thoughts had quickly switched from the grotto's mysterious message to my best friend. It had been two weeks since we had last seen each other, but it felt like an eternity. I grew even more agitated as the scenery faded from pine trees and lush green fields to houses and buildings. I squealed with excitement when Dad drove past a sign reading, Welcome to Newland! Kimmie's house was only a few more minutes away.

As soon as we pulled up in front of a cozy one-story house, I hastily unbuckled my seatbelt and leaped out of the car. I sprinted straight to the front door and rapped my knuckles on the wooden surface. Just seconds later, it flew open to reveal Kimmie's smiling face. "Rayne!" she exclaimed.

"Kimmie!" We embraced, laughing. "Wow, it's great to see you," I said.

"I know! I miss you so much. I felt miserable last week when the fog rolled in. It seems like we haven't seen each other in forever!"

"It's nice to see you again, Kimmie," Dad said, smiling as he came up to the front door. "How've you been?"

"Good! Thanks, Mr. Bennett." Kimmie stepped aside as her mother stepped forward.

"Rayne! Clark! Lovely to see you," Mrs. Winstrom gushed. "Please come in. I've made some sandwiches and a fruit salad for lunch."

As Dad followed her into the living room, Kimmie pulled me upstairs to her bedroom, where we plopped down on her bed. Her room looked the same as it always did—messy and colorful, with posters everywhere. Her laptop was sitting on top of multiple notebooks on her desk.

"So how do you like it?" Kimmie asked. "Living in Shady Cove, I mean."

"Oh, it's fine..."

"Do you wish you were back here?"

"Yeah." I winced, suddenly realizing I wasn't entirely sure of my answer. Of course, I did want to live near Kimmie so we could see each other every day, but then I would miss the ocean. After everything that had happened, I couldn't imagine myself living away from the coast.

Fortunately, Kimmie wasn't daunted in the least by my hesitation. "So how's the school? I bet you're still the number-one swimmer on the team, right?"

"The school's okay, but the swim team is actually pretty good," I said, partially skirting her question.

"Do you still have the same classes? How are the teachers?"

We went on and on, with Kimmie asking me questions nonstop for the next half-hour. I found myself zoning out during parts of our conversation, not really paying attention to what I was saying. I answered her questions vaguely and said nothing about the ocean or what strange things had happened to me over the past week. Something told me it wasn't right to spill my secrets to Kimmie. Even though she was my best friend, I couldn't bring myself to tell her about drinking saltwater, communicating with dolphins, and growing gills. It seemed fictional, somehow, now that I was farther away from the sea.

"—and then Zach was all, 'I'm gonna show him how it's done,' and he totally did show him up, and he was flying through the water! He's one of our best swimmers. You remember Zach, right?"

"Uh...I think so."

Kimmie giggled, lowering her voice. "I guess we're, like, friends now or something. I don't know what you call it. But rumors are going around the swim team that he might ask me out next week. What do you think?"

I suddenly jerked back to reality and ran Kimmie's words through my mind again. "Wait, so you have a boyfriend?" I asked, dumbfounded.

"That's the thing—I don't know! I guess we're technically 'friends' right now, but we have four classes together and I sit at his table during lunch, and we've hugged a few times, and people are saying we should totally be a couple, and there's a rumor that he might actually ask me out, so I guess he might be my boyfriend, but I'm not completely one-hundred-percent sure, because he hasn't said anything to me yet, so I don't know what to do." She took a deep breath, her eyes shining. "What do you think?"

"Me?" I was still shocked that we were talking about boys. It had never come up in our conversations before. It was just Kimmie and I and our love of swimming. There was never room for "boy talk."

"Yeah! Don't you have someone special?" Kimmie asked, wiggling her eyebrows suggestively.

I laughed dryly. "No way. I mean, there's this guy who tutors me in Spanish, but—" I quickly stopped myself from going any further. Telling Kimmie about my kind-of date with Luke was sure to bring another round of endless questioning. I opted to change the subject. "So have you made any other friends?"

"No, not really," Kimmie said vaguely, brushing my question aside. "Just Zach."

"Oh."

"What about you?"

"Well, these two girls on the Shady Cove High swim team be-friended me the first day of school. Their names are Marley and Sage."

"Cool." Kimmie grinned and quickly flicked her wrist, showing me a glittering bracelet. "So guess what Zach got for me yesterday? Isn't it beautiful?"

"Oh, yeah. It's really pretty." I suffered another ten minutes of nonstop chatter about gorgeous, talented Zach before Mrs. Winstrom marched in wondering if we were ever going to eat lunch.

"We're coming, Mom." Kimmie sighed dramatically. "We had a lot of catching up to do." As I followed them out the door, my gaze flickered over to a picture of Kimmie and another guy from the swim team, standing side-by-side on the deck making silly faces at the photographer. My stomach churned. When had things changed so much? Shouldn't I have been standing next to Kimmie on the Newland High pool deck, with my arm draped around her shoulders and laughing at our silly poses? And why did our conversation sound so forced? It seemed as though we had slowly drifted apart in the two weeks since I moved away.

I reached into my back pocket of my jeans, searching for my phone, but frowned when I remembered it was still in Dad's possession. I was almost positive that Kimmie and I had gone three or four days without texting or calling—something almost unheard of between the two of us.

"Rayne?"

I jerked my head up and realized Kimmie was staring at me. "Aren't you coming?" she asked.

"Oh, yeah. I was just thinking," I said lamely, quickly averting my eyes from the picture of her and Zach. I sucked in a deep breath before following her into the kitchen.

16

CHAPTER 16

Hundreds of miniscule raindrops streaked down my bedroom window. I had been cooped up inside the house all day yesterday thanks to the storm, but the rain had finally lessened and the lightning ceased just in time for school this morning.

"Wonderful," I grumbled as I shoved my feet into my worn Converse. Every bone in my body yearned to be back in the ocean. I wanted to return to the secret cave and see my mother's message again. Thinking about her made me both excited and sad at the same time. I knew she was alive, and that gave me hope that I would find her someday.

But for now I had to deal with reality. I sighed as I grabbed my backpack and headed downstairs, still sullen after my visit with Kimmie. It hadn't gone as planned—in fact, it had gone completely wrong. I had expected everything to magically go back to normal, as if I had never moved away and we were still close as ever, but that wasn't what had happened. The truth was inevitable: we had drifted apart. Two weeks with nothing but the occasional text and phone call had driven an invisible barrier between us. Kimmie was obsessed with this Zach guy, and though she was genuinely interested in my life at Shady Cove, she wasn't broken over the fact that I had moved away. Where I used to have an aching hole in my heart, I had filled it in with new friendships in Sage and Marley—and Luke. Had Kimmie done the same? Had we broken our promises to each other? Was that why everything had seemed so forced and indifferent on Saturday?

I was still deep in thought during my bike ride to Shady Cove High, and my mind continued to wander during my first four classes. I went through the motions of buying lunch, taking a seat in the cafeteria, and listening to the chatter of multiple conversations. Sage was as cheerful and bubbly as ever, completely oblivious to my strange behavior. I snuck in a few words here and there during our conversation with some girls from the swim team, but other than that, I remained silent.

The rest of the school day passed in the same manner, with most of my classmates assuming I was disconsolate because the authorities had suspended me on Friday. But that wasn't it at all—in fact, I could care less about my trivial punishment. What really made me anxious was a combination of my dwindling friendship with Kimmie and the mounting urge to swim in the ocean. Both were consuming my thoughts, but the closer the school day grew to dismissal, the more the desire for the ocean overpowered everything else.

I just need to wait until after tutoring, I told myself, knowing that Luke was counting on me to show up. But my throat was parched and my whole body tingled with the need for salt water. It was insufferable.

Finally, the last period of the day rolled around, and I joined Sage in the walk to the pool deck. She had been uncharacteristically quiet all day, and I had a feeling something important was on her mind.

"Well, I found out where Marley has been all this time," she said, surprising me with the sudden conversation.

"Where?"

"Sick." She shook her head sadly. "I guess she has a really bad fever."

"Oh," I replied, not knowing what else to say. We lapsed into another pregnant silence.

Sage turned to face me, wrinkles creasing her forehead. "Is something wrong, Rayne? You've been acting really sad lately."

"Nothing's wrong. But what about you? Is something on your mind?"

"You're still upset about the fight, aren't you?" she asked, skirting my question.

I laughed. "No, of course not."

"Then you're upset about getting suspended."

"It's not that either."

Sage sighed. "Well, it has to be something. What is it?"

I stared at her for what seemed like minutes. There were dozens of answers: I recently found out that my Mom never really died—she only disappeared before leaving me a secret message in an underwater cave. Then there was the fact that I'd developed some crazy and insanely abnormal features like gills and seeing underwater. Plus, my best friend from Newland was slowly slipping away from me, and there was nothing I could do about it except watch as she replaced me with some dream guy.

Sage blinked. "Well?"

"Like I said before, nothing's wrong." I continued walking to the locker room.

Sage groaned and jogged to catch up with me. "Fine—if you don't want to tell me, then you don't have to. But..." She paused, a strange look crossing her face. "Just know that I'm here for you, okay? We're friends, and friends help each other out."

"Thanks." I smiled as we headed over to our lockers and started undressing. "It's just that it's personal," I added. "Some crazy things have happened over the weekend."

"Oh." Sage frowned and glanced away for a second. "Does it have anything to do with...Luke, by chance?"

"Luke?" I started, but caught myself in time. "No. Why?"

"No reason," she said quickly, looking away. I felt my pulse pick up.

"What about Luke?" I pressed. "Sage..."

She closed her eyes, took a deep breath, and then turned to face me. "I'm not supposed to tell you this," she admitted, "but he texted me last Friday night, telling me that he had some big plans for the next day. Are you following?"

"Yes..."

Sage gave me an undecipherable look. I had no clue why she was acting so strange all of a sudden. "Look, Rayne, please don't tell him I said this—but he was going to ask you out."

"He what?"

But Sage was silent. I didn't know whether to shriek in excitement or blush like a fool, so I did both. "Oh my gosh, Sage, are you serious?" I gasped. "He's really going to ask me out?"

She gave me a wry smile. "I knew it. You do like him."

I blushed again and looked down at the floor. "Yeah," I admitted, "I guess I do."

"What a bummer. He was going to ask you out."

"What do you mean? Is he okay?"

"Oh, he's fine. Just suffering from a broken heart," she said melo-dramatically.

My head was spinning. "Okay, you lost me. What are you talking about?"

She gave me a disappointed look. "If you can't figure it out, then don't bother asking me. But I suggest you have a nice, long talk with him in tutoring today."

I gaped at her as she finished dressing and headed out of the locker room. I was completely, totally lost. Sage wasn't one to beat around the bush, and she certainly gave me more than enough hints for whatever she was trying to tell me. But for the life of me, I couldn't figure it out. And was she actually serious when she said Luke was going to ask me out? What could have changed his mind?

I shook my head and slipped my new racing suit on. It was nowhere near as pretty as my old one, but Dad and I had bought it at a sports shop in Newland the other day on our way home. I grabbed my new goggles and swim cap as well before hurrying out onto the pool deck. Sage gave me a sad smile but said nothing when I slipped into the same lane as her.

Something is definitely up, I thought, my mind racing with questions. I had the horrible feeling I had done something wrong to hurt Luke, but what? Why was Sage trying to catch me in a guilt trap?

For the first time since I'd moved to Shady Cove, I wanted to see Luke more than I wanted to swim in the ocean. If he honest-to-goodness liked me as more than a friend, then I wanted to find out why he had changed his mind. I had never had a boyfriend before, and the prospect of entering this uncharted territory thrilled me as it would any teenage girl. I had a sudden glimmer of light:

was this is how Kimmie felt about her relationship with Zach? Was she just as confused as I?

My attention was diverted when Coach Hansen strode onto the pool deck. He immediately launched into our warm-up and said we were going to be busy today. I was thankful for the hard workout that took my mind off everything, but as soon as I dragged myself out of the pool and headed back to the locker room, my worries came flooding back. Sage was still in her weird mood over Luke, so I didn't bug her with questions, even though I was drowning in them. She gave me an anxious smile when I left.

I immediately made a beeline for the library. Anxious and exhausted, I sat down at the first vacant table and watched as the librarian studied me over the rims of her cherry-colored glasses.

Five minutes later, Luke still wasn't here.

Thoughts swirled through my mind. What if something had happened to him—something that I should have known about, but was too blind to realize?

The next ten minutes were pure torture. I suddenly had a horrible feeling that this was all my fault. Maybe I had done something to hurt Luke, and Sage wanted us to talk things through. But what could I have done? I couldn't remember any times we had fought or yelled at each other. Luke was one of the kindest, most patient guys in the entire school, and I hadn't known him to hold a grudge.

I pulled out my water bottle and gulped down the remaining saltwater inside. It soothed my parched throat for the time being, but I knew that if Luke didn't show up within ten more minutes, I was going to have to leave. I couldn't stand the suspense any longer.

Finally, just as my mental breakdown was escalating, the library door flung open, and a composed-looking Luke Sanchez strode in.

He smiled casually at the librarian before shoving his hands into the pockets of his hoodie and glancing around the room. Since I was the only student in the entire library, his gaze automatically flitted over to me, and I felt the color rise in my cheeks. Should I smile? Wave?

Fortunately, Luke covered the distance between us quickly, leaving no time for minor complications. "You're here," he said, shocked.

"Well...yeah."

His surprise suddenly morphed into angst. "Well, could we talk for a minute?"

I gave a hesitant nod. His movements had become tense, his demeanor guarded. "Sure," I said.

Luke pursed his lips and glanced over his shoulder at the librarian. "How about we take this outside?"

"Oh. Right." I clumsily hoisted my backpack over my shoulders and followed him out the door, nearly tripping over a table leg in the process. My heart was beating so rapidly I was sure everyone within a fifty-foot radius could hear it. I swallowed nervously as Luke led me to the bleachers behind the football field. Once he was satisfied we would have some privacy, he cleared his throat.

"Look, Rayne, I don't know what you're thinking, but I can't handle this anymore," he said, exasperated. "I can't do this tutoring anymore, and I certainly can't keep following you around, even after—after—what promised to be a good friendship," he finished lamely.

"What?" I cried. "Luke, what are you talking about?"

His eyes narrowed. "Oh, so now you're going to play dumb?" He seemed flustered, dancing between anger and desperation. "I was expecting an apology, even an excuse, but to stay indifferent about the whole situation? That's pretty low, even for a nice girl like you."

His words stabbed my heart. He had never been sarcastic and angry before—especially not with me.

"Luke, please believe me when I say I don't have the faintest idea of what you're talking about," I pleaded.

"Really," Luke scoffed.

"Yes!"

"I can't believe this." He shook his head. "I thought you were different."

"Luke, I honestly have no idea what you're talking about! Can you please tell me what's going on?" Hot, frustrated tears sprang into my eyes. "What could I have done to make you so upset? Why are you so angry with me? I don't know what's going on!"

His gaze softened for a second. "Then you really don't know...?"

I shook my head vigorously.

"Rayne! Don't you remember our plans? The Café?"

I ran his words through my mind a few times, but still came up empty. "I don't know," I spluttered. "Luke, I honestly don't know! What—"

"You don't even remember our plans for Saturday?" He gave me an incredulous look. "Are you serious?" He threw his hands up in the air. "Rayne, how could you forget our date at the Shady Cove Café on Saturday? I had everything planned out—everything—but you never showed up. I texted you a dozen times and called you until midnight, hoping something wasn't wrong. I even called you on Sunday, too, but you never answered even once. And then you showed up to school this morning like nothing even happened!"

Oh no! How could I have been so forgetful? Our rendezvous...our meeting...our date. Luke had called it a date! Sage was right; he had been planning to ask me out! I had crushed his hopes, the poor guy. What had I been thinking?

"I'm so sorry!" I exclaimed as sincerely as possible. "Luke, I had no idea. I completely forgot about meeting at the Café. I'm so, so sorry!"

For a second, Luke looked like he was going to forgive me. But his jaw stayed firm and his eyes flashed with hurt. "So you went and hung out with some friends from your old town instead?" he retorted. "First of all, you never came to school on Friday, and then you pulled another fast one by not showing up to the Café on Saturday. As if that wasn't bad enough, you didn't answer your phone for two whole days! Do you even realize how panicked I was? Sage called you at least a dozen times too! Both of us were worried out of our minds wondering if you were okay. So when you showed up this morning like nothing had happened, I couldn't believe it. You had actually ditched me on Saturday and ignored me all weekend. That hurts, Rayne, especially when—" He paused, his face flushing between light pink and dark red. "Well, I guess my feelings don't matter now," he said bitterly.

Remorse hung heavy on me like a dark cloud. "Luke, I'm so sorry," I said again. "I completely forgot, and that was terrible of me. But honestly, I wasn't ignoring you!"

"Then why didn't you answer your phone?" he demanded.

"My dad grounded me and took it away."

He gave me a look of disbelief. "So your dad's version of 'grounding' is taking you to Newland to hang out with friends?"

"No, no—it's hard to explain!"

"Whatever," he muttered. "I hope you do well in Spanish."

"Wait, I'm serious!" I grabbed his arm before he could turn away. "This weekend was disappointing for me too. I haven't visited my best friend in almost in a month, but now I'm not sure we're really friends anymore...and before that I actually found out the truth about my mom, and even more things—crazier, unbelievable things—have happened to me in such a short time that I don't know what to do anymore!"

I sucked in a deep breath. My cheeks were stained with tears and my eyes pleaded for Luke to believe me. He had to believe me. As our gazes locked, I could see the hurt swimming in his chocolate-brown eyes, and I hoped he could see the remorse written in mine.

"Luke, you know how I feel about you," I said boldly.

"I don't know what to think anymore." He wrenched his arm out of my grasp. "And where were you on Friday? You didn't even show up for tutoring. Oh, wait, let me guess—you were hanging out with your friends from Newland on that day too."

"No!" I exclaimed. "Can you stop making accusations and just listen to me?" I was getting fed up with his attitude. Couldn't he understand that I was going through a hard time right now?

"I got in a fight on Friday," I explained. "With Madeleine Hansen. And it wasn't even my fault—she was the one who attacked me. But I got suspended on Friday anyway."

"You got in a fight?" Luke raised his eyebrows.

"Yes! I thought the whole school knew!" I sighed angrily.

He folded his arms across his chest.

"Luke, I'm sorry," I said, my voice breaking. "All of this has been one big misunderstanding. I know it's my fault that I forgot about Saturday, but—"

"But nothing. It's over." He glanced over his shoulder toward the parking lot. "Look, I don't know what to think anymore, or what to believe, or what to expect...it's all one huge mess. But we were never going to work out anyway."

He turned and started to walk away. "Luke!" I cried. "Wait! You don't understand..."

He ignored me and continued walking until he had turned the corner, out of sight. I clenched my fists and angrily wiped my tears away with the hard ridges of my knuckles. Fine. I guess we never were going to work out, not if he couldn't talk through a simple misunderstanding.

I knew it was my fault for missing the big "date" on Saturday, and I also knew Luke's high hopes had been absolutely shattered by my absentmindedness. He had legitimately planned on asking me out, so I deserved his accusations and yelling. But couldn't he take the time to see my side of the story, too?

I abruptly pushed off the ground and headed to the bike rack at the front of the school. There was only one place I wanted to go—only one place that could heal me and my broken heart.

I started to run.

17

CHAPTER 17

The private beach came in sight after one last turn of the trail. I flew down the flight of steps that had been carved out of the cliff and dashed across the sand. I tore off my sweatshirt, shoes, and socks before plunging into the water.

As soon as the cold enveloped me, I closed my eyes and glided under the breaking waves, letting the ocean work its magic. Within a few moments, my anxious thoughts subsided and my racing heart slowed. I placed my hands near the gills protruding from my sides and marveled at their tender beauty. It felt amazing to be back in the ocean.

I drifted with the swells for a little while, but my body craved something more. As if on instinct, I found myself swimming toward the secret cave until I found myself underneath a familiar large stone arch. I raised my eyes and glanced at the glittering cliff walls before swimming upwards and breaking through the surface of the water.

All around me were the familiar sleek, glossy walls of the cave. Reflections of the water bounced off the walls and created fluctuating blue lines across the ceiling. I smiled, already feeling much better. I kicked up my legs and let myself float on top of the water, watching the reflections shimmering above my head. For the first time in what seemed like forever, I let out a sigh of contentment. Being here just felt so right. Surrounded by nothing but nature put my mind at ease and relaxed my entire being. I couldn't imagine living away from the sea. I wouldn't be able to handle it.

Mom loved the ocean too, I reminded myself. Dad said she went for daily swims and loved to be at the beach.

The thought brought the mysterious message back to mind. I swept my gaze over the glittering walls, searching for the little cleft where it was written. As soon as I spotted it, I eagerly swam over and peered inside. It took me a second to make out the familiar words, but as soon as I did, they warmed my heart.

The sea holds many secrets. – Miranda B.

Once again, I felt that odd sense of mystery and excitement. Mom was still alive, and she had written this message for me and me alone. I just knew it.

Why? Where are you? I asked as the hand-carved letters shimmering in front of my eyes. Why did you leave us? What are you trying to tell me?

Suddenly, I realized my legs felt stiff. I glanced down and tried to shake them out, bending my knees this way and that, but it felt like they had fallen asleep. I bit back a giggle at the strange feeling. It tingled and ran up and down my spine, wrapping around my gills and back down to the tips of my toes.

And then the pain hit.

I no longer felt like laughing; I felt like crying. My legs were suddenly glued together; the thick material of my jeans stuck haphazardly them. I held back a scream when the pain intensified so much that it felt like jolts of electricity shooting through my limbs.

My first thought was that I had been stung, either by a stingray or a jellyfish. But one glance at my surroundings told me that there were no sea creatures to be found.

I gripped the cave wall with both hands, my fingers trembling. Please stop, my mind pleaded. Though I tried to move my legs and reach a more comfortable position, it was to no avail. I was paralyzed. Tears began streaming from my eyes and floated upwards, lost in the deep blue of the water. I bit back another scream as the shimmering letters swam front of me.

The sea holds many secrets.

The pain was mounting. It was so intense that it felt like my bones were popping and snapping. My knuckles were turning white from gripping the wall so hard. I doubled over and hugged my knees to my chest, surprised at the feeling of something rough and prickly instead of my jeans.

Just when I thought I couldn't bear it any longer, the pain disappeared as quickly as it had come. I opened my eyes and realized I was still floating halfway between the surface and the seafloor, hugging my knees to my chest—or, more accurately, what used to be my knees.

In their place was a long, shimmering, brilliantly blue tail.

It took me a few seconds to realize that, yes, the scale-covered tail was indeed attached to my body. With trembling fingers, I ran my hands over its rough surface. The glittering scales reminded me of those of a fish.

No way. I rubbed my eyes, part of me hoping that I was dreaming or merely delusional, but when I reopened them the tail was still there. I glanced down and saw that the scales came up over my gills before melting into my skin. No matter how hard I tried, I couldn't find a fine line where the gills separated into skin.

I felt lightheaded. After everything that had happened, from drinking saltwater to holding my breath to growing gills, I should have been used to abnormality. But this—this tail—was completely different.

It appeared to be one huge, strong muscle. I performed similar motions to bending my knees and moving my legs, and the tail acted correspondingly. This definitely wasn't a dream. It was just unbelievable.

An object caught my attention out of the corner of my eye. The movement was awkward with my long tail, but I eventually managed to see what was floating beside me—my jeans. The inseams had been completely obliterated during my transformation.

For some reason, the thought terrified me. As my jeans sank to the seafloor, I felt like my last shred of humanity sank with them. I had become a freak—a monster. I grabbed one of my scales and tried to pull it off, but a sharp streak of pain made me stop. The tail was a part of me, and there was nothing I could do to change it.

Exhausted, I let myself sink to the seafloor. As soon as I hit the cool, soft sand, I closed my eyes. The transformation from human to mermaid replayed itself over and over again in my mind's eye. What was I going to do? How could I explain this?

My fear soon gave way to acceptance, and I slowly sat up and opened my eyes, prepared to face reality.

First, I gingerly ran a hand across the end of my tail. Its entire length looked to be about six feet, including the tip where it branched off like a dolphin's flukes. Every inch was covered in shimmering turquoise-blue scales before fading to the natural hue of my skin just above my gills. My T-shirt was still on, thank goodness, but now that my jeans were ripped in half, I couldn't walk home even if wanted to.

But what did I want...?

The corners of my lips turned up into a smile. Now that I thought about it, my tail was kind of cool. It didn't bend like knees and ankles did; it was one long, thick muscle that moved whichever way I wanted it to. I felt tall and powerful. I felt fast. And I realized that maybe this transformation wasn't so terrible after all.

For the next half hour I practiced swimming around the secret grotto. I was clumsy at first, but the more I swam, the more I got the hang of using my tail. Once I was confident that I could swim in the "real" ocean, outside of the calm water of the grotto, I cautiously headed out of the cave. As soon as I passed through the giant underwater arch, a slight current began pulling me along the face of the cliff. My tail writhed anxiously as I fought the current, trying to swim back to the private beach. I concentrated on moving my body in an S-motion, "mermaid style," so I could make the most of my flukes. As soon as I felt my tail pounding the water a little bit harder, I launched forward.

It was exciting to be able to swim this fast. However, I felt awkward swimming with my arms at my sides, so I reached forward and glided through the water in a streamline position instead. At this pace, I realized I was going about three times as fast as I could with normal legs. My powerful tail propelled me against the current at amazing speeds.

I was exhausted by the time I finally reached the private beach. My tail, like an unused muscle, was already sore. I wanted to drag myself onto the sand in order to rest, but pulling myself out of the surf was trickier than I expected. My huge tail kept getting in my way and pulling me down. Army crawling was nearly impossible with the sand dunes and the heavy weight of my tail behind me. Just as I was about to give up, a huge wave suddenly crashed behind me and rolled me onto shore. Water poured into my nose and my mouth, but inwardly I was pleased. I had made it.

With a little sigh of relief, I collapsed onto the sand. My wet T-shirt was plastered against my skin while the scales on my tail were glistening like thousands of miniature crystals. But now that I had succeeded in getting onto shore, what was I going to do? Going home was entirely out of the question.

I debated with myself for a few minutes, wondering what to do, when I suddenly felt a familiar tingling sensation. I quickly sat up and stared at my tail. "Oh no," I muttered. "Not again..."

I winced when the pain hit. I dug my hands into the sand and clenched my fists, anchoring myself to the ground. My eyes squeezed shut as I willed the pain to stop. If it increased...

But to my surprise and utter relief, the pain wasn't nearly as bad as the first time. I still had to grit my teeth and tough it out, but as soon as my bones finished popping and snapping into place, it was all over. I opened my eyes and nearly fainted with relief.

My legs were back.

"Yes!" I exclaimed, pushing off the sand and reveling in the feeling of having my legs again. I wiggled my toes and bent my knees until I was satisfied they were real. But how was this possible? I lifted up the corner of my shirt, only to see that all my scales were gone. Though my gills remained, there was no sign that I ever had a tail.

I scampered over to my sweatshirt and shoes, which were lying at the base of the trail where I had left them. I wrapped my sweatshirt around my bare legs to cover myself before making the long trek home. I was brimming with excitement from my newfound discovery.

Swinging my backpack over my shoulders, I whistled a happy tune as I climbed the steep trail. What had been terrifying at first was now thrilling in every way. The impossible had happened, yet in retrospect, it made sense. All the other strange things that had happened to me were only leading up to this one crucial moment. It was like the final piece to the puzzle. As unbelievable as it was, I knew that there was no mistaking what I had become.

A mermaid.

It was insane, delusional, preposterous. Yet I threw back my head and laughed. I was giddy with excitement. Was this what Mom had been trying to tell me? That I was actually a mermaid? So did that mean she was a mermaid, too?

"Wow," I breathed. My skin tingled. If my mother was a mermaid, just like me, then her parents had to have been mermaids too, right? And if her parents were mermaids, then their parents must have been mermaids...Wait, did that mean there was an entire secret race of mermaids living in the ocean?

The idea was staggering. To think that all this time, I had been living life like a normal teenager, when in fact I carried this huge secret. Why hadn't Dad told me? Had he known the truth about Mom? Had he known this whole time what I was capable of?

I was even more tired and sore by the time I finally made it home. I wanted to sit down at the kitchen table and talk all this through with Dad, but to my dismay, he was nowhere to be found. I rushed upstairs, surprised at finding my phone on my dresser, and remembered that I was no longer grounded. I immediately checked my messages and saw that one of them was a text from Dad saying he was going to be late from work today.

I sighed and flopped onto my bed. While scrolling through the rest of my messages, I realized most of them were from Luke. In addition to those, he had also left three voicemails.

I immediately felt a pang of guilt. The fight with Luke was still fresh in mymind. It had been temporarily pushedaside from the excitement about my tail, but it was still there. And I had to do something about it.

18

CHAPTER 18

"**W**here are you going?"

I paused and turned at the sound of Dad's voice. He watched me, arms folded over his chest, while I stood awkwardly in the doorway.

"Um...nowhere?" I replied.

"Rayne—"

"I was just going to hike the trails and do some schoolwork," I explained, the lie rolling off my tongue smoothly. I patted my backpack for emphasis, though in reality it contained a large towel and a few snacks.

Dad mulled this over in his head before speaking. "All right," he said after a few seconds. "But call me as soon as you get there."

"Okay." I headed to the door.

"And when you leave!" he added.

"Dad..."

He took another step forward. "Please be careful. I don't know if you heard, but there was a kidnapping the other day."

Now he had my attention. "A what?"

"A kidnapping," Dad repeated.

But this was Shady Cove. I couldn't imagine anything happening other than a small-scale theft, vandalism, or minor traffic violation. But a kidnapping...?

"Make sure you stay within sight of the house, okay?" Dad instructed.

"Sure," I said before he could change his mind. "You don't have to worry about me, I'll be safe."

He sucked in a deep breath. "I know all those crisscrossing trails are fun to explore, but please stay close."

"Yeah. I'll be back soon." I gave him a reassuring smile before heading out the door and making a beeline for the nearest trail. Knowing that he might be watching me from a window, I stopped at the edge of the cliff. I dialed his number, as promised, but as soon as our call ended, I leaned over and gazed down at the ocean.

There was no way I was staying up here. With one last guilty look at the house, I scurried down the rest of the trail, my whole body buzzing with excitement until I reached the private beach.

I dropped my backpack onto the soft, golden sand before making my way to the water's edge. I let the tide tickle the bottom of my toes as I stood precariously at the shoreline. I winced when I remembered the intense pain from yesterday, but my excitement quickly won over. I wanted to experience the thrill of swimming as a mermaid once again. A little pain wasn't going to stop me.

I shimmied out of my jacket and tossed it onto the sand behind me. Goosebumps immediately sprouted on my arms, but I tugged my shorts down anyway. Then I quickly darted into the water and dove under the first wave that came my way. The freezing cold pierced my skin, but only seconds later, it was followed by a familiar tingling sensation. I hurriedly swam out to deeper water where the waves didn't break. Then I closed my eyes and prepared myself for the excruciating transformation.

It was certainly painful, but not nearly as painful as the first or second times. Though my bones popped and snapped as they rearranged themselves, it hurt significantly less. I smiled with relief when the transformation was over, leaving me with my shimmering blue tail once again.

I stared at the beautiful turquoise scales that adorned my tail. When I turned around, the scales glistened as they reflected the sunlight streaming through the water. It was amazing—wonderful—unbelievable!

I aimed towards deeper waters and pumped my tail furiously. I immediately shot forward like a bullet, stirring up clouds of sand with my powerful flukes. My long black hair streamed behind me and glided over my tail in waves. No human could ever experience what I was experiencing. The sensation of swimming underwater, unhindered by legs and feet, was a sensation like no other.

Swimming with a tail was still a little tricky, of course. I had trouble picking up speed from a complete stop, but once I did, it felt like I could glide through the water forever. Unfortunately, stopping or slowing was also a problem. My huge tail felt awkward when I was positioned right side up, with my head near the surface and my tail near the seafloor. Only when I stayed parallel to the ground could I easily float in place.

After an hour of swimming, my tail started to grow sore again, so I headed back into shore. I had to time my exit perfectly, since it was nearly impossible to drag myself out of the water. I pumped my tail in rhythm with the waves before shooting forward just as one broke overhead. The foaming whitewash carried me straight to shore, where I washed up onto the damp sand with the tide. I laughed and shook my hair out of my eyes.

Now my legs should come back, I thought. But after about a minute with no sign of my tail transforming into legs, I started to grow worried. What if I had stayed out longer than I was supposed to, and I wasn't able to change back?

Technically, I didn't mind staying in the ocean longer, but that was beside the point. Dad still didn't know I could transform into a mermaid, and I had no idea how to tell him. But if I was stuck with a tail, would he ever find me?

Suddenly, just as I was debating whether or not to slip back into the water, the tingling sensation began. I let out a sigh of relief, and within half a minute my tail had magically transformed back into legs. I quickly grabbed my shorts and jacket and pulled them over my wet, shivering skin.

"Wow," I breathed. I sat in the sand for a few minutes, quietly watching the waves breaking on the shore. The ocean glimmered in the warm afternoon sunlight. Everything looked so peaceful and breathtakingly perfect. I closed my eyes as a soft breeze tousled my hair.

Suddenly, my ringtone blasted through the thin material of my backpack, jerking me out of my reverie. I quickly stood up, brushed the remaining sand off my shorts, and darted over to my backpack. I pulled out my phone, desperately hoping the caller wasn't who I thought it would be.

"Rayne!" Dad exclaimed as soon as I answered the call. "Where are you? It's been nearly two hours—"

"I'm sorry, Dad," I said, cringing. "I wandered out on another trail, but I'm fine. Don't worry."

He heaved a long, relieved sigh. "I thought I told you to stay within sight of the house," he said.

"I know, I got a little carried away," I admitted. "I'm heading home right now."

As Dad rambled on about kidnappers and being safe, I reached down and grabbed my towel, then proceeded to dry myself off. "Bye, Dad," I mumbled when he finally finished his lecture. After shoving my towel and phone into my backpack, I took one last wistful glance at the ocean before heading up the trail.

It was Wednesday—the day Madeleine Hansen came back from her three-day suspension. I had a mild suspicion that she would be even angrier with me than before, but I had other things to worry about—things like quitting the swim team. I had given it a lot of thought, and I figured that it was the saltwater that had caused my legs to transform into a tail. Only when I was fully immersed in the ocean did the transformation take place. On the other hand, nothing happened when I simply showered or bathed, because that wasn't saltwater. Unfortunately, the Shady Cove High pool was filled with both chlorine and salt, so I didn't want to take any chances.

I had mentally prepared a little speech to give to Coach Hansen. At the same time, I hoped my absence would get Madeleine off my back too. Sage and Marley might be disappointed that I was leaving them, but I would still see them at other times during the school day. I knew it was all for the best.

I coasted to a stop in front of Shady Cove High School on my bike. But no sooner had I chained it to the bike rack that whispers began sprouting all around me. I couldn't even walk to my locker without students murmuring about me behind my back. I began to grow anxious. What if someone had spotted a mermaid yesterday, saw the familiar long black hair, and figured it was I? Did the entire school know?

Fortunately, my suspicions were denied when I slammed my locker closed, revealing Marley standing directly behind. "So I heard the Mad Hansen's going to beat you up!" she declared brightly.

I jumped. "Goodness, Marley, you scared me!"

"Yeah, it's my first day back in a long time," she said with a grin. "I'm finally getting over my cold."

"Rayne!" Sage came barreling over to us through the crowd of students. "Oh my gosh, Rayne, is it true?"

"I heard it's gonna happen during lunch," Marley butted in.

"What? What's going to happen?" I asked, confused.

"No, I heard it was all going down after school, behind the gym," Sage countered.

"You really think so?" Marley asked doubtfully.

"What are you guys talking about?" I repeated, lost.

"But I heard it from Madeleine herself," Sage demanded.

"Heard what?" I asked.

"But why would she wait all the way until after school?" Marley argued. "That doesn't—"

"GUYS!" I hollered. My two friends paused and turned to look at me. "Can you please stop talking and explain what's going on?"

The girls exchanged a look. Then they said in unison, "Madeleine's going to beat you up."

I narrowed my eyes. "There's no way—"

"After school," Marley added.

"No," Sage corrected, "I overheard her talking with her friends. She's going to beat you up during lunch."

"I don't care when she's going to beat me up, okay? I just want to know if this is for real," I said, massaging my temples worriedly. "Are you guys serious about this? Is Madeleine really that angry at me?"

"Yeah. She's probably mad because you were the one who got her suspended," Marley said.

"Whoa, whoa, that was totally her fault, not mine. She's the one who started the fight."

"That's not what she says," Marley pointed out.

I sighed and buried my head in my hands. "Look, guys, can we stop talking about this? I mean, school hasn't even started yet and rumors are already going around about Madeleine wanting to beat me up. Well, I say she's not going to beat me up. She's just a troublemaker with a big mouth. I'm not even scared of her."

Marley narrowed her eyes. "You don't know who you're dealing with here, Rayne. The Mad Hansen is completely psycho! You're going to get your butt kicked."

"Not me," I said firmly, with more conviction that I felt. "I already stood up to her once, remember?"

"Yeah, and she was all in your face before the teachers had to pull her off! You can't handle her. You just can't." Sage stared at me with wide, pleading eyes. I suddenly remembered the story she had told me about what happened between her and Madeleine years ago.

I sighed. "Okay...so maybe I can't take her by myself."

"Well, don't ask me to fight her with you," Sage said dryly.

"Oh, no, of course not. If Madeleine's going to pick a fight with me, then it's only between the two of us."

Sage sucked in a deep breath. "I think I should tell the authorities about this."

"But what if Madeleine finds out you tattled on her?" Marley pointed out.

Sage's face paled. "Oh. No way. I am not going through that again. You're right, I can't tell the authorities. If they find out through the grapevine, then so much the better. But if they don't..." She gave me an apologetic look. "I guess you're stuck, Rayne."

"Whatever." I shrugged, even though my heart had started to beat faster at the thought of confronting Madeleine again.

Sage gave me a weak smile. "Okay. See you in Spanish."

"See ya."

"Oh, wait." She suddenly paused. "Have you seen Luke lately?"

I cringed. "No, the last time I saw him was Monday."

"Oh no." Sage bit her bottom lip worriedly. "I haven't heard from him in two days. I've texted him quite a few times, but he hasn't replied."

She paused, and I knew that we were both thinking the same thing: the roles had been switched. First I had unintentionally gone incognito, and now Luke.

But the way Sage had asked her question made my stomach flip. I glanced down at my shoes, shame written all over my face. "You were right, Sage," I said quietly. "I tried talking to him, but it was useless."

"I'm sorry, Rayne," she said sincerely. "But that still doesn't explain why Luke would ignore me. I wonder...?"

The thought was like a knife to the heart. With no other words to exchange, I said goodbye to Sage and Marley and headed to my first class. I couldn't stand to look them in the eye after what Sage had implied so delicately. Luke was ignoring her because of me. Ever since I had missed our "date" last Saturday, things had spiraled into chaos. Was Luke seriously so upset that he wouldn't even talk to his friends?

I felt sick to my stomach. I sulked through my first few classes and felt even worse when I entered Spanish and found Luke's seat empty. My heart ached to see him again, if only to tell him I was sorry. My mind was a whirlwind of emotions, and the added stress of having to confront Madeleine later today made it even worse. I was a wreck.

Fortunately, lunch passed uneventfully, while Sage and Marley tried to cheer me up and make conversation. But news was buzzing: Madeleine was still on the move.

Upon reaching the pool for swim class, I ran into Coach Hansen on the deck. He seemed rather unnerved to see me, especially since I still hadn't changed into my swimsuit. "Rayne," he said, "how are you?"

"Good, thanks," I rattled off. "Well, I actually have something to tell you..."

I sucked in a deep breath, but Coach beat me to the punch.

"Rayne, you don't have to apologize," he said warmly. "I forgive you."

"Ah..." My face scrunched up in confusion. "Thank you?"

"I'm truly glad that you're a part of this swim team, and I know that you're a hard worker and a kind person," he continued.

"Wait," I blurted out. "I—um—I'm actually not going to be on the swim team anymore."

Coach's amiable countenance quickly dissolved into one of surprise. "Not on the swim team?" he echoed.

"I'm—I'm—quitting." My voice wavered a little when I said it, but it had to be done.

Coach was dumfounded.

"I'm so thankful for all that you've taught me and for all the time you've invested in me, but I can't swim on the team anymore," I added.

"You can't? But of course you can! You're the star swimmer!"

I lowered my eyes. "But my heart's not in it," I said truthfully. "I'm sorry, Coach, but it's not going to work out."

Coach Hansen opened and closed his mouth, but no words came out. He resembled a goldfish trapped inside its bowl. "Let's talk about this," he finally said. "Don't make this mistake, Rayne. You have so much talent, so much passion—"

I saw a few girls trickling onto the deck, and for fear that Madeleine was one of them, I swiftly interrupted Coach. "Okay," I assented, "let's talk about this later. But—please—just know that my answer is final."

He shook his head sadly. I took a deep breath, partly from relief and partly from nervousness, before heading back to the locker room. I walked with my head down, ignoring the stares from some of the swimmers who were still getting ready. Only when I was a safe distance away from the pool deck did I raise my head and brush away a stray tear.

There. I had done it. I never thought I would quit a swim team, but I did. I let out a deep breath and collapsed onto a bench next to one of the classrooms.

Great. As soon as Dad found out what I'd done, he was going to have a long talk with me. He wouldn't understand why I suddenly wanted to quit. And even worse, I still had no clue how to tell him everything that had happened to me.

"Rayne Bennett!"

The smug voice made a chill run down my spine. I glanced up and squinted into the glaring brightness. "Huh?"

"Don't play stupid with me. We have some things to settle, and you know it."

My heart beat a little faster as the Mad Hansen's figure came into view.

She glared at me. "I'm tired of your games," she said bluntly. "You've gotten away with things for too long."

I almost laughed at the irony, but had enough sense to keep my mouth shut.

"So what do you say?" she called. "Or are you too scared to have a little chat with me?"

"I'm not scared," I replied coolly.

"Then prove it."

Sage's words flashed through my mind: "You can't handle her. You just can't." I gulped and rubbed my sweaty hands on my jeans. My eyes darted from side to side. There was nobody around; only the occasional bouts of laughter coming from the pool deck gave away my classmates' presence.

I swallowed nervously. If I did this, I'd be playing right into her hands. I would probably earn another suspension, or worse. But as Madeleine continued to ridicule me, my anger started to boil. What right did she have to keep hassling me? Obviously her father and the school authorities weren't going to do anything about it. Someone had to put her in her place.

I clenched my fists. So what if I got in trouble? Right now, I didn't care.

With a deep breath, I slid my backpack off my shoulders and stood up.

19

— ◦ —

CHAPTER 19

"**W**hat do you want with me, Hansen?" I asked, resorting to her last name in the hopes that it would make me sound tougher.

Madeleine smiled smugly. "You know why."

I narrowed my eyes. "Humor me."

When she realized I wasn't going to budge, she rolled her lips into her mouth, frustrated. "Fine," she spat, "if you're too stupid to figure it out for yourself."

I resisted the urge to roll my eyes.

"It's because you think you can waltz in here and take whatever you want."

I had guessed as much. "Madeleine," I sighed, "I've been here for less than a month. What have I taken from you? When have I ever given you a reason to hate me?"

"You've given me plenty," she retorted, her smile morphing into a glare. She advanced a few steps, but I stood my ground, even though every nerve in my body was screaming at me to make a run for it. "You took my dad from me," she continued. "You took the swim team from me. You took the spotlight from me!"

Now I really couldn't help but laugh. "Attention? What are we, in kindergarten?"

Madeleine's glare deepened, and she took a massive step forward. We were only a few feet away, and I was seriously scared by now. Why did I have to sass the school's biggest bully? It was like hammering the nails into my own coffin.

"I think it's time I taught you a lesson," she said, clenching her fists.

My eyes darted from side to side, but there was no one within sight. It was too late to back down now.

"You'll be sorry you ever crossed paths with me," she threatened.

I was petrified. What had I been thinking? I couldn't take the Mad Hansen by myself. This wasn't who I was.

Suddenly, a thought came to me. I was more than a newbie. I was even more than a swimmer. I was a freaking mermaid!

"You're wrong," I said with a smile. "You should be sorry that you ever crossed paths with me."

The punch came in a heartbeat, but I had been expecting it. As Madeleine's fist lunged for my nose, I swiftly ducked and side-stepped to the right. Then I brought my arm back and slugged her right in the gut. She let out a grunt and stumbled backwards a few feet.

I grinned. "Guess you weren't expecting that one, were you?"

She glared at me. "You'll regret this, Rayne." With one hand still clutching her stomach, she reared back and aimed for my nose again. I blocked her punch easily, though it hurt my arm a bit. I countered her punch by throwing one of my own, much faster than she expected. I popped her right in the lip, causing a thin stream of blood to begin trickling down her chin.

"That one was for Sage," I growled, my fist stinging from the hit.

By now, Madeleine was beyond wounded. She was breathing hard and surprised by my agility. While she was taller and bigger, I was smaller and faster. She put her hand to her lip and glared at the bloodstains on her fingers.

"You were asking for it," I reminded her. My entire body was now buzzing with adrenaline. A few students came trickling outside from the pool deck, wondering what all the ruckus was about.

Madeleine suddenly lunged towards me again, arms swinging. I ducked one of her punches, but the other hit me square in the jaw. I stumbled backwards, my head throbbing from the pain. I could already feel a bruise beginning to form.

"Girls!" someone yelled. I assumed it was Coach Hansen, but I didn't pay him any attention. I brought my right arm back again and swung with all my might. It hit something soft and odd-shaped, and Madeleine yelped in pain when she realized I had punched her in the eye.

I heard footsteps rapidly approaching. I glanced up, my suspicions confirmed: Coach Hansen was barreling towards us at full speed. Madeleine, doubled over, glared at me with a murderous look in her eye.

"Girls!" Coach Hansen exclaimed. He ran in between us and grabbed me by my shirt collar, nearly yanking me off the ground.

"Put me down!" I said angrily. "It's not my fault!"

He glared at me, but released his hold nonetheless. "What do you think you were doing? How dare you attack my daughter like that!"

I calmly smoothed out my shirt and pointed to Madeleine, whose bloody lip and teary eyes made her a sorry sight. "It was in self-de-fense," I pointed out. "She was the one who started it." I glanced up and noticed the entire swim team was staring at me with wide eyes. Marley and Sage were among them, but the faintest of smiles were on their faces. Some students began chattering eagerly amongst themselves.

"Enough!" Coach Hansen hollered, causing the crowd to scatter. "Go to the office right this instant, Rayne," he ordered. He then bent down and helped Madeleine to her feet, not sparing me another look.

I set my jaw, grabbed my backpack, and headed straight for the office with my heart pounding in my chest. Students immediately parted to let me through. The chattering died down slightly as I marched past them.

"Rayne!" Sage cried, jogging up next to me. "How did you do that?"

"I'm not really sure. I was angry, I guess."

"Well, it's about time someone put the Mad Hansen in her place." Sage smiled, but it quickly faded into a grimace.

"Don't worry about me," I reassured her. "I doubt the school authorities will do anything drastic."

She sighed. "It's not that," she admitted. "I actually have something really important to tell you." Her voice shook as she paused to collect her thoughts. "I know this isn't the best time, but...you've probably heard about the kidnapping."

I nodded.

"Well, I found out who it was." She swallowed, looked around to make sure no one was listening, and then leaned in to say, "They took Luke."

My heart stopped. "Wh-what?" I stammered. My hands trembled as I echoed what Sage said. "They took Luke?"

"Yes," she confirmed, her voice cracking.

"But how—why—are you sure?" I stammered.

Sage nodded violently. "He hasn't been answering his phone, his parents don't know where he is, and...and...oh, Rayne, what are we going to do?" She began to cry, a few tears sliding down her cheeks. Her normally bright blue eyes were now a watery gray.

Something snapped inside me. My anger at Madeleine was now gone, but so was my sadness over losing Luke. I'd already lost him a first time, and I was determined not to lose him again.

"I'll be right back," I said.

"Where are you going?" Her voice rose to a concerned pitch.

Somehow I knew—I just knew. I gave my friend a reassuring smile before taking off at a full sprint towards the front of the school.

"Rayne!" Sage cried again. "Where are you going?"

Coach Hansen called after me as well, but I never stopped or slowed as I hollered over my shoulder, "To find Luke!"

The ocean's beautiful stillness contrasted sharply with the whirlwind of emotions in my heart. The sight of the shimmering blue water and foaming waves had a calming effect on me, so I kept my gaze on the sea as I made my way down the steep trail. As soon as I reached the sand, I breathlessly sprinted to the water's edge, clumsily taking off my jeans and shoes as I did so. I didn't want my clothing to get ripped when my legs turned into a tail.

With my heart racing, I dove into the water. I welcomed the cold as it pierced every inch of my body, washing away my sweat and tears. This had been one crazy mess of a day, so I let the saltwater do its healing while my legs magically transformed into a tail. The process, other than a slight tingling and tugging, hardly hurt at all by now.

As soon as I had regained my brilliant blue tail, I shot forward into the deep. I headed in the direction of the underwater cave, not really knowing where I was going beyond that, but merely trusting my instincts. A few minutes into my swim, I sensed a presence rapidly approaching ahead of me. I slowed and squinted into the water, trying to make out the two silhouettes that were coming. Once they were close enough to see clearly, a large smile broke out on my face. It was the dolphins!

They clicked excitedly when I rushed forward to greet them. You're back! I exclaimed, reaching out to stroke their rostrums. Their eyes seemed to dance with joy and excitement at the sight of my tail. I swished it this way and that to show them that I had flukes just like they did.

You're ready! You're ready! they clicked, turning happy somersaults in the water. Come, they urged, suddenly taking off in an unexpected direction. I frowned and followed them curiously.

Where are we going? I asked.

To the current. You are ready.

The current? I didn't know what they were talking about. As soon as we reached the underwater cave, though, I remembered. A short swim away from the cave was a fast-flowing current leading off into the deep. A chill ran down my spine.

You want me to take the current? I clicked, even though I already knew the dolphins' answer. Instead of replying, they eyed me curiously, as if letting me make up my mind for myself. I sighed and watched their movements—a flick of the tail here, a toothy smile there, and an occasional flap of the dorsal fin.

Where will this take me? I asked, turning my attention back to the streaming current. It made a few looping turns off in the distance until drifting out of sight. What if I became lost and couldn't find my way back?

You are ready, the dolphins clicked, a grave tone to their words.

That wasn't what I asked, I replied irritably.

They merely repeated their phrase once more: You are ready.

I sighed and ran a hand down my chin. The saltwater was rapidly healing my bruise, but it still throbbed with pain. I rubbed it tenderly as I scrutinized the situation. Was I really about to do something as risky as follow this current? I had no idea where it led. What if it took me so far away that I didn't have the energy to swim back?

But the strong feeling in my gut told me that it was the right thing to do. Somehow, someway, this current would lead me to Luke. And if not to Luke, then to another clue that would help me find him.

Okay, I clicked reluctantly. I carefully undid my bun and let my long hair stream out behind me. I'll go.

The dolphins clicked excitedly. They flapped their dorsal fins and swished their tails, creating a frothing whirlpool of bubbles around us.

See you soon, I said, giving them a nervous smile before swimming forward. I gingerly reached out my hand into the fast flow of the current. The speed of the water immediately tugged my whole arm forward, and I marveled at how fast clumps of sand and seaweed drifted past me.

Well, here goes nothing...I took a deep breath and launched my entire body into the current. I was immediately sent flying forward, hurtling at speeds faster than I'd expected. I glanced over my shoulder and saw that the dolphins were already a good distance away, clicking happily and waving goodbye with their flippers.

Meanwhile, I was on an underwater roller coaster. I flipped and turned, nearly crashing completely out of the current at some points. But once I started moving my tail and swimming with the fast-moving water, everything changed. It was like I had stepped onto a moving walkway in an airport terminal.

I couldn't help but smile as I shot forward at lightning speed. I banked around turns and sailed over underwater boulders. One time the current took a sharp dip and sent me flying over whirlwinds of sand that fanned out on all sides like a magic carpet. I smiled and waved to a school of fish outside the current as I zipped by them. This is awesome!

But the trip was all over too soon. The current began slowing and spreading out in width, causing the water to stop moving as fast. Before long, I was swimming at my normal speed again. I frowned and let myself glide to a complete stop. Where was I?

With my underwater vision, I scanned my surroundings. My gut told me Luke was somewhere nearby, but there was nothing around except water, sand, and rocks. High above, where the sunlight came streaming in through the surface of the ocean, I spotted a lone buoy floating overhead.

But that wasn't where I wanted to go. Something was pulling me down—down towards the seafloor, to a large pile of underwater boulders stacked on top of the sand. I swam over and studied their rough, jagged surfaces carefully. Something told me that I needed to go inside, but the feeling was also accompanied by a hint of fear. I needed to be careful; I was treading in unfamiliar waters.

I cautiously swam to the other side of the rocks, where to my surprise I found a small hole. It looked as if someone had drilled straight through the rock, creating a perfect-sized peephole. So

I pressed myself up against the rock, closed one eye, and peered through.

What I saw was so startling that I immediately gasped and reeled backwards in surprise. I waited until my pulse slowed down before approaching the hole once again. I nervously closed one eye and peered into the cave-like structure. But no—it couldn't be.

I saw her with my own eyes—my mother. There was no doubt that it was her who sat only a few yards away, her beautiful black hair floating in a halo around her head, her face still and serene, just as elegant as she appeared in Dad's photo albums. Yet there was one problem.

She was dead.

20

CHAPTER 20

"**M**om?" I managed to whisper. But my words were lost to the deep blue of the ocean as the sound escaped my mouth in a plethora of bubbles.

Who's there? a voice suddenly asked, piercing my thoughts. It sounded like a frightened young girl.

Once again, I reeled backwards in surprise. Where had that voice come from?

I said, who's there? the voice repeated, even more frightened than before.

It's just me, I replied uncertainly, forming the words in my mind like I had communicated with the dolphins. My name is Rayne. Do you know what happened to my mother?

I waited impatiently for a reply. When none came, I mentally kicked myself for being so gullible. I was going crazy. Maybe I was only hearing things...

All of a sudden, a young mermaid emerged from around the corner of the cave. Her eyes and tail were brilliantly blue, just like mine, and she had dark hair that streamed in waves down to her waist. She was wearing a dark green top that exposed just a glimpse of her stomach. What are you talking about? she asked, her frightened tone suddenly replaced by one of confusion. That's my mother!

I was at a loss for words. I was staring a mirror image of myself, only younger. What in the world was going on?

Well? the mer-girl asked impatiently. What do you want with us?

I'm here to rescue my mother, I declared.

The mer-girl frowned. It's not funny!

I tried a different tactic. Is she dead?

Mom? The mer-girl opened her mouth and laughed, letting a stream of air bubbles float to the ceiling of the cave. No, she's just sleeping.

I closed my eyes and let a sigh of relief. Sleeping! I nearly laughed at my inanity. Mom was only sleeping...

I beheld her figure for another moment, this time with an optimistic, rather than a mournful, gaze. Listen, I said quickly, is there any way to get inside this cave?

The girl's smile drooped. I've been here my whole life and I've never found a way out. Even if I did, they would be sure to find out.

Another question surfaced on my tongue—who are 'they?'—but I bit it back. This wasn't time to get carried away by technicalities. I had to focus on getting Mom—and this mer-girl—out of the cave.

I turned my attention to my mother's sleeping form. Wake up, I urged, pleading for her to hear me. Please, Mom, wake up! If it's really you, wake up!

The beautiful mermaid suddenly stirred. She lifted her head and sat up, her eyes fluttering open. Mara? she asked the mer-girl sleepily. What's wrong? When she felt an extra pair of eyes staring at her, she suddenly swung her gaze to the peephole. Our eyes met, and she immediately sat up, surprised.

Mom...it's me, I said quietly.

She clasped her hands together. Rayne? Is that really you? she cried, swimming right up to the cave wall and peering through the peephole to get a closer look at me.

As soon as she said my name, I felt a rush of exhilaration. It was true—it was really true. Mom! I exclaimed. A single tear fell from my eye and faded into the blue of the ocean. Yes, Mom, it's me! It's really me!

Oh, Rayne! She smiled and reached through the hole with a finger. I clasped it in my hand, letting my tears flow freely now. It's been so many years, she continued. Her voice, even in my mind, sounded thick with emotion. Just look at you now...all grown up, and so beautiful.

By now I had backed away from the peephole, allowing her to look through and see my entire figure. We were silent. As the water quietly swirled around us, I realized that more was to be said in our silence than in our words. All the time we had been separated, all these years of lost memories—we would probably need a few more years just to catch up on everything we had missed!

For now, though, I was merely trying to process that my mother was still alive.

I'm so proud of you, honey, she finally said. Did Nora and Nicky show you to the cave?

My confused expression must have clued her to explain, so she added, The dolphins. I sent them to come find you, and I told them not to let you take the current until you were ready. She swept her gaze down the length of my tail, smiling happily through her tears. Which you clearly are.

I was overjoyed. Somehow, the fact that I was a mermaid, like her, made our reunion that much sweeter. And Mom was just like I had imagined her—beautiful and kind, amazing and wonderful. Yet her eyes seemed to have taken on years of weariness. And what about the mer-girl stuck inside the cave with her?

Mom, I said hastily, I need to help you escape. I pressed my hands against the boulders, feeling their cold and rough surface. How is it even possible that you've survived in here for so long?

It's not what you think, she replied gravely. The tides have changed. Even you must leave before it is too late. They will be coming soon, and I can't let them find you.

Who? I demanded, my gaze flickering from her to the mer-girl.

Not now. Mom reached through the peephole once again, and I gripped her finger as if it were my last lifeline. I'll explain everything in due time. For now, get away from here as fast as possible. Do not get caught. If you do, all is lost.

My head was spinning. Could Mom be a fugitive? Was this some sort of mermaid prison?

You can come back between the seventh and ninth hours, she added.

I nodded, even though I barely understood what was happening.

I'll explain everything in due time, Mom repeated, as if reading my innermost thoughts. Please, Rayne, stay safe. I love you so much.

She slipped her finger back into the cave and pulled away, her eyes watering with tears.

Wait, Mom! I have so many questions! I persisted, my own vision becoming clouded with tears as well.

Not now, she said firmly. I love you, Rayne. Never forget that. Now go—and hurry!

I instinctively reached up to wipe away my tears, but they had already slipped away into the surrounding water. I now sensed another presence, but for some reason, it was laced with fear. I immediately swam straight up for the surface, but not before giving my mother one last glance. I wanted to savor what she looked like so I would never forget. My heart broke at having to leave her like this, trapped and in danger for some strange reason, but I trusted her too much to break her word. I love you, Mom, I said as I swam rapidly to the shifting surface above.

When I broke through, I let myself bob up and down for a few seconds as some remaining tears trickled down my cheeks. I couldn't believe I had actually found my mother after all these years! But while Dad and I had been living our lives on the surface, Mom had been trapped in an underwater cave. Only a few rays of sunlight reached into her rocky prison. And how did she eat? How did she have the will to keep living? I was determined to get to the bottom of it all. I had to rescue her and the mer-girl from the cave. Then the three of us could swim to safety, and Mom could tell me everything I wanted to know.

Exhaustion settled over me. I had survived a fight with Madeleine, ran two miles to the beach, and swam even further through the ocean—all in the space of just a couple hours. Relaxing in my bed and kicking my feet up on a pillow sounded like a wonderful idea at the moment, but that meant swimming all the way back to the private beach. With no swift-moving current to take me there, it would probably take even longer to reach home.

I raised my head and glanced up at the sky, which was tinted a soft pink from the pastel sunset. Watching the clouds lazily drifting overhead gave me a sense of peace. An idea suddenly came to mind when I spotted the buoy floating a short distance away. If I pulled myself onto the buoy, I would be able to rest my tail and enjoy the sunset at the same time. It would be the perfect way to relax before the long swim home.

I headed towards to the old, rusty piece of equipment bobbing up and down with the waves. But before I could attempt to climb on, I suddenly spotted a mop of shaggy brown hair on the other side.

I immediately ducked back underwater. That was human hair—I was sure of it. Or could it be another mermaid? Either way, I had to careful. I gulped and cautiously swam over to the other side of the buoy, making sure to remain underwater. When I peered through the surface of the water, I was surprised to see that it wasn't a mermaid sitting on the buoy. Instead, I saw a sunburnt boy lying facedown, clinging to its rusted surface. He was motionless.

I slowly swam closer to get a better look. As I did so, my hand flew to my mouth. It couldn't be...

But I saw the brown hair and the familiar T-shirt and immediately knew it was Luke. My mind was awhirl with thoughts. What was Luke doing out here, miles from shore? There were no major shipping lines in these waters, and any boats that launched from Shady Cove Harbor typically sailed much further south.

I swallowed nervously and slowly raised myself out of the water, my tail working overtime to keep me afloat. "Luke?" I asked quietly.

He didn't move. After a few more futile attempts to wake him up, a horrible realization dawned on me: was he dead?

"Luke?" I asked, louder and more frightened this time. "Luke, please answer me."

To my surprise and utter relief, he suddenly twitched and raised his head. His shaggy brown hair was matted and sticking up in random places, and his skin was red and splotchy from sunburn. But the wild, frightened look he gave me after turning around was more than I could bear. If he wasn't dead, then he was close to death.

"R-Rayne?" His chapped lips could barely form the word. He suddenly flung his arm in front of his eyes and murmured, "I must be hallucinating again."

"No!" I said quickly, grabbing the buoy and pulling myself up. "No, you're not seeing things. I'm really here. It's really me, Luke."

He blinked a few times before scooting over to get a closer look. I reached out, nearly slipping off the buoy in the process, and gripped his hand with all my strength. "I'm here, Luke. I'm going to save you."

"Rayne..." His voice was hoarse, but suddenly infused with energy. "Rayne, I can't believe it's really you! I've been stuck here for two days...for two whole days..."

As he rambled, he collapsed onto his stomach again, causing an interruption in the buoy's rhythmic bobbing.

"Let's get you home," I said, wriggling closer. "I need to get you into shore."

"How?" he rasped. "I thought you were captured and left here too."

"I wasn't kidnapped, if that's what you're talking about."

"Then you have no idea what's happened," he said, struggling to sit up. "They gave me a water bottle, but I drank all of it on the first day. Then they started to bring me some seaweed every few hours. But I couldn't answer their questions. Those—those things give me the creeps." He shuddered and glanced at the ocean warily.

A chill ran down my spine. The pieces were suddenly starting to fall into place. "So...these creatures captured you?" I asked carefully. "As in, merpeople?"

Luke nodded stiffly.

"Oh no. This is bad. This is really, really bad." I gave a shudder of my own, suddenly realizing that Mom was right. I needed to get as far away from here as possible, and fast. I couldn't let these merpeople catch me. But if they had kidnapped Luke and brought him here as bait, I was playing right into their hands!

"Luke," I exclaimed, "we have to hurry. Climb onto my back and hold on. We need to get of here."

"Go without me," he said wearily. "I can't even stand up, let alone swim."

His eyes started closing. I was losing him.

"I know you can't," I said, determined. "But I can."

The flukes of my tail suddenly broke through the surface, sending arcs of glittering spray flying high above our heads.

Luke's mouth dropped open. "You're—you're one of them!" he said hoarsely.

"I'm on your side, not theirs," I reassured him. I turned around so that my back was facing him. "Now come on; let's get out of here."

Luke swallowed and hesitantly swung his legs over the side of the buoy. Frail as he was, he managed to hop into the water and climb onto my back. When his legs accidentally brushed against my scales, he recoiled.

I was hurt, but I knew that Luke had gone through almost as much as I had in the past few days. "Hold on tight," I said.

With a powerful movement of my tail, I suddenly lurched forward. Luke's fingernails dug through my T-shirt as we darted through the water. I was careful to stay near the surface so Luke could continue to breathe. Despite my exhaustion, adrenaline (and fear) pushed me to keep going. Though all my muscles screamed from exertion—especially with Luke's dead weight on top of me—I was forced to push the pain aside.

The entire swim took over an hour to reach the private beach. Finally, when a wave carried us to shore and dumped us onto the sand, I allowed myself to fall limp.

"We made it," I gasped. "Oh, thank goodness we actually made it!"

Luke, who had been tossed a few yards away from me by the wave, collapsed onto the sand. "W-water," he rasped.

I saw his eyes, pleading, hoping. I nodded. As soon as Luke's head hit the sand and his eyes closed, I felt the tingling sensation beginning. Once my transformation was complete, I pulled on my jeans and hurried over to my backpack. It was still lying in the sand where I had left it, and I eagerly sorted through its contents until I found my uneaten snacks and half-empty water bottle.

"Here," I said breathlessly, sprinting back over to Luke. "I have water."

Luke cracked open his eyes. He seemed surprised to see that my tail had been replaced by legs, but his thirst overpowered his curiosity. I handed him the water bottle and watched as he pulled off the cap and guzzled every last drop.

"Careful," I laughed.

Water dribbled down his chin, but he merely sighed with relief. "Rayne," he murmured, "you're a lifesaver."

I waited patiently as he ate. Once finished, I saw that his eyes contained their familiar friendly glow again.

"Satisfied?" I asked with a smile.

"You have no idea," he said. "Though I have to admit that I'm still pretty thirsty."

"Don't worry," I reassured him, "you can come home with me." I knew that Dad would flip when he found out what happened, but I had no other choice. I was too far into this mess to go back.

Luke nodded gratefully. His gaze flickered down to my legs. "Well, before that, can I ask you a few questions?"

"Oh," I said awkwardly. "Right."

He cocked his head to one side. "Since when can you grow a tail?"

My cheeks reddened. "I found out I was a mermaid only a few days ago."

"Yes, but..." He seemed at a loss for words. "But how? I didn't even know mermaids existed until—"

"Until you were kidnapped?"

He nodded, but his eyes had suddenly drifted to another world. "I had been walking on the beach," he said absentmindedly. "It was after our fight. I just wanted to clear my head. I was nearing Shady Cove when—when those things suddenly appeared out of nowhere and dragged me into the water. Before I knew it, they had turned from humans into half-men, half-fish. It was a living nightmare. They strapped me to their backs, took me into the middle of nowhere, and left me stranded on that buoy. They spoke with a strange accent, and the questions they asked didn't make sense."

I stared at him. "What kind of questions?"

He took a deep breath. "I know this sounds crazy, but...Rayne, they were questions about you."

My heart sank. "I'm so sorry," I whispered. "Oh, Luke, this is all my fault. Those mermen were after me, not you. They were just using you as bait."

"But why? I thought you said you've only been a mermaid for a few days."

"I know, but it's a long story." I shifted in the sand, trying to avoid his gaze. The sky overhead was almost entirely dark, casting shadows across the browning sand. I didn't want to admit that I was almost as clueless as him. Why was my mother being held in that prison-like structure? Why would the merpeople capture Luke, knowing that he was connected to me in some way? The answers were beyond what I could fathom.

"It's getting late," I finally sighed, "and we still have a long walk ahead of us."

I stood up and headed over to my backpack. I quietly brushed the sand off my jacket and shoes before pulling them on and slinging my backpack over my shoulders.

Luke watched me with an indecipherable look in his eyes. "Yeah, I'm coming," he said, slowly getting to his feet and walking over to the start of the trail.

I felt my cheeks flush again. Now that we were back on solid ground, the whole concept of mermaids and kidnappings seemed a world away. Had it all been a weird and frightening dream?

As I studied Luke's countenance, I realized that there were still many questions he had yet to ask. He saw me as a stranger, a freak—a creature with the same characteristics as the ones who kidnapped him.

Oh, Luke, I thought. But his eyes bore a blank expression. He couldn't communicate in the same way that mermaids and dolphins could. Oh, Luke, what have I gotten us into?

21

CHAPTER 21

Luke stumbled up the trail, and it wasn't until I came closer to steady him that I realized his feet were bleeding.

He heard me gasp, and immediately turned around with a sour expression on his face. "Don't worry," he said, following my gaze. "It's only a few blisters."

But upon closer inspection, I realized his feet were cracked in multiple places—and on top of that, they were horribly sunburned.

"You need to rest," I said, motioning for him to sit down.

"But it's getting dark," he argued, "and you said we still have a ways to go."

"Never mind what I said, we can rest for a few minutes."

Too tired to argue, Luke collapsed onto the dirt and stretched his legs out in front of him. I placed my hands on my hips and gazed down at the churning ocean. It was barely visible now, save for a few hot flashes of white where the waves broke on the shore. When I turned back to face Luke, I saw that he was staring at me wide-eyed.

"Um...you do know you're glowing, right?" he asked after an awkward silence.

I self-consciously reached up and touched my hair. "Oh. Yeah. About that—"

"It's a mermaid thing?"

I laughed. "Yes."

"Well, after everything I've been through lately, I have no trouble believing that." He smiled, closed his eyes, and leaned his head against one of the rocks behind him. "Oh, Rayne," he murmured, "I'm so sorry."

"What?" I kneeled down next to him. "Luke, if anyone should be sorry, it's me. If it wasn't for my dumb mistake of missing our date, you would have never—"

Luke shushed me by placing a hand on my arm. "No," he said simply, his gaze flickering up to mine. "No, it's not your fault at all. Two days stranded in the middle of the ocean gave me a lot of time to think. I realized I had gotten worked up over a simple misunderstanding, like you said. I was so blinded by my crushed hopes that I didn't listen to you. I'm sorry for hurting you, Rayne. I care for you—I really do."

I glanced away, hoping the darkness would hide my flushed cheeks.

"Anyway," he said after a few moments, "we can get going."

I gave him a hand up, and we continued our hike. Luke never stumbled again, though it may have been to the fact that we were clinging to each other in case we tripped over an unseen ditch or boulder.

Finally, just when the last traces of sunlight had fled the sky, my house came into view. It was a huge, looming object barely distinguishable from the surrounding gloom.

"Wow," Luke breathed, "is that your house?"

"It looks more like a castle from here," I laughed, "but yeah, that's my house."

I helped him across the rough, weed-choked ground to the front door. We made it, slightly out of breath but smiling from our adventures. The worst was over—or so I thought.

With a relieved sigh, I turned the knob and pushed the door open.

"Rayne!" Dad nearly attacked me as Luke and I stepped into the hall. "Oh, honey, I was so worried! You have no idea how long I've been waiting for you! Why haven't you answered your phone?"

I took a few steps backward and held up my hands in surrender. "Whoa, Dad, relax. I'll explain everything in a few minutes."

"I think you need explain everything now," he corrected me.

I nodded slowly. He deserved as much.

"Who's that?" he suddenly asked, peering over my shoulder at Luke, who was standing uncomfortably in the doorway.

"This is Luke," I explained. "He...uh...he was kind of stuck on a buoy in the middle of the ocean."

A bewildered look crossed Dad's face, but I pleaded, "He's dehydrated and exhausted. Can't we help him first before you deal with me?"

Dad scratched his head, but finally gave a small sigh and held out his hand towards Luke. "Of course. Just follow me."

"Thank you." Luke smiled, relieved that he was now officially accepted into the Bennett household. "You know, your daughter saved my life, sir."

"She did?" Dad gave me a suspicious look.

"It was nothing, really," I said.

"Nothing?" Luke scoffed. "I was kidnapped by evil mermen and stranded on a buoy for two days. Rayne is a hero—she carried me all the way back to shore."

Dad raised his eyes at the word "mermen." I cringed, expecting an outburst, but the calm silence that greeted me was somehow even more terrifying. "Well," he said after a tense few seconds, "I guess we all have some catching up to do."

I headed upstairs to take a shower while Dad helped Luke get situated. The two seemed to be getting along fine, and I didn't want to spend any more time with my father than I had to. I knew the impending discussion between us was going to be very, very uncomfortable.

I hoped a warm shower would help clear my head and reorganize my thoughts, but one look in the bathroom mirror was enough to send my anxiety overboard. My hair was matted, tangled, and sandy. I looked horrific. Even my face resembled something from a crime scene—dark circles under my eyes, sand clinging to my eyelashes, dirt smeared across both cheeks, and a purplish bruise forming on my jaw. To make matters worse, I even had a dried trickle of blood across my knuckles and forehead.

"How embarrassing," I muttered. How could Sage have looked at me with a straight face after my fight with Madeleine? How could my mother even say I was beautiful? I suddenly burst out laughing. What a strange first impression I must have made! And Luke...well, Luke technically looked worse than I did.

It was a small consolation while I showered. Once I was thoroughly clean and rejuvenated, I stepped out and slipped into some dry clothes. Upon walking downstairs, I found Luke and Dad already chatting at the kitchen table. Two empty glasses of water and a large plate with some sandwich crumbs sat in front of Luke.

He looked like a completely different person. His eyes were still full of life and energy, but they were now greatly accented by his smooth, unblemished skin. His lips curved up into a friendly smile when I entered the room, and as he leaned forward, his perfectly combed hair fell slightly in front of his eyes.

I slid into the seat across from him and self-consciously adjusted my bun. Aside from Luke's sunburn, he looked nothing like the boy I had rescued from sea just hours ago. As for me...well, I'd been unable to scrub away the last traces of my bruise and dried blood, and probably looked only slightly better than earlier.

"Well," Dad said slowly, placing his arms on the table, "I guess we should get started."

I nodded. The sooner we began, the sooner I would have it other with.

But the tactic Dad chose was different from what I had been expecting. Instead of lecturing me, he settled back in his seat and said, "I guess you've figured everything out, right?"

I nodded again.

"You know about the mermen, so you must know the truth about your mother."

"Well...yeah." I shifted nervously in my seat. "But that's not all."

Dad raised an eyebrow. "It's not?"

I glanced at Luke, then back at my father. Luke clearly hadn't told him much. Did Dad even know that I could transform into a mermaid myself?

"Rayne," he prodded, "what else do you know?"

I didn't know where to begin. Everything was a tangled mess. I knew I had to tell Dad about all my adventures, including the dolphins, secret cave, mysterious message, and discovering Mom. But where did I start?

Dad and Luke were staring at me expectantly. I decided to start from the beginning—from the moment I discovered the private beach. After taking a deep breath, I dove in.

By the time I finished telling my tale, nearly twenty minutes had gone by. Dad was sitting thoughtfully in his seat, staring at something far in the distance, something I couldn't see. Luke, on the other hand, was staring at me with wide eyes, as if he couldn't fully digest my story.

Not that I would blame him. I felt like a huge weight had been lifted off my shoulders—there were no more secrets; no more hiding behind lies and pretending everything was normal. Because my life was obviously anything but normal.

I was a little surprised that Dad was acting so calm, though. It was actually quite unnerving. I had expected him to bombard me with questions and demand why I had been keeping so many secrets from him. Moreover, I had expected him to express some sort of emotion after hearing that Mom was still alive!

When no one made a move to answer, I awkwardly cleared my throat. "It's crazy, right?" I chuckled nervously. "I still have a hard time believing it myself."

"It's insane," Luke agreed. "Like something straight out of a fairy-tale."

Dad shifted in his seat. "And yet it must be true," he said. "Oh, honey..." He suddenly took my hands in his. "I'm so sorry for not telling you right away. I didn't want to tell you the truth about Miranda because I wanted you to live a normal life. That was her one wish, that you would grow up as a normal, happy girl, not having to glance over your shoulder for fear that your mother's kidnappers would be after you too."

The words came out in a rush, but emotion—trembling, overwhelming emotion—poured out with them. "Then you knew," I said softly. "You knew why Mom disappeared."

"Not really," Dad admitted. "Though she had often warned me her own race was after her, there was no clue as to whether or not that was the cause of her disappearance."

"But why would her own race capture her?"

"She had broken an ancient law—a law that said merpeople must never have relations with humans. And that's why they are after you, Rayne: you are the evidence of that broken law."

I felt a chill run down my spine. "What's the penalty?"

Dad glanced away, and his silence spoke volumes. Though I was horrified at the extent the merpeople would go to keep their race a secret, I identified with them. The fear I felt about hiding my own secrets was nothing compared to the fear of hiding an entire race of creatures.

"So why is Mom still alive after all these years?" I asked quietly, hoping my voice didn't waver. "Why haven't they—you know—killed her?"

"They're using her as bait." An angry look flashed across my father's eyes. "Just like they used Luke as bait, they've been using Miranda as bait, too. Their ultimate goal is to capture you, Rayne. The merpeople want to keep their race a secret. They don't want to become known to humans. And you are their number-one threat."

I swallowed nervously.

"Do you see why I've been so protective of you all this time? I used to be so paranoid, I would have doubts about letting you join the swim team. I didn't want your past to become known, because then you would be stolen from me, just like your mother was. But when

I saw how happy and talented you were in the water, I let you go. Miranda had told me that, depending on which genes you inherited, it was possible you could transform. However, only saltwater could bring about that transformation."

I let that sink in for a moment. "Then why did we move back here to Shady Cove?" I asked skeptically. "If you knew the ocean would make me turn into a mermaid, why did we come back?"

Dad seemed to struggle with this question, but he finally replied, "Because it felt right. It had been over a decade since your mother's disappearance. I honestly thought the threat was gone, that the merpeople had forgotten. I had an inkling of doubt in my mind, but for the most part I was willing to take the risk. I loved your mother so much that I never wanted to forget her. She had changed my world."

I let out a deep breath and propped my elbows up on the table. This was too much information to take in, but it all made sense—why I had never known about merpeople, why I could never grow a tail before, and how serious this situation really was: life or death serious.

"Um, can I say something?"

Dad and I both swiveled our heads to stare at Luke.

"So, I don't really understand all this," he said slowly, turning to face my father, "but I get that your wife is being held captive in the ocean, and these merpeople are after Rayne because she's the evidence of some ancient law being broken."

Dad nodded, and his silence cued Luke to continue.

"Since this all sounds pretty serious, aren't you going to do something about it?"

My stomach twisted into a knot. "Of course!" I exclaimed. "I know exactly where Mom is and what kind of danger she's in. But since I'm the only person who can go get her, how is this going to work? I can't rescue her all by myself while the entire race of merpeople is out for my blood."

"Rayne is right." Dad fixed his steely gaze on Luke. "We are not putting my daughter in danger."

"So you're just going to leave your wife down there? She's been trapped for over a decade, Mr. Bennett. Isn't it time someone came to her rescue?"

"We are not putting Rayne in danger," Dad repeated. "Stay out of this, Luke."

Luke held Dad's fierce gaze with a fiery one of his own, but he clenched his jaw and remained silent. The tension in the room had suddenly become suffocating.

"Actually, Dad, Luke is right." I surprised myself by speaking my thoughts aloud, but once the words were out of my mouth I had no choice but to endure Dad's glare and press on. "I mean, I've already swam to Mom's cave and back without getting caught. I can easily do it again. And this time I won't have to swim all the way into shore while carrying someone on my back."

Luke smiled faintly, but Dad still wasn't amused. "This is serious, Rayne," he said sternly. "You were lucky that there weren't any mermen guarding your mother's cave. You could have been killed, and I would have been left with another disappearance to grieve over."

His words stabbed my heart, but I took a deep breath and continued. "Look, Dad, I understand how serious this is. I really do. But if you'd just give me a chance, I promise I can save Mom and bring her back. She's counting on me, remember? She left me that secret message in the grotto and had two dolphins show me to the current. She wants me to save her because she knows I can."

Dad was quiet for a few seconds.

"I know where you're coming from and how hard this is for you, but please trust me," I pleaded. "I can do this."

He stood up and walked over to the kitchen window. He studied the scene outside for a few tense moments before turning back to me. "Fine," he sighed reluctantly. "But before you get too excited, I have a couple rules."

I sat up straighter.

"First of all, you have to let me help you," he said sternly. "This is not all fun and games. We need a plan."

"Understood."

"And secondly," he added, "I am not letting you go right this minute."

"Of course not."

"How about tomorrow?" Luke suggested, much to Dad's chagrin.

"Early,"I confirmed, remembering what Mom had told me. "Operation Rescue Mom starts at seven o'clock sharp."

22

─ ● ─

CHAPTER 22

old was an understatement. Frost covered every inch of the ground, coating plants and bushes in a thin veil of white. The ground was hard and pale, still damp in a few places from the chill morning air. Even the ocean looked gray and disheartening underneath the gloomy overcast skies. Freezing was more like it.

Dad and Luke jumped up and down in their oversized coats to keep warm, their breaths coming out as white puffs in the air. "It's too early," Luke grumbled.

"It's only seven," I pointed out. "Would you rather be getting ready for school?"

He shook his head vigorously. Last night, we had decided it would be best if Luke stayed with Dad until I got back. Even though his parents were still worried about his whereabouts, Luke desperately wanted to help with my dangerous mission. He already knew so much about merpeople, my mother, and my background that he was an invaluable asset to Dad and me.

"Are you sure you want to do this?" Dad asked, his voice rising against both Luke's and mine.

"Yes, I'm sure." I allowed myself to melt in his embrace as he hugged me close.

"Be safe," he murmured. "I love you."

My heart went out to him. "I love you too," I said softly. Then, with a deep breath, I stepped away and walked to the shoreline. I dipped a toe into the icy-cold water, and goosebumps immediately sprouted on every inch of exposed skin. I was clad in a mere tank top and shorts because it was easier to swim in light clothing. And I had to be prepared to swim fast in case a mob of angry merpeople decided to chase after me while I attempted to rescue Mom.

The thought was dispiriting, so I shook myself out of my trance and focused on the shifting gray water in front of me. Somewhere out there, Mom was waiting for me—somewhere beyond these foaming waves, out in the still deep of the ocean.

I turned around to face Dad. He looked awfully grim compared to Luke, who smiled and gave me two thumbs up. I laughed and turned back to the water. Here goes nothing...

I ran straight towards the first wave that came my way. Jumping over its foamy crest, I stretched out my arms and dove smoothly underneath the surface. The water was biting cold, but I soon grew used to it as the transformation took place. I quickly shimmied out of shorts before my tail engulfed my legs. Then, breaking through the surface again, I flung my shorts onto the wet sand.

"Hang on to those for me!" I called.

Luke laughed, but Dad gave me a skeptical look. Only when I flicked my tail above the surface of the water did he break out into a wide smile.

"Good luck, Rayne!" he called. "I love you!"

But I barely heard his cry as I dove underwater and began my swim to the current. My entire body buzzed with adrenaline. I was thankful for the rush, because I needed to stay on high alert if I wanted to avoid any unfriendly merpeople. If the mermen had somehow ventured on shore to kidnap Luke, then they might be stationed near the coast again. Fortunately, I sensed no presence in the water around me until I neared the entrance to the current. I could barely make out two silhouettes in front of the cave, their flukes swishing back and forth in the dark water.

My heart began pounding. Had the mermen figured out that I had used the current? Maybe they posted two guards in order to keep an eye out for me. I slowed down and floated precariously in one spot, not sure what to do. The silhouettes weren't moving, so I could only hope they hadn't sensed my presence yet. I was about to turn around and make the roundabout swim to Mom's cave, but then I realized it would take much longer. Time and energy were of the essence.

With shaking limbs, I cautiously swam closer. All my senses were on high alert, and my hands were trembling in anticipation. Just as I was about to chicken out and head back to Dad and Luke, I suddenly heard a familiar series of clicks.

Come, Rayne! What are you waiting for?

The dolphins! I smiled and laughed with relief, immediately chasing away my fantasies of two mermen guarding the entrance. Sure enough, as I eagerly approached the current, Nora and Nicky somersaulted in excitement at the sight of me.

I'm so glad you're here! I clicked. I need to rescue my mother from her trap. Can you come with me?

Nora and Nicky showed matching toothy smiles in reply. Of course.

The three of us quickly darted into the current and took off at full speed. We raced through the water, banking around turns and flying over the seafloor until the current dispersed. My tail was weary from so much swimming in such a short time, but I pressed on, determined to save Mom.

Do you know how to get inside the cave? I asked the dolphins as we neared the pile of boulders off in the distance. As we rapidly approached, I scanned the surrounding water for any sign of mer-people.

The rocks are too heavy, the dolphins replied sadly.

But with three mermaids and two dolphins, it had to be worth a short. I was determined to try.

My heart pounded rapidly in my chest when I finally reached the cave where Mom was imprisoned. I pressed myself up against the boulders and peered through the peephole. Mom! I clicked anxiously.

My mother, along with the mer-girl, had been reclining on the sandy floor. But at the sound of my voice, they both turned. Mom was the first to dash over, a hopeful smile on her face. You're back! she exclaimed. Oh, Rayne, I knew I could count on you.

I brought Nora and Nicky to help me, I replied, warmth rushing through me at the sight of her. We have to hurry, but I think I know how to get you out of here. If all five of us work together, we might be able to push one of these boulders aside.

Mom nodded. Yes, that's how the mermen bring food to us. They always move aside this boulder to give us our rations. Mara and I have tried to move it ourselves, but it won't budge with just the two of us.

I glanced over at the mer-girl. Mara was certainly too small and light to do any heavy lifting—especially if the boulder had to be moved aside by full-grown mermen.

Mom motioned me to watch before swimming over to the opposite side of the cave, where a medium-sized boulder was lodged in between two larger ones. Here it is, she said.

I clicked rapidly to the dolphins, explaining the situation to them, and the three of us swam around to the outside of the boulder. Okay, Mom, I clicked, hoping she could still hear me even though she was now out of view. How many mermen usually move this rock?

Six, she replied automatically.

My hopes plummeted. Maybe my plan wasn't going to work after all.

Alright, I said reluctantly, let's give it a try. On the count of three, you and Mara push, and the dolphins will help me pull.

Nicky and Nora swam over, their flukes positioned inside a crevice between the boulders to help lift the rock. I did the same, my tail wedged in one of the crevices while my fingers gripped the top of the boulder. One...two...three!

I groaned as I pulled with all my strength. The dolphins struggled to lift the rock, and I heard Mom and Mara grunt as they pushed as hard as they can. I gasped when the boulder began to move a little, allowing a tiny crack to grow wider. But we quickly gave up when our muscles began to shake and the boulder became impossibly heavy.

Let's rest for a few, I suggested. I waited a couple minutes, letting everyone catch their breath, before going at it again. We grunted and groaned as we worked with all our strength, and the boulder moved slightly farther this time. But the strain quickly became too much, and we were forced to let the rock slam back into place once again.

It's too heavy, Mara clicked, her young voice piercing my thoughts.

We need to try again, I said determinedly. Come on!

Nora and Nicky were breathing hard from their efforts, and their tails shook as they pulled with all their strength. I was growing weary as well, but I knew this was Mom's only chance of escape. She and Mara groaned as they pushed their combined body weight against the boulder.

One of the cracks began to widen. Keep going! I urged. It's almost there!

Pain rippled through my tail, and my arms throbbed. My body was on the point of exertion. But I knew our efforts were working as the crack suddenly grew wide enough for a small fish to swim through.

Keep going! I commanded. The dolphins let out a serious of high-pitched clicks. Meanwhile, the crack continued to widen.

Almost there! I squeezed my eyes shut, focusing all my energy on lifting the rock. I gripped it tighter with my fingers and pulled harder with my flukes. As soon as the gap between the boulders became big enough for a small mermaid to swim through, I clicked, Hurry, Mara! Now's your chance!

Mara gave one last push before eagerly swimming through the crack. She turned sideways so her shoulders would squeeze through and made it out it in less than a second. Her eyes shone. Mother, mother, we're free!

But Nora and Nicky were struggling to hold the rock in place. I gritted my teeth and ignored my screaming muscles. Mara swam to my side and helped me lift the boulder while Mom struggled to fit through the opening. She succeeded in getting her head and arms through, but her shoulders were too wide. We all made one last redoubled effort. The gap widened a tad more, and with a slight scrape, Mom was able to force her shoulders through. Her tail writhed as she swam quickly to freedom. Then Mara, the dolphins, and I all ceased our efforts and let the boulder slam back into place, sending a mushroom cloud of sand floating through the water.

You made it! I cried, wrapping my arms around Mom's neck. She laughed and returned the hug, capturing me in a long embrace. When we pulled away, we both had tears of joy in our eyes and wide smiles on our faces.

My mother looked even more beautiful up close. From her shimmering blue tail to her dark, wavy hair, she had the grace and perfection of a queen. Though her skin, like Mara's, was extremely pale from lack of sunlight, the glow in her eyes showed that she was still healthy and radiant.

Come, she said, taking my hand and squeezing it tenderly. I sense someone coming. We had better leave.

Someone's coming? Frightened, Mara whirled around and scanned the water for any sign of approaching merpeople. But it's only the eighth hour!

They must be coming early to check on us, Mom replied, a sense of urgency creeping into her voice. We must go.

Nora and Nicky clicked anxiously, their eyes dark with worry. By now, I sensed another presence too. Without another word, the five of us began swimming rapidly away from the cave and toward the coast. Since it was the first time in years that Mom and Mara were in the open sea, they swam a little awkwardly at first. Their tails were much weaker and more easily prone to exhaustion, but neither of them complained.

How far do we have to swim? Mara asked after a nerve-wracking ten minutes. I could tell we were still in danger because Mom kept checking over her shoulder every few moments.

If we keep going at this pace, we'll make it to the beach in a little over an hour, I replied. We quickened our pace and remained silent for the next twenty minutes, with the only sound being the rush of the water as we sprinted by. Nora and Nicky were the only ones who seemed tireless, their eager eyes rapidly darting all around. But after nearly a half hour of swimming, even my tail was starting to grow sore.

Faster, Mom suddenly urged, her voice piercing everyone's thoughts. I looked at her in surprise, wondering why she sounded so paranoid all of a sudden. But when I glanced over my shoulder, I realized why.

A hazy mob of silhouettes was approaching. My eyes grew wide in horror. When I looked back just seconds later, their forms were now distinguishable—five mermen with murderous expressions on their faces.

Mara let out a sharp cry and the dolphins clicked urgently when they realized what was happening. We still had a ways to go, but the mermen were swimming so fast that they would overtake us before we could reach the shore.

Don't worry, Mom clicked, though the fearful look in her eyes said otherwise. They're still far away. We can make a distraction. She glanced over at the two dolphins, who clicked in understanding.

My heart broke at the thought of separating from my two friends, but Nora and Nicky gave me toothy smiles. They paused and turned around, swimming rapidly in the opposite direction toward the mermen.

Meanwhile, the three of us pressed on. I knew the private beach was still a good distance away, but something else was bothering me. Mom? I asked anxiously. How many mermen usually give you and Mara your rations?

Six, she replied, glancing over her shoulder. Her eyes widened when she realized that there were only five mermen following us. One must have turned around to get reinforcements. We would soon be terribly outnumbered.

I forced myself to swim faster. Mom did the same, one of her hands gripping Mara's so she wouldn't fall behind. The three of us shot through the water at full speed. I glanced over my shoulder and saw Nicky and Nora approach the mermen as a distraction. When that didn't work, they attacked them. But the mermen were carrying spears and a large net, and the dolphins were helpless in their attempts to give us a bigger head start. The mermen didn't even flinch as they pushed past Nicky and Nora and swam even faster. Their scales glittered menacingly in the sharp light.

I glanced upwards and realized that the sun was indeed already out. Dad and Luke were probably still standing on the beach, wondering where I was, hoping everything was okay. I wasn't about to let them down—not when we were so close to safety.

The private beach was only ten minutes away. The underwater cave where Mom had carved her secret message was directly in front of us. I could see the large arch marking the entrance to the grotto.

Rayne! Mom exclaimed, her eyes suddenly growing wide with fear. I looked behind me and gave a sharp cry of astonishment. The mermen were even closer.

I knew immediately what Mom was thinking—we weren't going to make it. They would overtake us in a matter of minutes, and the three of us were already exhausted as it was.

What are we going to do? I cried. The private beach is the closest strip of land, and it's still ten minutes away!

We're not going to make it, Mara said sadly.

Wait, Mom instructed. There is another way. She nodded in the direction of the secret cave.

I raised my eyebrows questioningly. Behind us, the mermen were getting closer. They were nearly upon us.

You have to trust me, Rayne. We need to swim inside the cave and block the entrance.

But how are we going to get out again? I argued, perplexed. We were just running from one trap to another. My mind was already coming up with multiple scenarios of what would happen when the mermen caught us. Would they kill us on the spot? Would they drag us back to a new, darker, deeper prison and lock us up forever?

Trust me, Mom repeated, her eyes filled with urgency. I nodded numbly, and we changed direction to make a beeline for the grotto. We sprinted underneath the arch and reached the cave in less than a minute.

As soon as we were enclosed on all sides by the sleek, glistening walls of the cave, Mom swam over to the side of the grotto where a large pile of rocks was resting on the seafloor. She grunted as she began rolling rocks from the top of the pile toward the entrance to the cave.

Mara collapsed onto the sand in exhaustion. I wanted to do the same, but Mom needed my help. I followed her lead and helped move the pile of rocks, which was situated on an uphill slope. It was fairly easy to send the rocks tumbling downhill to block the entrance, but the mermen would certainly have a harder time trying to move them.

Mom and I rolled the last stone in place just as the mermen rounded the corner. Their dark expressions and glinting spears showed that they were indeed bent on capturing us, but they were surprised to see that we had created a dam.

The rocks were wedged firmly in place. As the mermen scrambled to pull them aside, I slumped onto the ground, exhausted. My entire body felt numb. It hurt to move any of my muscles, so I lay quietly on the sandy bottom of the grotto, staring up at the glossy ceiling until my rapid breathing slowed to normal. Mara lay next to me, her skin covered in light beads of sweat, while Mom sat thoughtfully across from us.

I glanced over from my mother's worried expression to our temporary blockade of rocks. We were now entirely surrounded on all sides. There was no way out, not even from the surface—the only light that flooded in came from small holes in the ceiling, none of which were big enough for even Mara to fit through.

Mom's plan had worked to a certain extent. But now, as I swept my gaze over the sleek cliff walls and our makeshift dam, I realized we were stuck. We had escaped, only to become trapped once again. There was no way out, not until the mermen succeeded in moving the rocks. And when that happened...

I shuddered.

23

⸻ • ⸻

CHAPTER 23

What are we going to do? I groaned, burying my head in my hands. I knew our makeshift dam wouldn't hold us for long. We're trapped!

Mara sat up, her hands trembling. Are we, Mom?

Shh. We'll be all right, girls. Mom swam over and wrapped us in a large hug, the flukes of her tail covering our smaller ones. I asked you to trust me, remember?

Mara bit her lip to keep herself from crying. Yes, I remember.

Then how are we going to get out this mess? I asked.

Mom opened her mouth to reply, but a loud boom suddenly erupted from beyond the dam. The rocks shook and quivered, causing a few to topple to the floor. A large hand suddenly reached through one of the gaps and clutched at the water in front of us. We lurched away.

Well, there is one way, Mom replied, pulling away from Mara and I. She swam over to one the cave walls, her fingers lightly tracing over the bumps and ridges as she scanned her surroundings. Here! she exclaimed when she found a small cleft. She eagerly beckoned Mara and I forward.

I pushed off the sandy seafloor and headed over to the cleft, with Mara following. When I realized it was the exact spot where Mom had carved her message, my eyes widened in surprise.

Does it look familiar, Rayne? Mom asked with a smile. I nodded, and she scooted over to make room for Mara and I to peer inside. Sure enough, the message was still engraved into the cliff wall: The sea holds many secrets. – Miranda B.

I used to play in this cave with my friends, Mom explained, gesturing to our glittering surroundings. We would come here without our parents knowing. It was our own secret grotto, sheltered and protected from humans. Only later, after I met Clark, did my entire world change. Mom suddenly looked straight at me. We thought long and hard about the risk we were taking by starting a family. Without Clark knowing, I spent hours carving this message into the wall, thinking that if something ever happened to me—which it did—then our children could come to this cave and find this message.

But you kept it a secret, I replied. I never even knew I was a mermaid. What if I never found this message?

Ah, but I knew you would, Mom said with a smile. Once you were old enough, Clark and I agreed our children should know the truth. Once the time was right, we would let you swim in the ocean, and the transformation would officially begin.

I paused to let the information sink in. So Mom and Dad had obviously put a lot of thought and effort into their marriage. They had gone to huge risks to protect themselves and me, but after everything we had been through, it was hard to believe that it had all been for nothing. We were about to be captured—and most likely killed—by a race of merpeople I hadn't even known existed until a few days ago. I briefly wondered if Dad had been right after all. I couldn't rescue Mom, not even with all of us working together.

So what are we going to do? Mara asked quietly after another resounding boom came from behind the dam. The three of us watched in horror as even more rocks toppled over. We would only have a few minutes before the mermen broke through.

Mom immediately burst into action. Mara and I scooted aside as she reached through the cleft, twisting her body this way and that as she reached blindly for something. She grunted as she strained to grab onto the roof of the small opening. When her fingers finally latched onto a slight rock, she smiled and triumphantly pulled it out. The three of us backed away as a dozen other rocks suddenly came flying out of the hole. It was like she had unplugged a giant drain.

There, Mom exclaimed. That's our way out! Now all we have to do is remove these rocks.

I could hear the mermen working hard to break through our dam, so I quickly joined my mother in pulling the rocks out. Before long, we had a huge pile at the bottom of the seafloor, adding some width to the dam we had already created.

Now, to make the hole wider, Mom instructed. She glanced worriedly over her shoulder as her fingers flew over the cliff wall. She pulled and pulled with all her strength until one finally came loose, crashing down on top of the pile below us.

Mara and I smiled with relief. The small cleft that used to be impossible to see through was now a gaping hole, just big enough for us to squeeze inside one at a time.

Go! Hurry! Mom cried, pushing Mara through. The mergirl quickly forced herself into the hole and disappeared out of sight. I could hear the mermen toppling even more rocks behind us, so Mom pushed me through next. I scraped my back against the cliff wall as I struggled to fit through the hole, but I finally made it. I swam rapidly towards the glimmer of light ahead. Mara's silhouette cast shadows along the narrow tunnel. Before long, I saw her reach the surface and pull herself out of sight. I reached the surface a few seconds later, my heart pounding in my chest, and let out a cry of excitement when I realized the tunnel was an exit to the world above. It was a secret corridor connecting the beach to the underwater cave.

I gripped the rim of the hole with both hands and heaved myself up, my arms straining from the immense weight of my tail. Mara, lying on the rocky ground a few feet away, coached me out. Once I had shimmied onto dry land, I laughed with relief and wrapped her in a large hug.

"We made it!" I exclaimed breathlessly. We both cried tears of joy, knowing that we were finally safe.

But moments later, when we realized Mom still hadn't surfaced, we pulled away.

"Oh no," Mara gasped, the words sounding a bit funny coming from her mouth. She blushed in embarrassment. "Sorry, it's my first time talking above water."

"You've never been above water before?" I asked incredulously. The two of us leaned over the hole and gazed worriedly at the swirling water below. There was still no sign of Mom.

"I've been stuck in that cave with Mother my entire life," Mara said softly. "She taught me how to form words with my mouth, but I could never get it quite right because it sounds awkward underwater."

I nodded, even though in the back of my mind I wondered why she still referred to my mother as hers. Could she have been adopted?

That wouldn't explain the striking physical similarities between her and Mom, but maybe all mermaids looked that way.

The two of us waited in nerve-wracking silence. The only sound was the crash of waves in the distance, pounding against the cliffs that rose on either side. We were in some sort of valley, surrounded by nothing but ocean and cliff on all sides. I had a sudden feeling that we were trapped once again, and the mermen would climb out of the water and capture us in any second. But when I turned and saw a few steps carved out of the cliff behind us, I breathed a sigh of relief. There was a still a way out—we could head farther inland.

I ignored the tingling sensation that had started in my tail. Even though my legs were about to return, I continued peering into the hole. "If Mom doesn't surface in another five seconds, I'm going down there," I announced.

"No!" Mara cried, more tears springing into her eyes. "You can't."

"But she's in trouble!" I argued. I winced when I felt my bones snapping into place. Before long, my tail had transformed back into legs.

Mara suddenly doubled over in pain. She let out an ear-piercing scream as she rolled away from the hole, hugging her tail.

"What's wrong?" I asked urgently, stretching out my legs before crawling over to her. Then my eyes widened in realization. "Oh, no...Mara, have you ever transformed before?"

She gritted her teeth from the pain and shook her head fiercely.

"Then it might hurt a little," I explained, putting a reassuring hand on her shoulder.

"A little?"

"Okay, a lot." I cringed when she let out another scream. "Just let your tail change naturally. It will only last a few seconds."

Suddenly, the sound of water splashing jerked my attention away from Mara. I gasped when I saw Mom struggling to pull herself out of the tunnel, her arms wobbling from the strain. I helped her climb out of the hole before wrapping my arms around her in a tight embrace. "Mom!" I cried happily. "You made it! What took so long?"

She wrapped her arms around me as well, her long ebony hair intertwining with mine. "We're safe," she repeated, crying tears of joy. I was overwhelmed with emotions—relief that Mom was okay, happiness that we were finally reunited, and hope that we would finally get to live as a family once again. We continued to cry into each other's shoulders until Mara suddenly cleared her throat from behind us.

"Oh, honey," Mom sobbed, wiping a few tears from her face. She gently pulled away from me and grabbed Mara's hand, squeezing it tightly. "Look at you!" she exclaimed, giving a little laugh. "You finally get to know what it feels like to have legs!"

Sure enough, where Mara's sparkling blue tail used to be was now a pair of white, wobbly legs. Mara wiggled her toes uncertainly and smiled a bit at her new motor skills.

"I'm sorry to have to say this, girls, but we're not completely safe yet." Mom glanced worriedly at the hole. "The reason I took so long getting up here was because I covered the entrance with more rocks. Once the mermen figured out we swam up to the surface, they'll try to catch us by swimming onto the beach." She pointed at the waves crashing on the shore a good distance away.

"Then we better get out of here." I quickly stood up and made my way over to the side of the cliff, where a flight of steps had been crudely carved out of rock. It was a dangerous slope, but it was our only chance of escape. Since the mermen could transform just as easily as us, they could swim around to the beach and catch up with us.

"Go ahead, Rayne. I'm going to help Mara," Mom called. I suddenly realized Mara was in no condition to walk—it was only her first time with legs, after all.

"Are you sure?" I called back, watching as Mom hoisted Mara onto her back. Though Mara was thin and light, Mom wasn't all that much bigger. I could tell it was going to be a long trek home.

"Don't worry about me," Mom said rather breathlessly as she stumbled towards me.

"Okay, but if Mara gets too heavy, just let me know." I took a deep breath before heading up the makeshift staircase. I nearly slipped a few times, but since I had a lot of practice going up and down the goat-trail by the private beach, I made it to the top of the cliff in no time. As soon as I was back on flat ground, I closed my eyes and relished in the cool sea breeze that tousled my hair, whipping it behind me and rustling my tank top. There was nothing to see for miles around except the glittering ocean, the endless stretch of rocky ground, and a few distant lights that marked the town of Shady Cove.

"We're almost there, Mara."

I glanced down and saw Mom huffing and puffing as she struggled to finish the climb. I reached out a hand to help her up, and within a matter of minutes she and Mara made it to the top.

"Wow!" Mom smiled and shook out her long hair, causing Mara to giggle as it blew in her face. "I'm winded! It's been ages since I used these old legs." Though there was a carefree tone to her voice, the threat of being captured still lingered over us like a daro cloud. We silently glanced down at the outcropping of beach. Somewhere over that rocky ground was the secret tunnel to the underwater cave, but there were no sign of the mermen.

"Mom," I said softly. "We're never going to be one hundred percent safe, are we?"

A faint smile was on the corners of her lips. "No," she admitted. "No, we'll never be completely safe, especially not in the ocean. But here on land, we are as safe as we'll ever be."

"What?" The news was both delightful and puzzling. "But won't the mermen just run after us? I thought all merpeople can transform."

"Oh, we can. But most have never set foot on land or experienced what if feels like to have legs. I certainly never did, not until my curiosity became too overwhelming to handle." Mom smiled. "You see, the merpeople have a fear of becoming known to humans. We prefer to keep our race a secret. Even now mermaids are considered a myth among humans, and we intend to keep it that way."

"But Luke—I mean, one of my friends—was kidnapped by the mermen. They ambushed him on the beach before transforming and carrying him through the water."

Mom's smile faded. "Then this is more serious than I thought," she murmured. "Only in rare cases do merpeople have an excuse to go on land, but even then we never go farther than the beach. We prefer to stay as close to the water as possible."

I grinned. "So we are safe."

"Yes." Mom hoisted Mara higher up onto her back. "Unless the merpeople suddenly decide to overcome their fear and try to find us on land, then we are safe. The odds against us being captured on land are too big for us to worry about."

A wave of relief washed over me. I could tell Mara was pleased, too, because she rested her chin on Mom's shoulder and smiled. My nerves were still jumpy from being so close to danger, but now I could finally relax. Home was only a mile or so away. The mermen could never catch us. But most importantly, I had my mother back.

"I love you," I murmured, suddenly rushing over and embracing Mom in a large hug. I wrapped my arms around Mara, too, fingering her long hair as she rested her head against my chest.

Our emotions quickly became too much to bear, so the three of us sank to our knees, still wrapped in our embrace. We cried tears of joy and relief as we kneeled on the rugged, rocky ground. Safety had never felt so sweet.

24

CHAPTER 24

I had never been so weary, exhausted, and hungry in my entire life. My back was bruised and scraped, my feet were scuffed and dirty, and my body felt like it had been tossed in a blender at high speed. My hair, still sopping wet, was plastered against the nape of my neck and soaked through my tank top.

"Are we almost there?" Mara groaned, resting her chin on top of Mom's shoulder. I glanced over and saw Mom grit her teeth, hoisting Mara higher up on her back. Though I had offered several times to carry her, Mom refused every time, even though it was clear she was on the point of exhaustion.

"I think the trail is just up ahead," I announced, pausing to survey our surroundings. I reached up and shielded my eyes from the bright sunlight with one hand. All I could see was an endless stretch of rough, rocky terrain to our right, and the glittering ocean hundreds of feet below to our left.

"Rayne!" Mom suddenly gasped. Her lips curved up into a slight smile. "Is that what I think it is?"

I strained to see what she was looking at, but the blinding sun made it nearly impossible to make anything out. The harder I stared, though, the more I thought I could see a dark shape in the distance.

"It's been years," Mom murmured, "but I wouldn't miss that sight anywhere."

"Our house!" I exclaimed. "We're almost there!" I let out a cry of excitement and pressed on with renewed strength. With each step I took, freedom seemed more tangible in the sultry afternoon air. It felt like days had gone by since I left Dad and Luke standing on the private beach, watching me disappear underneath the waves in hopes of rescuing Mom. I had dreamt of returning to the private beach with Mom and Mara in tow, proudly showing off our shimmering tails from the water, but hiking a few miles after a frightening underwater chase worked just as well. As long as we get home safely, I thought with a smile.

The three of us were exhausted yet overjoyed by the time we finally reached our destination. I had never been happier to see that pathetic little goat-trail winding its way down the cliff face.

"Finally," Mom sighed, relieved. She carefully slid Mara onto the ground before plopping down next to her. Meanwhile, I peered over the edge of the cliff in search of Dad. I spotted him sitting on the private beach directly below us, with Luke pacing the sand next to him.

"Dad! Luke!" I hollered. At the sound of my voice, the two of them suddenly whirled around, wondering where I was.

"Up here!" I called. Mom and I waved as Luke and Dad got to their feet and stared up at us, raising their hands to shield their eyes from the glaring sun.

Dad let out a cry of excitement that ricocheted up the walls of the cliffs. He sprinted over to the goat-trail with Luke on his heels.

They made it to the top of the cliff in record time, looks of pure joy on both of their faces. Dad's brilliant smile overpowered everything else, lighting up his countenance with a glow I hadn't seen since Mom disappeared.

"Wait!" I giggled as the three of us quickly ducked behind a nearby bush. Mom placed a hand over her lips to keep herself from laughing. Apart from our scanty tops, we had no clothing.

"Wait," I repeated breathlessly. "I know we're all excited to get this reunion going, but can we put some clothes on first?"

The guys immediately froze in their tracks. A slight blush crept up on Dad's cheeks. "Oh!" he said, laughing nervously. "Right. Of course."

Fortunately, Luke had had the sense to grab my clothes before making the trek up the cliff. He tossed my shorts and overcoat behind the bush, where I unsnagged them from a few branches. Then I quickly slipped my shorts on while Mom helped Mara pull on my coat. It was so long that it nearly reached her knees. Meanwhile, Dad tossed his own coat over to Mom for her to wear. As soon as the three of us were presentable, we emerged from behind the bush.

I immediately rushed over to Dad, who wrapped me in a tight embrace. "Rayne," he sobbed, squeezing me securely against his chest. "I'm so proud of you. I was worried out of my mind, but you did it. You really did it." He pulled away and stroked my hair lovingly. "Thank you, honey."

I smiled, but quickly wiggled out of his arms. "Don't mention it. Besides, I think there's someone else you really want to talk to right now."

Dad gently pulled away, and his gaze automatically locked onto Mom's. She smiled and tried in vain to stop the tears that were streaking down her face. "Clark...it's been ages," she half-murmured, half-sobbed, suddenly overcome with emotion. She rushed over to Dad and wrapped her arms around his neck. They embraced for a long time, crying and laughing, not even pulling away after a good thirty seconds had passed.

Dad finally took a step back and pressed his forehead against hers. With gentle smiles, their lips met in a tender kiss.

I was beyond happy. When I turned away from parents, my gaze suddenly met Luke's. It was an awkward moment, and we immediately glanced in opposite directions.

Mara, who had been sitting on the ground the entire time, suddenly cleared her throat. Mom and Dad pulled away with soft smiles, blushing like two high school sweethearts. "We have a lot of catching up to do," Mom told him. "But I almost forgot—you need to meet Mara!"

Mom helped the girl to her feet, and she stood with her whole weight leaning against Mom's. "Hello," she said shyly.

"Hello, Mara." He bent down and embraced the shivering girl, but an indecipherable look had crossed his face. His gaze flitted from Mara, to Mom, and over to me. "You're right, Miranda," he said after a moment. "We have a ton of catching up to do. Let's head over to the house and get you girls some fresh clothes. Then we can all eat a big lunch and talk things over at the table. How does that sound?"

"That sounds perfect," I said automatically.

Dad carried Mara in his arms while the rest of us walked to the house. We meandered down the narrow trail in a comfortable silence.

My heart was overflowing with happiness. I felt like I was in a dream as I entered the house. I floated upstairs, into the shower, and into my bedroom. The remainder of the day was spent around the dining room table, with everyone sharing stories about the events from the past few days as we snacked on turkey sandwiches, chips, and lemonade. Mom was horrified (and Mara enthralled) upon hearing Luke's tale of being stranded at sea. Mara was especially curious about everything, from staircases to electricity to bathrooms. Because her entire childhood had been spent trapped in the underwater cave with Mom, dry land was a foreign world to her. She explored every inch of the house with childlike fascination while my parents chatted away for hours at a time.

Well, Mom did most of the talking. Dad hardly spoke. He had this goofy smile on his face as Mom and I took turns explaining our dangerous escape from the mermen. He never once looked at me, though—he had eyes only for Mom. Every chance he got, he would wrap her in a hug and place a tender kiss on her forehead, as if to make sure she was really there.

Luke and Mara also remained quiet throughout most of the day. I was still a little puzzled over Mara herself, since Mom had never told me the full story about her. So before I headed off to bed, I pulled Mom aside to satisfy my curiosity.

By now, nighttime had descended on Shady Cove. Millions of stars were scattered across the inky black sky. A sliver of moon barely illuminated the scenery outside as I stared out the window, quietly stirring my hot chocolate.

Mom stepped over to me and gave me a quick hug. Her scent lingered in the air for a few moments before she pulled away and took a seat on the couch. She was wearing a pair of my sweatpants and one of Dad's large sweatshirts. Her long, sweeping hair was pulled back in a tight bun just like mine.

"I was just thinking," I said, "about Mara."

"Yes, I've been meaning to talk to you about her, too."

I glanced up. "You have?"

Mom nodded, her eyes flooded with concern. "I have a feeling you don't quite understand."

I stared down at the clumps of powder swirling in my hot chocolate. "No," I admitted. "I don't know why she calls you her mother."

Mom let out a deep sigh. A ghost of a smile was on her lips. "Honey, she doesn't call me that because I adopted her or because we were imprisoned together, but because I am her mother."

My jaw dropped. "Really?"

She smiled. "Yes."

"So that makes Mara and I—?" I couldn't finish the sentence. A tiny part of me had suspected as much, but it was too unbelievable to be true.

"Sisters," Mom finished for me.

"No way," I exclaimed. "But how is that possible? Is she my half-sister?"

"She's your legitimate sister, Rayne. Clark's daughter. The reason she's alive is because I was pregnant when I was captured."

My breath caught in my throat. "What? Are you serious?" That meant, if Mom had never been captured, the two of us would have grown up as normal sisters. It was staggering—all my life I had believed I was an only child.

"I gave birth to her and raised her inside the cave with me," Mom explained. "She had never experienced what it felt like to swim in the ocean, unrestricted by walls. She had never even seen humans or completed her first transformation. She was despised as a traitor to her race, just like I was. But, against all odds, they never killed her."

Mom trailed off into silence. She stared out the window, deep in thought. "But all that's over now," she continued in a brighter tone, tears sparkling on her cheeks. "Thanks to you, Rayne, your little sister can experience life to the fullest. We can truly be a family again."

I smiled. The thought of having a younger sister was overwhelming, but somehow it made sense. I felt as if a bridge had been crossed—I felt like Mara and I were closer than ever, even as I heard her light voice laughing from the other room. "You're right, Mom," I said. "We are a family again."

Mom laughed as I plopped into her lap, nearly spilling my hot chocolate in the process. When Dad, Luke, and Mara trailed into the room a few moments later, the joy on everyone's faces was indescribable. Even Luke shared in the happiness that surrounded our family. Everything was finally falling into place.

"Hurry up, Rayne! You're going to be late for school!"

I sprinted down the stairs, grabbed my backpack, and dashed out the door. Dad was sitting impatiently in the driver's seat with his hand on the gearshift.

I breathlessly slid inside. "Sorry! Mom wanted some last-minute details about school."

"I don't blame her for prying into your academic life, but she has to understand that school starts at eight." Dad shook his head at his wife's antics before pulling out onto the dirt road.

I glanced over my shoulder at Luke, who was sitting in the back-seat. He was staring thoughtfully out the window.

"Hey," I said.

He turned and smiled at me. "Hey yourself."

"You look sad."

"Yeah, well, after everything that I've been through, it's hard to leave your family. You guys are so inspiring...and you have way too much fun together."

I grinned. That much was true. "But your own parents are worried sick. They haven't seen you in days."

"I know. I miss them terribly." Luke sighed as he shifted in his seat. We had all gotten so caught up in this adventure that we hadn't given as much thought to Luke's parents as we should have. But we finally decided that our safest route was to come up with a story to tell them. We couldn't exactly say that Luke had been kidnapped by a group of mermen, stranded on a buoy as bait, and rescued by a mermaid. Instead, the past few days had gone something like this: Luke had walking on the beach, and when it became too dark to see, he accidentally slipped and hit his head. I had found him the following morning, unconscious, so I brought him back to my house to treat him from his concussion. Since Dad had been on away on a business trip, I was unable to retrieve any information from Luke or bring him into town.

So maybe it wasn't the most believable story, but we were banking on Luke's parents being so worried that they would believe anything.

As we sped down the dirt road into town, Luke gave my father directions to his house.

"Rayne, why don't I drop you off at the school on the way?" Dad suggested.

"No, we still have plenty of time," I said. It's not that I minded being early to school, but I wanted to talk to Luke and thank him for...for...

I frowned. Luke had certainly helped around the house these past few days, especially by encouraging me to go after Mom and rescue her, but why else were my thoughts so focused on him?

"I just don't want you to be late," Dad warned, jerking me back to reality. "You've already missed three days of school in a row."

But our conversation was cut short—we had reached Luke's house. Dad pulled over the curb. "You can walk him to the door, Rayne, but you have three minutes," he instructed.

"Okay!"

Dad said a few more words to Luke, and they shook hands warmly. Then Luke and I filed out of the car and onto the sidewalk. Dad had accidentally parked a tad too far down the street from Luke's house, so before I could turn around and head toward the front door, Luke suddenly grabbed my arm.

"This way," he said, pulling me in the opposite direction.

"Where—" My question was suddenly cut short as Luke took off running towards the pier, which was at the end of the street. Caught off guard, there was nothing I could do but run after him, glancing over my shoulder at the little blue house waiting expectantly for us.

"What are you doing?" I cried breathlessly, my bun bobbing against the top of my head. As soon as we hit the wooden planks of the pier, our footsteps became loud enough to attract the attention of some fishermen going about their business.

"Just wait!" Luke called.

We slowed our pace to a walk. Our cheeks were warm from the short sprint, and my heart was beating rapidly in my chest, though it wasn't necessarily from running.

Luke leaned against the railing and beckoned me over. I stood in front of him, trying to catch my breath, my thoughts awhirl.

"Rayne," he said, so quickly that his words ran together, "after staying with your family, I've had a lot of time to think."

We stared at the shimmering ocean before us. The glistening whitecaps sparkled like millions of crystals in the pink morning glow. "So have I," I said truthfully.

"Well, I've been thinking about us," he clarified.

Oh. This was something that I had wanted to think about, but never actually had the courage to pursue. "Right," I said lamely.

The faintest of smiles appeared on his face. "Well, about that..."

His smile suddenly disappeared. My stomach twisted into a knot when I realized he looked sad. Maybe spending time with my family hadn't been such a good thing after all—maybe what he meant to say was that this had all been too overwhelming for him.

"Rayne, I don't know to tell you this, but..." He seemed at a loss for words. "I've never really had a friend like you before. I've never clicked with someone so soon, so easily. And I think we get along really well. I—"

The corners of my lips curved into a smile. "What are you saying?"

"I'm trying to say that I value your friendship," he laughed. "There!"

I laughed along with him, but inwardly I wondered why that had been so hard for him to say. Had he been meaning to tell me something else?

I immediately thought of Sage. "Luke, I'm so sorry for letting you down," I apologized. "It was a terrible move on my part to ditch you at the Café."

He shook his head. "No, no, don't even think about that. It's in the past. I think we've grown a lot closer since then—a lot closer—and we have more important things to think about."

I studied him carefully, but the friendly twinkle in his eyes betrayed no other emotion than sincerity. Luke certainly was an invaluable friend. He had proved himself in many ways, especially as the only outsider who knew my family's deepest secrets. We were all indebted to him.

Suddenly, a loud splash from the water below jerked our attention to the ocean. We rushed over to the opposite side of the pier and leaned over the railing. Water swirled and foamed below us, hinting that whatever had made that splash was now below the surface.

Fear suddenly gripped me. I had imagined this scenario before, many times, over the course of the past few days. What if it was one of the merpeople? Had someone been sent to spy on me? I swallowed nervously as Luke and I continued to peer at the water, searching for any sign of a creature.

Just as we were about to turn away, a large, gray animal suddenly burst out of the ocean. I pulled back in surprise, but a huge smile lit up my face when I realized it was a dolphin—and not just any dolphin, but Nora! A few seconds later, Nicky also breached the water in a glittering spray that arced above his flukes.

"Whoa!" Luke exclaimed.

"It's them!" I cried happily. They were safe after risking their lives against the mermen.

The dolphins continued to splash in the water, putting on an entertaining show of acrobatics. A few fishermen glanced over and frowned at them for chasing away any potential catch.

Suddenly, my phone pinged from my back pocket. I pulled it out and groaned when I read the text from Dad: Time's up.

"I have to go back." I sighed and shoved my phone away. I waved at Nicky and Nora, who were lazily floating in circles below us. They clicked happily and waved their flippers in return before disappearing underneath the water.

"You never fail to amaze me," Luke chuckled as we headed back to the car.

"What do you mean?"

"The dolphins. How you can communicate with them."

"Oh, it's nothing," I said quickly, but deep down I was pleased. Luke had handled everything in stride, never backing away from a challenge, and certainly never leaving my side. His friendship was worth more than all the secrets and abilities that came with being a mermaid.

Once we were in front of his house, we both paused.

"Good luck," I said. "With your parents, I mean."

He smiled. "Thanks."

Quickly, awkwardly, he reached out and squeezed my hand. Then he let go and turned back toward his house.

"Bye, Luke," I called after him.

"Rayne!" Dad thundered from behind me. "You're going to be late!"

As Luke stepped up to the front porch of his house, I turned away and jogged over the car, resisting a glance over my shoulder.

25

— ◆ —

EPILOGUE

I could feel Dad's steely gaze on me as he pulled away from the curb. "Are you mad at me?" I asked hesitantly after a rather uncomfortable silence.

"No," he sighed. "No, I just have a lot to think about. And don't pretend you're off the hook about the fight at school."

"It wasn't my fault," I said automatically.

"I never said it was."

We turned the corner, and Luke's little blue house vanished from sight. "Madeleine had it in for me," I declared. "There were rumors going around school that she was going to beat me up."

"But that's not what happened, is it?"

I paused. I'd been prepared for another argument, but Dad didn't look angry in the slightest. "What's wrong?" I asked as his face grew redder and redder. He was clearly trying to hold in his laughter. "Dad?"

He suddenly laughed so hard that the car swerved just a bit into the other lane. "The school counselor called me a few days ago," he explained as soon as he caught his breath. "She said you had beat up Madeleine Hansen. The first words that came to my mind were, 'What? My daughter beat up another girl?' Then your swim

Coach called me a short time later and said you had attacked her. Attacked her."

I was now thoroughly confused. "But that's a lie. I was only acting in self-defense."

He laughed again.

"Dad, how is this funny?" I cried, frustrated.

"I just think the whole thing is ironic! I mean, the bully who picked a fight with you ended up losing," he chuckled. "Madeleine didn't know what she signed up for."

"So you're proud of me?" I asked hesitantly.

He gave me a warm smile. "How could I not be proud of a daughter who stood her ground at school and risked her life in the ocean? You're beautiful, you're strong, you're—" He reached over and tweaked my nose. "You're just like your mother."

I smiled. Just a few moments later, we pulled into the school parking lot.

"It's been a crazy few days," Dad sighed.

"Try a crazy few months. This all started when we moved back to Shady Cove, remember?"

He nodded thoughtfully. "Are you glad we made the move?"

"Not at all," I said immediately. Upon seeing Dad's surprised expression, I added, "In the beginning. But now..."

I looked out the window at the students walking to their classes. Somewhere, beyond the buildings of the school, lay the Shady Cove Café...the pier...the ocean.

"Now I can't imagine myself living anywhere else," I said honestly.

"Not even if we moved back to Newland?"

I immediately thought of Kimmie, but she seemed like someone whom I had known ages ago. My life was filled with new, more intimate, relationships.

"I guess it doesn't matter where we go," I said finally. "As long as our family sticks together, I don't care where we move."

Dad smiled gratefully. "Well, you don't have to worry about that. I don't think we'll be moving for a long while."

Happiness welled up within me. Shady Cove had been my childhood home, and now it was my home to stay.

"Well," he said, unlocking the car doors, "I guess you better head off to class. Have a good day at school, honey."

I pushed open the door, but Dad stopped me with one last reminder. "And don't pull another fast one on your swim coach," he warned.

"What do you mean?"

He gave me a stern look. "The school said that you quit the swim team."

"Oh." I suddenly felt like a deer in headlights. "Yeah, about that..."

"I don't blame you one bit, Rayne," he reassured me. "But your mother reminded me that only saltwater causes a transformation. You don't have to fear growing a tail unless you're in the ocean."

Hope bubbled up within me. "Really?"

"Really," he confirmed. "You might have to straighten things out with Coach Hansen, but I'll be right by your side."

I grinned. After everything I had been through, another conversation with Coach seemed no more daunting than winning a swim race. "Thanks, Dad," I said.

He gave me another tweak on the nose as I scooted out the door. "Have a great day."

Once my feet hit the pavement, Dad pulled away, leaving me standing with an amused smile on my face. I couldn't wait to tell Sage and Marley that I was still on the swim team—and that Luke and I were back together, closer than before. My heart was content.

"Rayne!" a voice called as soon as I stepped into the school hallway.

I turned around and saw Sage barreling towards me with Marley right on her heels. "You're back!" she shrieked.

"Of course I'm back." I chuckled as Sage slammed into me, trapping me in a tight hug. Marley wrapped her long arms around both of us, and we all laughed.

"Rayne, you were gone for three days! Everyone's been wondering where you went!" Marley exclaimed as soon as we pulled apart. "You left right after punching Madeleine's guts out—which was pretty awesome, I might add."

"Well, thanks...but the strangest thing happened to me." As Marley and Sage listened with wide eyes, I told them the fictitious story about how I had found Luke lying unconscious on the beach. "Once my dad got home," I continued, "he helped treat Luke for his concussion, and then we brought him to his parents."

"No way," Sage gushed once I'd finished. "I'm so glad you found Luke! When I heard he was the person who had been kidnapped, I just couldn't stop thinking about him."

"Yeah, while the rest of the school couldn't stop thinking about you," Marley added. "Everyone was shocked when you beat up Madeleine. We thought for sure you would get suspended, or even expelled."

Sage grinned, and I knew she had something juicy she wanted to tell me. "But guess what happened?" she said. Without waiting for an answer, she blurted, "Madeleine's track record finally caught up with her, and she got expelled!"

"You're practically a legend now," Marley added. "The whole school thinks you're a black belt in karate."

"Karate?" I rolled my eyes. "Come on, all I did was throw a few punches."

"Plus an awesome ninja kick to the stomach," she pointed out.

The three of us laughed. It felt good to finally be back with my friends. We slowly made our way towards our classes, chattering excitedly the whole way.

"So are you and Luke back on good terms now?" Sage asked. "I mean, he should have forgiven you after you saved his life."

"Yeah." I smiled at the memory.

Sage gave me a knowing look. "And...?"

"And what? There's nothing more to say."

"Sage is the ultimate matchmaker," Marley teased. "I wouldn't question her judgment."

"I bet he's planning to ask you out," Sage declared. "He already tried once, and he's going to try again! Just watch."

"Not a chance," I said, heading into my first class.

"Rayne..."

"See you at lunch!"

"This conversation is not over yet, Rayne!" Sage called.

I merely ducked my head, slipped into my seat, and tried to hide the pleasant blush that had blossomed on my cheeks.

Time flew by quickly. I was thankful that Dad was picking me up today so I didn't have to ride my bike. Though my body was still sore and bruised from the past few days, my heart was practically overflowing with happiness. School had passed like normal, aside from teachers and classmates wondering where I had been. A few students even congratulated me on beating up Madeleine. It was weird, and not to mention a little awkward, but I quickly got used to the unwanted attention.

Meanwhile, Dad spent every waking moment with Mom. They were practically inseparable. The love between them was more tangible than any other emotion I had ever experienced. Dad seemed to be a whole different person now—more patient, understanding, and definitely more energetic. He and Mom would stay up late at night just talking about whatever was on their minds.

Though the ocean continued to call to me, inviting me back in, I knew I had to fight the urge. It simply wasn't safe to go swimming in the sea, not with a horde of merpeople out for our blood. Mom and Mara especially struggled with this desire. We all wanted to lose ourselves in the water and feel free again. Dad, in an effort to satiate our desire, promised to drive us up the coast so we could swim in one of the nearby lakes. It wouldn't be anything close to swimming in the ocean, especially since we wouldn't have our tails, but at least we could get wet. We were all looking forward to it.

As soon as I got home from school, I tossed my backpack onto my bed and peeked over into my sister's room.

"Hey," I said softly.

Mara glanced up from where she was flipping through a magazine. Mom, like the ingenious woman she was, had taught Mara how to read and write while they lived in the underwater cave. She had passed on as much of her knowledge as she could to the young girl. But even before that, Dad was the one who taught Mom how to read and write in English.

"Hey," Mara chirped. She patted the empty space next to her on the bed, and I gratefully took a seat.

"How are your exercises going?" I asked, referring to Mara's daily routine of practicing walking. She was definitely getting better, but she wasn't quite up to skipping or jogging yet.

"I'm doing good. Mother even says I might be enrolled in school next week."

"What? Already?"

"Oh, I'm not talking about public school," Mara said with a small smile. "Mom has been thinking of homeschooling me. I still have a lot to learn now that I'm going to live mostly out of water."

My eyebrows shot up in surprise. "Homeschooling is a great idea."

"Thanks. I'm glad you think so." She smiled up at me with her wide blue eyes. "You know, ever since Mother told me that I had an older sister, it was hard to imagine what she would be like. But when I finally met you, it made sense."

I blushed. "Does that mean I've met your expectations?"

Mara laughed. "Yes, yes, yes! You're the best older sister a mermaid—I mean, a girl—could ever have."

I wrapped my arm around her shoulder and hugged her close. "And you are the best little sister a girl could have," I replied.

For the next few minutes, Mara and I chatted with a casualness I hadn't even known existed between us. It was like we had sealed the final bond between us, and we were officially sisters now.

"Do you want to play in the game room?" she suggested. "I can climb the stairs pretty well now."

"Sure." I grinned and followed her out the door, guiding her upstairs with my hand on the small of her back. She walked slowly, concentrating on each step, but never once stumbled or fell. As soon as we reached the top of the stairs, she headed in the direction of the game room.

"Hey, I'll meet you in there in a second," I told her, my gaze flitting over to a familiar light blue door.

"Alright," she said, heading around the corner.

Once she had disappeared, I took a deep breath and approached the light blue door. After twisting the old, dusty knob, I pushed the door open and entered my old bedroom.

It was still the same as I had left it. In a way, I was glad Mom and Dad hadn't moved anything. As I walked inside and traced my fingers over the wallpaper, I realized the room no longer brought any feelings of sadness. Though it reminded me of Mom, I no longer had any reason to grieve because she was now alive. If I listened carefully I could hear her talking with Dad downstairs. It was almost as if she had never disappeared—she had been with me the whole time, living in my memories until I finally had the chance to see her face-to-face again.

I smiled as I pushed aside the faded curtains and peered out the window. The ocean was just as beautiful as ever. I felt a tug at my heart, immediately wishing I could be out there diving under the waves, but I quickly pushed the urge away. For now, I was content with being with my family.

Suddenly, my ringtone blasted through the room, and my fingers fumbled to slide my phone out of my back pocket. I didn't even glance at the caller ID as I whipped the device up to my ear. "Hello?"

"Rayne!"

I was taken aback for a second. At first I thought it was Sage or Marley, but then I realized the voice was too high-pitched to be either of them. "I'm sorry, who is this?" I asked hesitantly.

"Rayne, it's me." After another awkward silence, the person on the other end of the line sighed and added, "Kimmie."

"Kimmie! Oh, gosh, I'm sorry!"

"No problem," she laughed. "So how's it going?"

I paused, but after a moment, I realized maybe this was Kimmie's way of trying to restore connection between us. I smiled and dove into an explanation of everything that had happened since we'd last met—minus the whole mermaid scenario, of course. I was surprised at how casually our conversation flowed. After visiting her in Newland last week, I was sure that our friendship was headed downhill, but Kimmie seemed to pick up on our relationship as if nothing had happened.

"Hey, we should totally get together soon," she said at the end of the phone call, after—thankfully—making only a few comments about Zach. "Are you able to hang out this weekend?"

"Of course," I replied quickly. "That would be great. We have a lot of catching up to do." I immediately thought of Mom, Mara, and my new status with Luke. We were still trying to come up with a believable explanation for Mom and Mara's sudden appearance, but as for Luke, that plan had already been settled.

"Awesome!" Kimmie gushed. "How about I come to your house this time? I've never been to Shady Cove before."

I swallowed. Yep, we would definitely need to come up with something fast. "Sure, that would probably be fine," I said vaguely. "I just need to ask my par—uh, my Dad first."

Kimmie and I talked for a few more minutes before hanging up. Just as I was about to slide my phone into my back pocket, a new text popped up on the screen. My heart did a little skip when I realized it was from Luke.

Lunch at the Café tomorrow?

My fingers flew across the screen. Of course, I replied. Then, on second thought, I added, And this time I won't forget!

When I glanced up from my phone, my gaze automatically locked onto the picture hanging on the wall next to the window. I moved closer, studying it carefully, sweeping my gaze over the figures captured within the frame: the beautiful woman and the smiling girl with bright blue eyes and long, black tresses.

The last time I had entered my old bedroom, the picture had brought back memories so painful that I fled. But that seemed so long ago. Things were vastly different now. Though the picture still brought back tender memories, I knew I was no longer the little girl who had lost her mother. I was the girl who had unlocked the secrets of the ocean and rescued her mother.

From the hallway, I suddenly heard Mom and Dad clatter up the stairs and past the bedroom. Mara called their names, and they plodded into the game room.

As my family chatted away, I took one last look at the picture. "I love you, Mom," I whispered, but my gaze had drifted from her face in the photo to the open doorway only a few yards away. I quickly darted out of the room and into the hallway.

Laughter erupted from the game room, and I smiled. "What's all the racket?" I called upon entering.

Mom, Dad, and Mara simultaneously glanced up at me with wide smiles. "It's a really fun game! Come play with us," Mara urged, patting the seat next to her.

I obediently plopped down on the couch. Mom immediately draped an arm over my shoulders. "You should see this game they're playing," she said. "I think it's called Wii."

"Dad and I are racing! We're off-roading," Mara interjected, proud of the new word she had learned.

Though my eyes were fixed on the TV, my thoughts were elsewhere. I was thinking about Mara's smiling face and Dad's booming laugh from behind me. I was thinking about the way Mom had drawn close to me, her warm breath tickling my cheek. But most importantly, I was thinking about how wonderful it was to finally be with my family.

The sun streamed down from a cloudless blue sky. I smiled as I soaked in the warm rays and dangled my feet in the cool water. The empty lane stretched before me in all its sparkling, refreshing blueness. All around me, the pool deck thrummed with activity. People weaved in and out of the crowd, cheering swimmers on while the announcer called out names through his microphone.

As soon as my heat was announced, I quickly hopped to my feet and made my way over to the starting blocks. I spotted Luke seated next to my family in the bleachers. As soon as they heard my name called, they started yelling and waving.

On the opposite side of the pool, I saw Sage and Marley jumping up and down, screaming my name. Behind them was the rest of the Shady Cove High swim team, cheering me on as well.

This was it. No, I wasn't about to swim in the qualifying rounds for the Junior Olympics. It was just another school swim meet, but to me and my friends, it was equally important.

As soon as it was time to step onto the starting blocks, I reached up and adjusted my goggles, making sure they were secured around my skin-tight swim cap. Then, wiggling my toes against the rough, grooved surface of the starting block, I mentally prepared myself for the all-consuming race.

"Swimmers, take your marks."

I bent over and gripped the starting block with both hands, fingering the bottom like an outlaw would finger his gun in a showdown.

I can do this.

Narrowing my eyes, I focused on the translucent turquoise water below. The thick black line on the bottom of the pool was visible as a fluctuating geometric design.

Bring it on.

Just before the buzzer sounded, Mom's words from this morning flashed through my mind: "Don't worry about anyone else. Focus on yourself and your swimming. When you leave this pool you should have no regrets. Just do your mermaid thing and win like you always do."

I closed my eyes and smiled. Though I didn't have my tail, I still had my speed. Mom was right—I would just have to do my mermaid thing.

I pushed off the starting block and flew through the air. Within milliseconds, I hit the water and dove beneath the surface, my legs automatically breaking out into a dolphin kick.

The race was on.